Praise for

Read this and prepare to be whisked away on an absolutely mesmerizing Christmas journey unlike any other imaginable. Through the agency of a magically ornamented Christmas tree which enables time travel you can capture genuinely fresh insights into the true meaning and historical significance of Christmas. Ancient Israel's first Hanukkah, Rome's Saturnalian feasts, Charlemagne's coronation celebrations, Puritanical Boston, and Dickensian London all have new life breathed into them. A wonderful voyage of historical discovery that puts Advent back into the Children's Adventure story!
—LARRY J. KREITZER
Tutor of New Testament and Tutor for Graduates
Regent's Park College
The University of Oxford

Bush has created a *tour de force* that weaves together strands of old stories, traditions, and the very heart of Christmas into a tapestry that will delight audiences of all ages. Equal parts imagination and information, THE MAILBOX TREE drips with history and heritage, whisking readers across centuries and cultures while returning to the present with a harvest of fresh understanding of Advent's deep roots in our awareness of Christ's birth and life. Light a fire, gather around the couch, and get ready for a Yule adventure!
—GENE C. FANT, JR.
Executive Vice President for Academic Administration
Dean of the Faculty
Professor of English
Union University

Christmas is in danger! The seed of the Serpent is once again trying to snuff out the light in our world and in Arboria. It's up to two boys, Alex and Grant, with angelic help, to uncover the truths about Christmas from the past in order to preserve Christmas for the present and future. This is a wonderful romp of a story, delightful fun saturated with deep truths. Amidst the fun and adventure, it is a primer on the interpretation of Christian symbolism in scripture and history. Randall Bush's previous two Christmas novels are favorites of our family so we were excited to hear of a third installment—and it did not disappoint! If you want to enrich your family's celebration while gathered around a fun book together, make Randall Bush's Christmas books a part of your family's tradition.
—RAY VAN NESTE
Professor of Biblical Studies
Director, R. C. Ryan Center for Biblical Studies
Union University
editor of *KJV400: The Legacy and Impact of the King James Version*

Praise for GABRIEL'S MAGIC ORNAMENT

No Christmas tree will ever look the same again after you have read Randall Bush's piece of Christmas magic. Among the branches of this familiar tree he creates a whole world of good, evil and salvation. Echoes of John Bunyan, C. S. Lewis and the Bible abound, as do humorous side-swipes at the absurdities of our present-day world, but it is the author's own vivid imagination that will keep the young reader turning the page. Randall Bush tells a good story, and I commend it as a way of sharing in the best story of love.

—PAUL S. FIDDES
D.Phil (Oxford), D.D. (Oxford)
Principal Emeritus
and Professional Research Fellow
Regent's Park College, Oxford

The family is delighted with [Gabriel's Magic Ornament]; I have re-read it; and a thirteen-year old church friend said that she could not put it down! A delightful fantasy tale, that carries the reader along within a world comparable with that of C. S. Lewis's Narnia books. It conveys an unobtrusive spiritual dimension, but will also entrance most especially young readers of between eight and fourteen, and will also be enjoyed by readers of all ages. The book is an ideal gift for children, especially at the Christmas season.

—ANTHONY C. THISELTON
Emeritus Professor of Christian Theology
University of Nottingham, England
Canon Theologian of Leicester Cathedral
and of Southwell Minster

THE MAILBOX TREE

—PART 1—

SPHINX ON THE LOOSE

THE MAILBOX TREE

—PART I—

SPHINX ON THE LOOSE

Randall Bush

D.Phil., University of Oxford

BORDERSTONE PRESS, LLC

2012

First Edition

The Mailbox Tree, Part I
Sphinx on the Loose

Author: Randall Bush
Editor: Mary Ellen Poe

Cover Art: D. Ellen (Kay) Ingle

Published by BorderStone Press, LLC,
PO Box 1383, Mountain Home, AR 72654
Memphis, TN

www.borderstonepress.com

Supervising editor: Brian Mooney

ISBN: 978-1-936670-44-4

Library of Congress Control Number: 2012919061

As of the time of the 1st printing: interior is acid free and lignin free.
It meets all ANSI standards for archival quality paper.

To Katie, the mother of Grant
And Meghan, the mother of Alex

TABLE OF CONTENTS

Part I

INTRODUCTION

THE MAILBOX TREE, LIKE the previous books in the series, *Gabriel's Magic Ornament* and *Widgmus World*, is intended to be a Christmas fantasy, but unlike the others it has interspersed amongst its fantasy portions a fictionalized account of the history of Christmas. For this reason, the more informed reader should be advised to distinguish between the portions of the books that are purely fantastical and those that are reflective of actual historical situations, events, and contexts. This can easily be done by thinking of the mailbox doors that open to past epochs as temporary exits from the fantasy world into historical episodes. This is sort of the reverse from the way Dorothy in J. Frank Baum's *The Wizard of Oz* leaves the real world of Kansas to enter the imaginary Land of Oz. In our novel, Alex and Grant leave the fantasy world of Christmas present to enter a "real world" of Christmas past.

In constructing the historical episodes, I have tried to adhere as closely as possible to real—and not invented—historical contexts. My reason for doing this is philosophical: the past is what it is and cannot be changed no matter how much we may wish it. Still, since the historical episodes in my book are fictionalized, one needs to know how best to discern between the factual and the fictitious elements in them. The historical and cultural contexts form the most factual elements of these narratives, and when actual names of places and persons are given in these episodes, they do refer to actual places and persons. I have tried as much as possible to avoid anachronism and to achieve authenticity by checking the history of the places and by representing as closely as possible the way these places would have looked at the times in question. Though most of the dialogue has been invented, I have tried to make the dialogue reflect to a high degree the actual viewpoints of the individuals involved. I have done this by consulting historical documents such as biographies, diaries, letters, and sermons. Though most of the dialogue is invented, I have intentionally constructed it in an effort to reflect the kinds of discussions that might have occurred during the epochs under question by taking into consideration actual historical, political, theological, cultural, and economic factors that we know did form their background. When specific names are not mentioned, I have tried to let the dialogues reflect the kinds of perspectives persons at the time were known to have had. Below are some specific examples of the distinctions between fact and fiction I speak of:

1.   The dialogue of the scribes in the scriptorium prior to Hanukkah is invented, but the fact that the scribes tried to deceive the Greek soldiers by hiding their scrolls and spinning Dreidels has its basis in Hebrew tradition. The words of the High Priest on the eight days of Hanukkah are invented, but they reflect the kind of theological thinking that was known to have existed at the time.

2.   Bishop Julius I established December 25 as the date for the celebration of Christmas for the Roman Church in A. D. 350. The historical events and cultural situations were all being faced by Christendom at the time. However, the council at St. Peter's is invented, and there is no evidence that such a council ever took place. The dialogues do, nonetheless, represent real perspectives that existed at the time.

3.   The political, cultural, and theological issues facing 17th century New England are historically factual as are the persons men-

tioned in the narratives, but the meeting of the town council is fictionalized. The perspectives of the persons dialoguing at the council meeting, however, are accurate.

4. The factual information on Charlemagne is for the most part derived from biographies about him (such as that of Einhart), but the boar's head feast and the description of the room in the Lateran Palace containing instances of Christ's victory over tree worship are fictionalized. Still, the tree worship among the people groups alluded to in the room is a known fact as is the church's struggle against it.

5. The historical information given on Charles Dickens, Angela Burdette-Coutts, Hannah Meredith, and William Simpson is accurate and is taken from biographies on Dickens and from letters written by him to Lady Coutts. Dickens's association with Ye Olde Cheshire Cheese is also historically accurate, though the meeting of Dickens with Lady Coutts and Ms. Meredith at the Cheshire Cheese on Christmas Eve of 1843 and their dialogue are fictionalized. The dialogue nevertheless represents what Dickens mentions in his correspondence with Lady Coutts in the autumn of 1843.

A final word should be said concerning some of the purposes I have had in mind while writing *The Mailbox Tree*. One purpose I envisage is to ignite in young people an interest in history by using the sparks of the imagination. As a college professor, I am saddened that many of my students come to me with no interest in history whatsoever. The reason, I think, is that teachers have taught them history in dry and unimaginative ways. This loss of interest in history, however, must be rectified or the immortal words of George Santayana will come true: "Those who refuse to learn the lessons of history will be doomed to repeat them." A second purpose is to help young people see how the past influences the present, and how the present influences the future. What happens in history has a real bearing on the world we live in today, and we curtail our ability to function as change agents in the world if we do not understand how history has made our world what it is. Furthermore, if we do not understand how the present is connected to the past, how can we understand how it connects to the future? Helping young people know how to identify these connections and understand them is one of my principle objectives. Third, my purpose is to help young people realize that our time in the world is short and that we must make the most of the time we are given in the here and now if we are to make a lasting contribution for good. We cannot change the past, but we can change the future. My own strategy of how best to do this should become apparent to the reader. The secular approach to positive cultural change has been weighed in the scales and found wanting. Restoring real meaning to Christmas not only challenges this secular approach but it also provides a better way forward.

In constructing this book, I have had considerable help and inspiration from others, particularly from my family. Family members have patiently read not just this manuscript, but also those of my other books. I should like to express my thanks to them at this time for their continued help. Mary Ellen Poe, the youngest daughter of my very good friends Hal and Mary Ann Poe, did the final editing of the book. I am grateful to her for catching the errors and inconsistencies that I had missed. Finally, I want to thank my colleagues at Union University where I teach philosophy and Christian Studies for encouraging me to pursue my writing of children's books. May all who read this book be enriched in their understanding and appreciation of Christmas!

—Randall Bush
Jackson, Tennessee
August 2012

—Chapter One—

NOT ANOTHER MAILBOX!

AS GRANT, ALEX, AND THEIR mother arrived at the retirement village where Nanny lived, Mom drove into the spot where Nanny had once parked her car. Now that Nanny, the great-grandmother of Grant and Alex, could no longer drive, her spot was always empty. Other spots might be empty, too, but Nanny warned all her visitors—sometimes as many as three or four times— not to park in any but hers.

Grant and Alex were sitting in the back of the car sulking when they arrived. Going to the 'Old Folks Home', as they called it, was always boring. Nanny had no toys, and the boys always had to 'behave. Occasionally, if she would remember, Nanny would let them play 'Battle' with a deck of her playing cards, but even then she would tell the boys to be careful not to damage her best deck. Playing Battle was never as fun as playing video games. Nanny, it seems, had never heard of video games. In fact, she did not have a computer. She did own a television, but it seemed to get only one channel. And the only programs that ever were on were game shows.

"Mom," Grant moaned, "how long do we have to stay?"

Mom was looking into the mirror attached to the car's visor and brushing her hair. "Not long," she replied. "Nanny has made us special ornaments for our Christmas tree. She's called me several times to come get them."

"I'll bet they are more of those mailboxes," Alex said unenthusiastically.

Mom was putting on a fresh coat of lipstick. "Probably so," she replied, "but making them gives your Nanny and her little friends a lot of joy. It keeps them busy and gives them a chance to make affordable Christmas gifts."

"There," she said, stuffing her cosmetics back into her purse. "Let's go see Nanny."

Grant and Alex scrambled out of the back seat. "We already have at least a hundred of those mailboxes," Grant went on. "Pretty soon we won't have room for any other ornaments on our Christmas tree. What is it about Nanny and mailboxes anyway? Did she used to live in a Post Office or something?"

"No, but her son, your grandfather, was a mailman. He was working at the Post Office when he died. He was young when that happened, and he was Nanny's only child. Losing him was one of the most difficult things she ever had to go through. She also was a good letter writer," said Mom as they started up the stairs. "And she always sent lots of Christmas cards to her family and friends. I suppose mailboxes are important to her because, for most of her life, she lived far away from everyone she loved. At least she lived far away from everyone until she moved here. In the old days, using the phone to call long distance was very expensive. There were no cellphones or computers then, and email had not yet been invented. I guess writing and receiving letters was the only way Nanny had to communicate with her family. Of course, letter writing is a lost art today, but as far as I know, Nanny still writes lots of letters to friends and family who live in other parts of the country."

When they arrived at Nanny's door, Mom said, "Okay, boys, remember to be on your best behavior." She rang the doorbell. Soon the door opened slowly, and Nanny peeked outside.

"There you are!" Nanny said smiling. "Come on in." Mom gave her a hug and then said, "Boys, give your Nanny a kiss."

Grant and Alex never really liked this part because Nanny had whiskers, and her kisses were always very wet. Mom had told them, however, not to wipe off the kisses until she was not looking, so the boys waited for the moment Nanny turned her head and then quickly wiped their faces with their arms.

"Sit down," said Nanny. "I've just been watching the local news. Did you hear a lion escaped from the zoo?"

"What?" Mom blurted with a startled look. She focused on the television. A news banner, telling about the escaped lion, was streaming across the bottom of the screen.

"It happened a little over an hour ago," Nanny told her. "They've got a section of town near the zoo cordoned off. They're warning everybody to stay in their homes until they catch it." Then Nanny asked, "Isn't that section of town pretty close to where you live?"

"Yes," Mom replied.

"It's settled, then," said Nanny. "I insist that you and the boys stay here with me for the remainder of the afternoon, or at least until we're sure the lion is back in its cage."

The boys looked at each other with a sense of dread. A whole afternoon? Surely it would be better to risk coming face to face with a lion than have to stay all afternoon at Nanny's!

"Well," said Mom. "We'll see how things go." Changing the subject, she asked Nanny, "How are the aunties doing?" The aunties were Nanny's sisters.

"Not too well," Nanny replied. She and Mom proceeded to chitchat about the aunties' health. This portion of the stay always involved Nanny's rundown on the long list of medical problems her sisters were having. Grant and Alex never had a clue about what medicines did what for what ailment, or why the aunties had to get off one pill and be put on another, or why they had to have their doses regulated and re-regulated by their doctors. The boys just sat there 'behaving' as the small talk went on and on.

When Nanny had finished her update, she slowly rose up out of her chair and said, "I suppose it's time now for me to give you what you came for." She left the room and returned with several shopping bags. "I've had time to make extras for everybody this year," she said, opening one of the bags and removing its contents.

"Oh, how lovely! More mailboxes!" Mom said enthusiastically. "Aren't these the cutest things?" she said to the boys, trying to coax them to react favorably. When they didn't immediately respond, she gave them "the look."

"Oh, yeah!" they each said haltingly.

"Nanny, how do you ever manage to make so many of these," said Mom. "It must take you so long."

"Oh, it's nothing once you get the hang of it," Nanny remarked.

"Sometime you'll have to show us how you do it," Mom said, trying to be polite. The truth was that she really did not want to know how to make them.

"Then hold on a moment, and I'll show you," said Nanny, slowly rising from her chair and going into her bedroom.

"Mom," Alex said when Nanny had left the room. "How much longer do we have to stay?"

Mom shushed him and said, "Just try to be patient a little longer."

CHAPTER ONE

A few moments later Nanny returned with a basket filled with yarn, a pair of scissors, a crochet hook, and the special kind of facing through which she wove the yarn.

"I've already got the facing cut out for this one." she said. "You start like this with the crochet hook, and you loop the yarn through the little squares on the facing—like this." She proceeded to demonstrate how it was done. "Now," she said, handing the materials to Mom, "you try."

Mom drew the yarn through the slots with the crochet hook. "Oh, I see," she said. The truth was that the mailboxes were not at all hard to make. "Boys," Mom said, "you would enjoy making these."

The boys frowned at each other when Mom and Nanny weren't looking. They had already been examining some of the mailboxes from the bag. In the past, Nanny had always crocheted the current year on both sides of the mailbox so people would know exactly which Christmas she had made them for. On their Christmas tree were mailboxes with dates going back at least twenty years, long before the boys were even born. However, on the boxes that Grant and Alex now were examining something seemed very wrong with the dates. Some of the dates on these mailboxes were way in the past, like 168 B. C. and A. D. 800. Grant, who was holding one that said 4000 B. C., whispered to his mother, "Nanny's done something weird with the dates on the mailboxes."

Mom shushed him, hoping Nanny did not overhear. Fortunately, she didn't, so Mom continued asking Nanny's advice as she made the mailbox.

"You boys must be a little bored," Nanny finally observed. "I have a deck of 'Old Maid' playing cards. Do you boys know how to play Old Maid? It's so much fun!"

The boys nodded, though they were not too thrilled with the prospect of playing a card game meant for girls. What would Nanny come up with next? Would she bring out a box of paper dolls and expect the boys to play with them as well?

Nanny went to her desk, fumbled through it, found the deck of Old Maid cards, and brought them to the boys. "I know you boys would probably much rather play Battle, but I'm afraid my new deck of playing cards might get scratched. Playing Battle is so rough on cards, you know. I'm sure you boys won't mind playing Old Maid, will you?" she asked. The boys politely shook their heads, took the cards from Nanny, and started playing.

Meanwhile, Mom was getting antsy, too. She had kept one eye on the news banner streaming across the bottom of the television screen, hoping that it would soon reveal that the lion had been caught. This, however, did not happen. What did happen was the same thing that always seemed to happen when they visited Nanny. Time did not flow quickly like water from an open faucet. At best time slowly dripped, dripped, dripped. At worst, it seemed to freeze solid like an icicle. Of course, it was not Nanny's fault that time slowed down inside her apartment. No one could blame her for being ill-prepared to entertain children, for her world revolved for the most part around her friends in the retirement village. Still, Mom and the boys knew that Nanny loved them and that she relished every minute she could spend with them. The truth was that she was enjoying herself immensely and was glad that time was frozen. If she could have her way, she would freeze this moment forever. She knew, however, that the lion would eventually be caught and returned to its cage. After this happened, time would again be let loose and would once more begin to flow by quickly. Like a rushing river, it would carry Mom and the boys away from her, and her wonderful moment of family enjoyment would have to give way to distance and loneliness. When that happened, more mailboxes would have to be made, and more letters would have to be written.

"Nanny," Mom said after a period of long silence. "You know what you need to do is learn how to work a computer. If you learned how to use email, you could be in constant conversation with your sisters and with your friends from all over the country."

"One of these days, maybe I'll do just that," said Nanny. "Then again, I just think I'm getting too old to learn new tricks."

"The boys would be glad to show you how, wouldn't you boys?"

They both nodded enthusiastically. They would be willing to do anything to bring Nanny into the modern age.

"Well, we'll see," said Nanny. About that time, Mom noticed on the news that the lion had been located. "Oh, look!" she said. "They've found the lion. They're saying it's just a matter of time before they capture it. That is great news!"

Nanny, however, seemed disappointed. "I guess that means you and the boys will have to be going. I can't tell you how much I've enjoyed this visit."

The boys leapt from the sofa and headed to the door, forgetting the shopping bags filled with mailboxes. Quickly, Mom retrieved them from the table so that Nanny would not have her feelings hurt.

"Just one more thing," Nanny said. "I've been collecting the desserts from my dinners in the freezer for you and the children. Let me get them for you."

"Oh, Nanny, that's okay," Mom told her. "We really don't need any more sweets."

"Nonsense," Nanny scolded. "I'm sure you will enjoy them, and I can't eat them. Doctor's orders, you know." Nanny returned with a bag filled with desserts on paper plates wrapped in tin foil. The truth was that the desserts were usually freezer burned and did not taste very good. This was because they had not been properly wrapped. However, Mom took the bag anyway and told Nanny, "Thank you."

As Mom walked toward the front door, Nanny followed. "We'll be seeing you for lunch tomorrow, then," Mom said cheerfully, "and of course, as usual, on Christmas Eve we'll celebrate your birthday!" She and the boys hugged Nanny and told her goodbye. When Nanny had shut the door, the boys felt a sense of relief, but they also felt a sense of sadness whenever Nanny's door closed. Neither Mom nor the boys could say exactly what it was about that door closing. Maybe they were just feeling the loneliness of the 'Old Folks Home' in general. Whatever it was, they would soon be able to shake it off as they returned to their car and started home.

—Chapter Two—

THE TIME LINE AND THE TIME LION

MOM SOON TURNED onto Robert Morris Boulevard. When the boys caught sight of their favorite home improvement store, they started jumping up and down in the back seat and shouting, "The Store! The Store! Can we stop? Can we stop?"

Grant and Alex always loved going down the Boulevard because this particular store offered 'do-it-yourself' seminars for youngsters. 'Grampy,' the boys' grandfather on their mother's side, always took them to these on Saturday mornings because he wanted his grandsons to learn how to work with their hands so that they could become good handymen when they grew up. The boys had learned how to construct various objects from wood, including a birdhouse, a coat rack, and yes, even a mailbox made of cedar! They loved the wood's fragrance because it always reminded them of their Christmas tree. Over the past month, they had used cedar boards to build a manger scene, and Grampy had used his jigsaw to cut figures from weather-resistant ply-board. Thus far he had produced Mary, Joseph, three wise men, two shepherds, a donkey, a camel, a cow, and three sheep. All they needed now was Baby Jesus, his cradle, the Star of Bethlehem, and a few angels. After Grampy finished each figure, he took time to instruct and supervise the boys on how to paint them.

As Christmas approached, Grant and Alex's excitement increased as they anticipated putting up the manger scene in their front yard.

Though the boys kept begging their Mom to stop at the store, she ignored them and kept driving. When they passed it, they groaned, "Awww!" but Mom seemed not the least bit phased. They hadn't driven much further, however, when they got caught in a traffic jam. About ten parked police cars and a fire truck had lights flashing blue, red, and white. Some policemen, scattered about in a field, stood with guns drawn while others conversed with bystanders and talked on two-way radios.

"What in the world?" Mom declared as she slowed down. Their car crept along at a snail's pace. A policeman directing traffic kept furiously signaling for the drivers to keep it flowing, but curious people couldn't help but slow down to gawk at the scene. When their own car crept past the officer, Mom slowed down a tad more. At first, the boys could not seem to discover what was causing all the commotion. Then suddenly they blurted out, "Look! The lion! The lion!"

Mom, who was trying to keep her eyes on traffic, stole a quick glimpse and said, "Thank goodness they've caught it. There's no telling what might have happened if they hadn't. I hope nobody got attacked."

The lion lay motionless on its side with eyes tightly shut. It became obvious that Animal Control workers wearing white suits had shot the beast with tranquilizer guns. They were now securing a harness around its enormous body. As they crept by slowly in the car, Alex, Grant, and their mother watched as one of the workers attached the harness to a hoist. Then the worker signaled the hoist operator to lift the enormous cat up. The operator set the gears into operation, lifted up the cat, and lowered its limp body into a large cage that was attached to the bed of a white truck.

CHAPTER TWO

"That is so cool!" Grant remarked. At that moment, the driver of the car immediately behind theirs honked for them to speed up, so Mom pushed down on the accelerator, and they were off.

"How did the lion escape?" Alex asked his mother.

"I have no idea," she replied. "Maybe we will find out later when we watch the local news."

They soon turned onto the freeway signaling the last leg of their journey home. Grant then noticed something strange happening to a very large clock in the tower standing in front of their bank. Its hands were running rapidly backwards. Now, they had left Nanny's at about 4:00 in the afternoon, and their trip home usually took about forty-five minutes. The clock on the tower, however, read 10:00, and there was no telling how long it had been behaving strangely. Next, Grant noticed a billboard with a digital clock that alternated between time and temperature. The temperature remained constant, but whenever the time would flash on, the minutes would fly by more quickly than seconds. On this clock the time was speeding forward instead of backwards.

"Mom," he asked, "what's going on with all the clocks?"

"Clocks?" she asked, a bit distracted by the heavy traffic.

"Yeah. The one in the clock tower of our bank and the one on that billboard we just passed."

"I didn't see them," she remarked.

About that time, Alex noticed that digital clock on the dashboard of their car was misbehaving as well. It would run rapidly forward for a while. Then it would reverse itself and run rapidly backwards. "Look!" he exclaimed. "The clock on the dash is acting weird, too!"

Mom glanced at it. "How strange," she said. "Why would the clock in our car do that? I can understand the other clocks. They could be affected by the electrical grid. But our car battery is not on the grid."

When they arrived home and turned into their driveway, they saw Dad collecting the mail from the cedar mailbox Alex and Grant had built with Grampy's help. After Mom pulled up and parked, the boys quickly opened their car doors, jumped out, and ran over to Dad to give him a hug. Dad, who had a small brown-paper-wrapped package in his hand, stooped down to hug and kiss them. Mom followed, and he hugged and kissed her, too.

"We've been to see Nanny," she informed him. "Guess what surprise I have for you?"

"Don't tell me. Let me guess. More mailbox ornaments, and Nanny's latest collection of freezer-burned desserts."

Mom laughed. "You must be psychic."

"How is Nanny?" he asked.

"Health wise, she seems fine, but I think she's lonely."

"We ought to visit her more often," he said. "I'm glad we've invited her for lunch tomorrow."

"Me, too," Mom agreed. "We did actually stay longer than usual, though. Did you hear about the lion on the loose?"

"Yeah, it was on the radio. I was listening coming home from work. They must have just captured it."

"We saw the whole thing!" Alex exclaimed.

"Really? You did?" Dad queried.

Mom continued her account. "They caught it over there on Robert Morris Boulevard close to the do-it-yourself store that Grampy takes the boys to on Saturdays. They had already tranquilized it and were hoisting it into the truck when we passed."

"You should have seen it, Dad!" Grant exclaimed. "It was gigantic!"

"Really," he stated.

"Do you by chance know how it escaped?" Mom asked Dad.

"No, but I can't wait to watch the news to find out. Nothing quite this exciting has happened around here in a long time."

Meanwhile, Alex had been eyeing the package that Dad was holding in his hand and inquired, "Dad, what's that?"

"I don't know yet," he answered. "The package is addressed to our family, but it has no return address. What puzzles me is this stamp. I think the writing is Hebrew."

"Hebrew?" Mom commented. "How unusual. We'll have to open it when we get in the house and see what's inside."

After Mom, Dad, and the boys had gone into the house, Dad turned on the television and sat down on the sofa. The boys joined him.

"Open the package, Dad," Grant said.

"Yeah, Dad, open it," Alex urged.

Dad shouted, "Mother, do you want to see what's in this package?"

"Okay," she shouted from the kitchen. But then they heard her say, "Oh, dear!"

"What's wrong?" Dad asked.

She popped her head around the corner. "The kitchen clock!" she said. "Now it's running backwards, too!"

"What?" Dad said, jumping up and running in to check it out. The boys followed him.

"All the clocks in town are messed up," Grant informed him. "Some are running backward and some are running forward! They're all running really, really fast, too."

Dad pondered. "I wonder how that could be."

Meanwhile, the evening news started coming on television, so they returned to the sofa and plopped down. The story of the lion's escape was first up on the report. "A suspect has been taken into custody," a lady news anchor said. A picture of a man in a long white robe with long white hair and a long white beard flashed on the screen.

"Hey," said Alex. "He looks a little like Grampy, but his hair and beard are a whole lot longer and a whole lot whiter."

"What's that he's carrying?" Alex asked.

Dad shushed them. "Boys, I can't hear a thing."

"The old man, who speaks no English, appears to be a Greek immigrant named Pater Kronos," the commentator continued. "For reasons as yet unknown he was carrying a sickle when he managed to enter a restricted area of the zoo undetected. The theory is that he somehow used his sickle to open the lion's cage and release it."

"Pater Kronos," Dad mumbled to himself. "I think I know what that name means. I took Greek in college, you know, but I've forgotten a lot of my vocabulary."

The news anchor went on. "Once the lion was captured, all the clocks in the city began behaving strangely. They started to run either backwards or forwards very rapidly, while others randomly did both. Now, some people are referring to the lion as the 'time lion', an obvious play on the word 'time line'. The clock problem has led to the suspension of all flights in and out of the city. Trains and subways will not run either until the problem is resolved. Buses everywhere are loaded to the max, and taxis are in short supply. Some fear a worldwide computer network crash is close at hand. Top scientists and technicians are already being recruited to resolve the problem."

Just then, Dad's face lit up. "Father Time!"

"Who?" Grant, Alex, and their mother asked.

"I remembered my Greek vocabulary. Pater Kronos means 'Father Time.'" By now, the news anchor was on to another news story, so Dad pushed the mute button on his remote.

CHAPTER TWO

Mom had been standing behind the sofa watching the news. "This is strange. It seems that, while we were at Nanny's, time had completely stopped. I know that always seems to happen when we visit her, but this time, it was as though time actually did come to a complete standstill. I'm worried."

"I'm sure they'll soon get it figured out," Dad said, trying to reassure her. "After all, only the clocks are messed up. Nothing else seems to be affected."

"All right," Mom said. "Why don't we do something to take our minds off it? The Christmas tree still needs decorating, and of course we have more of Nanny's mailbox ornaments to hang. We need to finish decorating before bedtime, so I'll make us something simple for dinner. I hope you guys don't mind having grilled-cheese sandwiches."

Dad and the boys agreed, but then Dad asked, "Don't you want to see what's in the package first?"

"Oh, the package," she remembered. "Yes, go on and open it."

Dad started tearing off the brown wrapping. "What's this?" he asked. Under the paper was a red velvet box covered with golden brocade.

"A treasure chest!" Alex shouted. "Open it, please, Dad!"

Dad slowly lifted the lid of a small jewelry box, revealing a golden angel nestled inside an indention made in the red velvet. He carefully removed it and held it up.

"Why, it's beautiful!" Mom remarked. "Surely the Post Office has made some mistake in their delivery. Who could have sent it?"

Meanwhile, Dad started opening a letter he'd found stuck inside the box lid.

"This could explain it," he said. He read quietly to himself at first, but Mom soon prodded him. "What does it say?"

"Listen to this. It says, 'Warning! You have been chosen! Do not hang this ornament until your Christmas tree is fully decorated!'"

"Things just seem to be getting stranger and stranger," Mom commented. "Do you think it's some kind of prank?"

Dad continued reading silently. "I don't think so," he said. "Listen to what this says. 'Gabriel's Magic Ornament, Ornament of Miracles. Made by St. Nicholas, Bishop of Myra from gold brought to the infant Christ by Balthazar the Magi. This ornament may be used only once. Then it will return home to the Church of the Nativity in Bethlehem.'"

"Why would they pick us to send it to?" Mom asked. "Did you order it over the internet?"

"No," said Dad. He again looked at the postmark. "And it couldn't very well be a hoax. The stamp is definitely from Israel."

Dad turned the letter over. "Oh, look. Here's more. 'Whoever places this ornament on the Christmas tree will have an enlightening Christmas adventure.'"

When the boys heard the word 'adventure,' they perked up. "Dad!" Grant exclaimed. "We want to hang that ornament!"

"Yes!" Alex chimed in. "Please, let us do it!"

"First we have to finish decorating the tree!" Grant reminded him. "Mom, you've got to hurry up and make the grilled-cheese sandwiches. We have to get those ornaments on the tree."

"Yes, Mom," Alex said. "You've got to hurry."

The boys each grabbed one of Mom's arms and guided her toward the kitchen.

"Okay! Okay!" she said. "Let go, or I won't have hands left to cook with."

The boys rushed back to their living room and started unpacking the mailbox ornaments from the Nanny bags.

"Dad, go up to the attic and get the Christmas decorations. Please! Please! Please!" Grant begged.

"I guess I could do that while your mom makes the grilled-cheese," he replied. "But promise me you both will eat your sandwiches and help me and Mom clean up."

"Yes! We promise!" the boys shouted, jumping up and down. Then they ran into the kitchen to check Mom's progress.

"Mom, we have to eat on paper plates tonight," Grant stated. He knew washing dishes would waste precious time.

"Good idea," she agreed. "I've almost got the sandwiches ready."

"Yea! Yea!" the boys shouted, and they hurried back to check on Dad.

In a short while, Dad returned from the attic with a large box of ornaments, and Mom brought their grilled-cheese sandwiches out to the table. Soon, the boys were wolfing them down.

"You boys might as well take your time," Mom told them. "You will have to wait until Dad and I have finished eating before any decorating begins."

The boys frowned. This was worse than having to wait to leave Nanny's.

—Chapter Three—

"TASTEFUL" AND "SCIENTIFIC" DECORATING

GRANT AND ALEX HAD already cleared off as much of the table as they could. Now they waited impatiently for Mom and Dad to finish their sandwiches. As soon as Mom was through eating, Grant snatched her paper plate and napkin, ran to the kitchen, and threw them in the trash bin. He hurried back, took her knife, fork, and spoon, and rushed away again. Mom and Dad grinned as they heard water running and silverware clinking. Alex, on the Dad front, stood poised to deprive him of his paper plate the minute he lifted the last crust of bread from it. The moment he did, Alex grabbed his plate and napkin, and when Grant appeared, away went Dad's utensils, too!

"Really, boys!" Dad hollered. "You don't have to be in such a rush! Can't a person eat in peace?"

Mom shook her head. "Wouldn't it be wonderful if we got this kind of service all year round?"

"Uh huh," Dad replied. "I wish I could thank whoever sent that golden angel."

The boys returned. "Now can we?" Grant begged.

"Very well," Dad agreed. "But let's try to get things organized, first. Do we have a decorating plan?"

"First, the lights, right?" asked Alex.

"Right, but let's make sure they're not tangled and are all working properly."

"Can I plug them in?" he asked.

"Sure," said Dad, rising from the table. Then he said, "Grant, unroll the lights. But be careful not to break any. I'll start checking to see if any bulbs are burned out or broken."

Together, they went to work, plugging in strings of lights, unwinding them carefully across the floor, checking each bulb to see if any needed replacing. On one string that they tried, only half the lights burned while the other half were dark.

"There always seems to be one like this," Dad commented. "I guess we'll have to throw it away."

"Don't do that," Grant countered. "A fuse may just be burned in two." Grant unplugged the lights, took the plug to Dad, and pointed to a little plastic tab. "See, you just take this off, like this." He lifted the tab from the plug and removed a tiny fuse. "Just as I thought," Grant said. "The fuse is blown."

Dad's mouth was hanging open. "How did you learn to do that?"

"From Grampy," Alex told him.

"Grampy," mumbled Dad. "I should have figured."

"You have to find out the problem by troubleshooting," Grant explained.

"Yeah, troubleshooting," Alex chimed in. "If one bulb is burned out, then you only need to replace the one, but if the whole string or half a string isn't working, it's best to check the fuses."

"Well," said Dad. "I guess I learned something. I'm glad your grandfather is teaching you boys something about electricity. Just remember that it's dangerous."

"We know that," Grant said.

"I don't want you playing around with it unsupervised. Is that clear?"

Grant and Alex both nodded.

"Do we have a fuse, Dad?" Grant asked, handing his father the burned out one.

Dad examined it. "Oh, that's what those are. There are several in the little plastic bags with the replacement bulbs. Let me see if I can find one."

Dad rummaged through the box. "Okay. Here it is." He tore open the bag. "Grant, do you want to put it in?"

"Sure," he answered. After Dad handed it to him, Grant lodged it into the receptacle and replaced the tab.

"Okay, Alex," Dad said, "plug them back in." Suddenly, a bright trail lit up across the living room floor, and the boys shouted, "Yea!"

"What do you know?" Dad remarked. "They work!"

At that very moment, Mom, who was in the kitchen, cried, "Well, how do you like that?"

"What?" Dad questioned.

"The clock is working again, too!"

Dad and the boys jumped up and ran into the kitchen. Sure enough, the hands on the clock were no longer zooming ahead at breakneck speed but seemed, for the time being at least, to be running normally.

"What a strange coincidence," said Dad. "The minute Grant and Alex repaired those lights and got them plugged in, the clock started working the way it's supposed to."

Dad and the boys returned to the living room and started stringing the tree with lights. Once the lights were in place, they called out, "Mom, we're ready to put the ornaments on now!"

"Okay!" she said. "I'm coming!"

Mom soon joined them in the living room and began sorting through the ornaments.

"Now," she said, "I know you boys are good at wiring and scientific stuff like that, but when you put the ornaments on the Christmas tree, you need to do so tastefully. This means that you should vary the colors of ornaments and space them properly so that they're not all crowded together. We've got more of Nanny's mailboxes, too, of course, so I guess we should get those on the tree first. After that we'll put on the regular ornaments." Then she added, "That is, if there are any places left for them."

Mom left the room for a moment to fetch the bags with the mailboxes. When she returned, she sat them beside the cardboard box containing the other mailboxes they'd gotten from Nanny over the years.

"Gosh, there are a lot of these," she remarked. "But they will look pretty on the tree, I'm sure." She handed a couple to Grant and Alex. "Okay, be careful to get the yarn hanging-loop completely around the branch so they don't fall off," she instructed. "And try to spread out the green and red ones as evenly as possible."

Grant remembered from earlier that day that he'd asked his mother why the mailboxes had unusual dates on them. Mom had not answered, so now he asked her again, "Mom, why did Nanny put these weird dates on the mailboxes?"

"I haven't a clue," Mom replied.

"Look!" exclaimed Alex, who had been rummaging through the mailboxes in the storage container. "These have weird dates, too!"

Mom grabbed a mailbox from Alex. "Why, that's impossible! Last year the dates on those mailboxes were normal!"

Dad began examining each mailbox carefully. The boys were right! The dates on all the mailboxes had changed!

CHAPTER THREE

"Is this some kind of practical joke?" Dad asked. "Who could have done this?" He glared at the boys and squinted.

"Don't blame us," the boys said, reading their father's face.

"Let me check these out," Dad said. He removed the red and green mailboxes one at a time. After he had spent a little less than a minute comparing them, he said, "There is a pattern here. All the red mailboxes have dates from the past, but all the green ones have future dates!"

Mom checked them, too. "You're right. Why do you suppose that is?"

"I have no idea!" Dad said with a puzzled look.

"Dad! Look!" Alex shouted, holding a mailbox up to Dad's face.

Right before their eyes, the date rapidly changed, just like the schedule flip boards do in a train station!

Dad felt of the mailbox's side. "This is impossible! The date is woven into it with yarn! It just can't do this!" He felt the date. It still felt like yarn. A perplexed look crept over his face, and he mumbled to himself, "I'll be a monkey's uncle."

"First the clocks, and now the mailboxes!" Grant blurted.

"What?" Mom and Dad asked.

"It all started happening when that lion escaped from the zoo," Grant reminded them. "Ever since then, time everywhere has been going bonkers."

"I would have guessed it to be all just a big coincidence," Dad ventured. "That is, if I hadn't seen the mailbox dates change before my very eyes!"

"Do you think we should call those scientists they mentioned on the news?" asked Mom.

"Too late in the evening for that," said Dad. "Maybe first thing tomorrow I can make a report. For now, I don't think it would do any harm for us to go ahead and decorate the tree."

Alex picked up one of the mailboxes. As he did, its date started spinning rapidly into the past. But the second Alex secured it to one of the tree branches, the spinning date abruptly halted at the year A. D. 1949.

"It stopped!" he exclaimed.

Grant, Mom, and Dad looked at it closely.

"You're right," said Dad. "I wonder if the others will do that, too."

Grant picked up one of the green ornaments. When he did, the dates started spinning forward wildly into the future. But when he secured it on a branch, it immediately stopped at A. D. 2525. "Weird," he remarked, his eyes wide with amazement.

"Let me try one," Dad said. As he picked up one of the red mailboxes, the date on it, too, began quickly to spin backward. Dad observed it for a short time, and then placed it on a branch. "Okay," he said. "This one now reads A. D. 200."

"The spinning of those dates reminds me of that game show, *Wheel of Fortune*," Mom stated. "That's the show Nanny watches every afternoon, remember? Do you suppose she was making these mailboxes while watching that show?"

Dad and the boys looked at her. Their faces revealed that they, too, believed Mom's suggestion lay within the realm of possibility.

As Mom, Dad, and the boys placed each mailbox on the tree, they continued to see the pattern they had seen before repeated. Though all the dates spun, the red mailboxes always stopped at dates in the past, while the green ones always stopped at dates in the future.

Then Alex asked, "I wonder, Dad. Why do the green ones go forward and the red ones go backward?"

"My guess would be that they are operating kind of like green and red traffic lights," he ventured. "Since 'red' means 'stop', the red mailboxes must stop at dates in the past—kind of like cars that have to stop at a red light. And, since 'green' means 'go', the green ones must go forward to dates in the future—sort of like a car going through a green light."

"What would happen if someone ran a red light?" Grant asked.

"Hmmm," Dad said, stroking his chin. "I suppose the Christmas tree police would have to pull them over and give them a ticket!"

The boys and their mom snickered.

"I still don't understand why the dates spin and only stop when we place the mailboxes on the tree," Grant said. "Why would they do that?"

"Maybe it has something to do with the lights," Dad replied. "Remember how the clock in the kitchen got straightened out when you fixed the lights?"

"Oh, yeah," Grant said. "But that's not very logical, Dad. Grampy would tell you that there has to be a logical reason. It can't just be magic."

"What?" Mom said. "No magic? It is Christmas, remember?"

"Oh, Mom," Alex remarked. "We're getting too old to believe that magic stuff."

"Yeah," Grant added. "There has to be some logical way of explaining it. I wish Grampy were here right now. He'd be able to figure it out. He'd explain it to us."

Dad held up *Gabriel's Magic Ornament*. "What about this? If you don't believe in that 'magic stuff' why are you so anxious to hang this ornament?"

The boys couldn't give an answer. They just stood there with their mouths hanging open.

"Okay, boys," said Mom. "We'll be sure to ask Grampy for the scientific explanation when we see him. I'm sure Nanny will give us a scientific explanation, too, for why her yarn makes the dates on her mailboxes spin like that wheel on *Wheel of Fortune.*"

* * *

As the boys hung the mailbox ornaments on the tree, their mother directed them. "I think you need one there," she would say. "And another one there," she would add. Soon, Grant and Alex had finished hanging all the mailboxes.

"Okay," Mom said. "Let's stand back and see how the tree looks thus far."

They took several steps back and surveyed the results. Mom, with her hands on her hips, then said, "I suppose it doesn't look too bad. I think we've got them spaced evenly enough. It just looks like a Christmas tree you might see inside a Post Office. I suppose we need now to balance it out with the other ornaments."

Mom started handing Grant and Alex the fragile glass ornaments, and they began hanging them on the tree between the mailboxes. In addition to the glass ornaments, they hung other homemade ornaments Nanny had made in the past. One was an airplane made with yarn in the same way as with the mailboxes. Embroidered on its sides were the words 'The Spirit of Christmas. Mom had also bought a special set of ornaments that featured characters from Charles Dickens's, *A Christmas Carol.* From the box the set came in, Mom removed Ebenezer Scrooge, Bob Cratchit, Tiny Tim, and Jacob Morley from their little molded indentions.

"Oh, look," she said, removing the Spirits of Christmas Past, Present, and Future from their indentions in the ornament box, "these will go great on the tree, especially with all the strange dates on those mailboxes."

From one of the containers, Mom then carefully removed an ornament that a dear friend had made her many years ago. "I love this one!" she exclaimed. "It's Old Man Winter!" She stroked its white beard of angel hair. "I can't believe I've had him so many years!"

"He sort of looks like Grampy," Alex commented.

"You know, he sort of does," Mom agreed. She carefully placed him on the tree.

"Are we ready to put the star on the top of the tree?" Dad asked Mom.

"Sure, go ahead," she told him, as she rummaged through a box containing some of their older ornaments. "I don't know about these," she said. "They're in pretty bad shape."

"There," said Dad, placing the top star. "How does that look?"

"Beautiful," Mom said.

"Let me see those ornaments," Grant said to his mother. He rummaged through the container and pulled out a lion. "What do you know!" he said. "The Lion King!" Alex ran over to see.

"Oh, dear," said Mom. "Is it that old thing I got at McDonald's years ago?" She took it from Grant. "Why, it's the very one. This belongs in the garbage can for sure!"

"No!" Grant countered. "He's one of my favorites."

"Mine, too," Alex added.

"You boys can't be serious," Mom said.

"Yes, we are," Grant assured her. "Please, please, let me hang him," he begged.

"Okay, if you insist," she agreed. "But next year I think it will be time for him to retire to the garbage can."

Grant hung the lion on the tree.

"I just thought of something scary," said Dad, watching him. "You don't suppose that lion will jinx our Christmas tree. Remember what happened to all the clocks when the lion escaped from the zoo earlier today?"

"That's not logical, Dad," Grant said. "I think you're being superstitious."

"Really," Dad returned. "Well don't say I didn't warn you. After all, you two are the ones planning on placing *Gabriel's Magic Ornament* on the Christmas tree—unless, of course, you've changed your minds and believe that's superstitious, too. Earlier, you both seemed pretty eager to hang that ornament."

"Just because it seems like magic, that doesn't mean that science can't explain it," Grant told him with an air of confidence.

"Is that so?" Dad asked. "Well, if you do get sucked in, I hope you don't have to deal with that lion."

"If the lion comes after us, we'll just escape into one of the mail-boxes," Alex assured him.

"I'm not certain that will help," Mom said. "He'll just wait until you come out. Then he'll eat you. Are you sure you still want that lion ornament on the tree?"

The boys sheepishly nodded their heads.

"Okay, don't say we didn't warn you," Dad said.

"The tree is decorated," said Mom. "Let's stand back and see how it looks."

The boys had something else in mind. "It looks fine," Grant said. "Can we hang *Gabriel's Magic Ornament* now?"

"Yeah!" Alex echoed. "Let us hang it!"

"Really, you boys are so impatient," Mom told them. "I will let you hang it, but first you've got to help me clear away these boxes."

"Oh, Mom!" they cried. They now had awful frowns on their face.

"You know, Mom," Dad said. "In the old days people waited until Christmas Eve to decorate their trees. Wouldn't it be nice if we let the boys wait until Christmas Eve when the whole family is here to watch them put *Gabriel's Magic Ornament* on the tree?"

"No, Dad!" they yelled. "We'll help Mom clean up. Just please, please let us hang the ornament when we're finished, okay?"

"We'll see," Dad replied. "I want you boys to try to learn to be patient."

—Chapter Four—

THE RIDDLE OF THE SPHINX

WHILE THE BOYS HELPED their Dad put away the storage containers in the attic, Mom vacuumed up bits of glitter, pine needles, and artificial snow from the floor. Soon, the boys returned with their father, and Mom ducked out for a moment to store the vacuum cleaner.

"Now can we? Please! Please!" they begged.

The moment Mom returned, Dad removed *Gabriel's Magic Ornament* from its little chest and held it up.

"Are you going to let them hang it after all?" Mom inquired.

From the expression on her face, Dad detected she had no objections. "Okay, guys," he said. "We'll let you try this thing out to see if it really works. But don't be disappointed if turns out to be a dud."

"Let me hang it, okay?" Grant demanded.

Dad noticed that Grant's request caused Alex to stick out his lower lip. "Now that wouldn't be fair to your brother, would it?" he asked. "There's no good reason why you can't both hang it. Each of you can hold one of its wings. Alex, you grab that branch while Grant loops the hanger around it."

"Yippee!" Grant shouted, taking the ornament from Dad and running over to the tree. "Come on, Alex! Let's do it!"

The boys each held on to one of the angel's wings as they hung it on the tree. In a split second, a wild and sudden spiral of golden light unwound from the angel's heart like a clock spring set loose.

Startled and speechless, the boys jumped back, rubbing their eyes in disbelief.

They watched as the spring expanded into a golden spiral sliding board.

"Whoa!" Grant shouted.

The sliding board, which now stuck out from the tree about four feet, continued on into the tree through a circular portal that glistened like silver glitter inside a snow globe that someone had just vigorously shaken. Beyond the portal, the sliding board spiraled into the distance as far as they could see.

"Okay," Grant said with a note of hesitation. "I guess we should slide on in. Why don't you go first, Alex?"

"Me? I'm scared there won't be anybody down there to catch me. You're older. Why don't you go first?"

"Don't be such a chicken," Grant scolded. "Go on. I know you can do it!"

Alex turned to his mother. "Mom, make Grant stop!"

But Mom said nothing. She and Dad were as still as statues.

"What's wrong with them?" Alex asked.

"It's probably the magic ornament," Grant replied. "We'd better not waste any time going in. That portal could close any minute."

Alex stood paralyzed, like a little child faced with jumping into the deep end of a swimming pool for the first time.

"I'll tell you what," Grant said, taking his brother's hand. "Remember how we used to go down the sliding board with you in front and me behind? Let's try it that way."

"Okay," Alex agreed.

"Climb on up, then. I'll be right behind you."

Alex frowned. "Promise you won't push me!"

"Cross my heart, I won't," Grant swore. Alex grabbed his brother's hand to be sure he didn't have his fingers crossed. When he saw that Grant was telling the truth, he climbed on to the edge of the board with Grant following right behind. After Alex sat down on it, Grant positioned himself behind his brother. They rocked, scooting forward a little at a time, until they were ready to dabble their feet in the mysterious portal. However, if they had thought they could jerk their feet out as people often do when a pool of water is too cold, they had another think coming. The second their feet touched the portal, they were sucked in at lightning speed.

Alex, in a panic, was now screaming and whimpering in quick succession.

"Don't be afraid!" Grant shouted. "I've got you! Alex, do you know what we're in?"

"Whatever it is, I don't like it!" he yelled. He was giggling one second and sobbing the next.

"A wormhole! Remember your sci-fi? Who knows, we might be traveling to a distant planet!"

"It's sure a lot faster than that roller coaster we rode at the beach last summer!" Alex hollered. "I want off now! Where does it end?"

"I don't see where it ends yet!" Grant replied. "Just hold on! Maybe we'll be there soon!"

The boys closed their eyes. Their stomachs had butterflies. After a few minutes, they began to slow down. Before they knew it, they came to the end of the sliding board and landed with an enormous splash in what seemed to be a municipal swimming pool. The pool and its walkways, however, were made not of concrete but of a soft, velvet-like material resembling Irish moss. The fence surrounding the pool looked at first like chain-link, but it was not made of galvanized metal. Instead it was composed of a kind of soft golden net.

When Grant and Alex surfaced, they wiped the water from their eyes. "Great!" Grant complained. "Our clothes are all wet!"

"Where are we?" Alex asked.

"I don't know," his brother answered. "But at least the water's not too cold. The weather here seems pretty warm in fact. I'm just glad we didn't fall through a hole in the ice."

Other people waded and swam in the pool, but they did not resemble normal human beings. They had metallic-looking skin. Despite this, a few were lying about on the green-velvet sides of the pool, or lounging in red- and gold-velvet lounge chairs as though they were trying to get a sun tan.

"Is it summer time?" Alex asked. "How can that be if it's so close to Christmas?

"I don't know," Grant replied. "It's not at all what I expected would be inside our Christmas tree."

Suddenly, they heard a whistle blow. They looked up. The lifeguard was motioning to them.

"Uh, oh, I think we're in big trouble," Grant said. "I don't think we're supposed to be in the pool with our street clothes on."

With guilty looks on their faces, they paddled over to the side of the pool. The lifeguard stood frowning down at them. He had a golden tan, and he wore white shorts down to his knees and a white sleeveless shirt. His face was round with a white moustache and long beard, and his white hair, which cascaded down the sides of his face, fell gently upon his shoulders.

"Okay, smart guys," he said, pointing to the pool rules. "What part of 'no street clothes allowed in the pool' do you not understand? Out, this minute!"

The boys climbed the ladder, which, strangely enough, was also soft and padded. "Sorry," they apologized.

"You'll have to sit on the benches for time out until your clothes are dry," he told them. "Then you will do like all the normal swimmers and change into your swimsuits."

"But we didn't bring our swimsuits," Alex stated.

"So, you think you can just come in here and swim in your clothes whenever you feel like it, is that the idea?" the lifeguard lectured. "For that stupid little act, you're barred from the pool for a week!"

"But we didn't want to swim, anyway," Grant told him.

"I can see you're a little smart aleck," the lifeguard stated. "Then why were you in the pool if you didn't want to swim? Explain!"

"To tell the truth, sir," Grant answered, "we slid in from another world."

"That does it!" the lifeguard growled, grabbing them by the backs of their collars. "You're out of here!" The lifeguard took them to the gate, gave them a gentle shove, and shut the gate with the words, "Don't bother to come back until you adjust your attitudes!"

The boys felt as though they had been exiled from paradise until they looked around them and saw shining green meadows covered with luminous flowers and bordered with trees ripe with glowing fruit. The shining flowers and fruit, which were every color of the rainbow, actually glowed with a kind of phosphorescent light. There was no sun in this world that they could see, but instead something looking like the Aurora Borealis spread a brilliant curtain of green, gold, and red light across the whole sky, reflecting onto the entire land beneath it.

The moment the lifeguard closed the gate, a terrible commotion ensued! Grant and Alex turned to see the metallic-looking people jumping out of the pool and running in every direction. Some slipped and fell because they were running with wet feet. Fortunately, most of them bounced gently when they hit the soft moss and remained uninjured, but a few hit too hard and cracked. Others were climbing the golden-net chain-link fence to escape. Then the boys caught a glimpse of what had caused the commotion. An enormous creature, that at first sight resembled a lion, lifted its head out of the water, and roared fiercely. Then unexpectedly, wings, looking like those of an eagle, peeled away from its side and started flapping, sending a shower of water everywhere. The boys had never seen or heard anything like it. Its face appeared human-like one minute and cat-like the next. Indeed, its appearance changed back and forth from one to the other, depending on the particular angle from which the boys viewed it. It reminded them of those wiggle pictures they had often discovered rummaging through their Cracker Jack boxes. If the wiggle picture was slanted one way, it would reveal one image, but if slanted the other way, it would reveal another entirely different image. The creature's roar cut through the air like a peal of thunder on a crisp winter day. Its golden fleece was so brilliant, they had to shield their eyes, and its teeth, like ivory swords, were so white they twinkled when the light hit them in just the right way. Its eyes, too, reflected light like the eyes of a cat on the prowl at night. The entire pool, which mirrored the great creature's golden coat, seemed to turn into brilliant golden liquid fire as it escaped.

Grant's and Alex's eyes widened, and Grant uttered in a hushed way, "Does that look like the Lion King to you?"

"Yes, when you look at it a certain way," said Alex. "Mom and Dad tried to warn us." Then he added with a trembling voice. "We should have listened."

"Too late now," Grant said.

The creature roared again. Like an icepick made out of sound, the roar caused some of the metallic creatures to break into pieces just like stem crystal-ware shatters when a soprano opera singer hits a high-pitched note. The lion-looking creature bounded out of the pool, flew around in a circle, and immediately started eating the pieces of the metallic-looking people his voice had shattered.

The boys together let out an "oooo" and cringed as they heard the glass fragments, like pieces of peanut brittle, being ground up by the creature's teeth.

Meanwhile, the lifeguard, who by now had managed to hurdle the fence, screamed at the boys. "The Sphinx is loose! Run if you value your life!"

Sphinx? Wasn't that some monument out of ancient Egypt? The boys wasted no time voicing their questions but sprinted as fast as their legs would carry them. The lifeguard followed close behind. Alex kept turning his head to see how near the creature was to them.

"Don't look back!" Grant shouted. "You'll lose speed!"

"It just flew over the fence!" Alex yelled, almost whimpering at the same time.

"Then you'd better run faster!" shouted the lifeguard. "He is still hungry!"

Panting, Grant managed to ask, "How many people will he eat before he's not hungry anymore?"

"There's no telling!" the lifeguard returned. "Only the answer to his riddle can stop him!"

"Riddle? *What riddle*?" Grant asked. He now felt stitches in his right side from all the running, and he was pressing it hard with his right hand to ease the pain.

"The riddle of the Sphinx, of course!" he shot back. "Don't you know anything?"

"What's the answer to it?" Alex asked, huffing and puffing.

"That can only be given to those who have been initiated. Why don't you know that?"

"Do you know the answer?" Grant asked.

"Yes."

"Then why can't *you* use it to stop him?"

"It doesn't work that way, boy!" the lifeguard answered impatiently. "Who was your teacher anyway? Didn't you learn that each person has to give the Sphinx the answer it requires? No one else can do it for you! Even giving it the proper words will do no good. The Sphinx will know if you try to fake it. Giving him the answer without understanding what it means will only make him eat you that much faster. How come you're so ignorant?"

Grant and Alex shot each other panicked glances.

"Quick!" exclaimed the lifeguard. "Our only hope now is to find shelter in one of the mailboxes! They are the only places where it's safe!"

"Look!" Alex shouted. "There's a green one not too far ahead!"

"I just hope you can figure out the combination and get it open in time," said the lifeguard.

"Combination? Don't you know it?" Grant asked, panting and fearful. "Why would anyone in his right mind put a combination lock on a mailbox anyway?"

"To keep the Orna folk out, of course," the lifeguard answered.

"Who?" Alex asked.

"The Orna folk," he repeated. "The people with metallic skin that you saw at the swimming pool. Do you boys have amnesia? Or did you just arrive from another planet?"

"I tried to tell you that we slid in from another planet, but you wouldn't believe us." Grant replied.

The lifeguard slapped himself on the forehead. "Of course!" he said. "That explains a lot!"

"Explains *what*?" asked Grant.

They now were very close to the mailbox.

"I'll tell you when you're safe inside," he answered.

"Look, Grant!" Alex shouted. "It has the date A. D. 2525 on it!"

"How are you boys at picking locks?" the lifeguard asked.

"I wish Grampy were here," Alex said. "He'd know exactly how to open it."

"There's not much time now!" yelled the lifeguard. "The Sphinx is circling overhead!"

When they looked up, they saw it, zeroing in on them. Like a brilliant lantern sailing through the sky, it abolished darkness wherever it flew. Then it landed and immediately bounded toward them like a living sunburst, its golden fleece radiating light across the landscape. Rushing toward them, it showed no sign of giving up its pursuit.

When they reached the mailbox door, Grant said, "Let me give the combination a try." Fortunately, Grampy had taught him a thing or two about listening to the tumblers click, and the lock did not seem terribly complicated. On the first try, however, Grant failed to open it.

"Hurry, Grant!" Alex fretted. "The Sphinx is almost here!" Indeed, the light shining from it was now reaching them.

"Time to pray," the lifeguard moaned.

Grant kept trying to open the combination. On the second try, he failed again.

"Grant! Hurry up!"

"I'm hurrying! I'm hurrying!" he returned.

The Sphinx, now only thirty feet away, was fast approaching. Just then, there was a click, the lock released, and the door to the mailbox sprang open. Grant, Alex, and the lifeguard quickly ducked inside, slamming the door behind them. The next thing they heard was a loud thud. It was the sound of the Sphinx's head crashing into the mailbox door.

"Wow, that was close," Grant said, wiping the sweat from his forehead.

"What was the combination?" the lifeguard asked him.

"5252," he replied.

"Okay, that's 2525 backwards. 2525 is the date on the mailbox. Try to remember that for the other mailboxes. Maybe they will be the same."

Alex fought to hold back tears. "I hope that stupid Sphinx knocked himself out!"

"Are you okay, boy?" the lifeguard asked him.

Alex nodded, though he was quite shaken up from such a close call.

Green wooden benches ran along each side of the mailbox. Clearly, this was not just any mailbox; it was built to double as some kind of a storm shelter as well. "Sit on those benches there and rest," the lifeguard said, so the boys sat on a bench on one side, while the lifeguard sat across from them on the other.

"I'm sorry I was so rough on you boys," the lifeguard apologized. "I didn't believe you at first when you told me you were from another world. You have to admit it sounds like a pretty lame excuse for jumping in a pool with your regular clothes on. But now I remember that I was supposed to meet you. I had just forgotten it was today."

"You mean you were expecting us?" Grant asked.

"Yes, I was told to expect a GMO. Stupid me!"

"A what?" asked Alex.

"A GMO. The initials stand for *Gabriel's Magic Ornament*. It's the way that we Time Guardians refer to travelers through the wormhole." The lifeguard could see from the boys' faces that they didn't quite know how to take him.

"Okay," he said. "I may look like an ordinary lifeguard, but it's just a disguise. I am really a Time Guardian. My name is Pater Kronos. But you can just call me Kronos if you wish."

"I remember you!" Alex exclaimed. "You were the man we saw on TV—the man who let the lion out of the zoo."

"I beg your pardon?" Pater Kronos questioned.

"He probably wouldn't know about that," Grant told Alex. "That was in our world, remember?"

"Oh, yeah," he replied, hanging his head.

"Okay," said Grant. "Can you tell us where we are?"

"Sure," said Kronos. "That is, after all, why I was sent to meet you. We call this Christmas Tree World you have entered 'Arboria'. There are a few very important things you should know about it. First, you need to know that it's the domain of one whom we call Tree King. He is not only the supreme Time Guardian. He is also the Time Lord because he is one who invented time. Have you boys ever played with Silly Putty?"

They nodded.

"Well, because Tree King invented time, he can play with it like you play with Silly Putty. He can stretch it. He can roll it up in a ball. He can bounce it against a wall. He can even use it to record events of the past just like you use Silly Putty to make imprints of cartoons in the comics section of your Sunday morning newspaper. Have you done these sorts of things with Silly Putty before?"

41

"Sure," Grant said. "Dad showed us how to copy newspaper comics like that. It was pretty cool, but after a while the Silly Putty turned gray."

"Well," Kronos continued. "Tree King dwells inside the Star at Tree Top. He is the one who made Arboria, and all dwellers of the Tree World, including myself."

"Then why does he allow that horrible Sphinx to be on the loose?" Alex asked.

"That's a good question," replied Kronos. "First of all, you should know that the Sphinx at this time of year looks very much like a lion, but he is no ordinary lion since he sometimes has a human face and can fly like an eagle. He is, in fact, one of the guardians of the throne of Tree King. Now, you should also know that, from Tree King's perspective, the Sphinx is like a big old pussy cat. Tree King has him completely tamed, and he loves to stroke his mane just to hear him purr. Though I find it hard to believe, I hear tell that the big cat's roar sounds more like a meow when he is in Tree King's presence."

"What's he doing down here, then?" Alex asked. "Did Tree King let him loose by mistake?"

"No. He is here on a mission. Summertime now has come to Arboria. It is the season when the Sphinx does most of his work, but there is something else you need to know. Summertime here is not like it is in your world where it only lasts for three months. Here summer can last a thousand years. During summer, the fruit growing on the trees ripens. When fruit is ripe, it must be picked and either eaten or preserved. Otherwise it will rot. Do you remember the folks with metallic-looking skin that you saw at the pool?"

They nodded.

"Those are Orna folk. In your world you know them as the ornaments on your Christmas tree, but here the Orna folk are something like fruit on a tree. Unlike regular fruit, however, it takes more than just three months for them to ripen. It usually takes many years. Still, they are only allowed a certain length of time to grow and ripen on the branches of our Tree World before they are either picked or fall off."

"Then why is the Sphinx after us?" Alex asked. "Does he think we are Ornas?"

"Maybe he does and maybe he doesn't," Kronos replied. "Or maybe he is just curious. Most cats are curious, and human boys like you would certainly be a curiosity to him. But really, we have no way of knowing whether he would pose his riddle to you or not. If he did pose his riddle, and you were unable to answer it, he could very well eat you. I would rather you be safe than sorry. One more thing, if he just so happens to wear his human face so that he doesn't look so much like a cat, don't let that fool you. He is still just as much a lion."

"Does he pose his riddle to every Orna folk he finds?" Grant asked.

"That's a very good question," said Kronos, "and the answer is 'no'. Sometimes when he poses his riddle to an Orna and it cannot answer, he simply walks away. At other times, when they cannot answer he devours them on the spot. The point is that when the Sphinx comes for you, you must be ready to face it and live with the consequences. Ornas who are filled with treasure have nothing to fear if the Sphinx devours them. For them, the Sphinx is but a gateway to the world of Tree King. Hollow and rotten Ornas, however, have a great deal to fear from an encounter with the Sphinx."

"Why is that?" Grant asked.

"When Ornas are born, they all start out hollow on the inside. Some over time become filled with the joy, light, and love of Tree King. When this happens, they become much more beautiful on the inside than on the outside. If you see how beautiful they appear to be on the outside with their glittering skin of so many colors, you would think that none of them could possibly be more beautiful on the inside. That, however, is not true. Some of them have treasures inside them that by comparison make their outside appearance look like ugly clay jars. When these Orna folk crack, the treasure inside them is carried by an invisible Eagle into the Star and into the presence of Tree King himself. At least the Eagle is invisible to the Orna folk right now. When autumn comes to Arboria, then the Ornas will be able to see him and wonderful things will be revealed."

"Do the Ornas get cracked open because they don't know the riddle's answer?" Alex asked.

"Sometimes, but not always," Kronos replied. "Sometimes they just die of natural causes. These are like the ripe fruit that drops to the ground and is gathered before it decays. Others are like fruit picked directly off the trees, and these are the ones the Sphinx decides to pose his riddle to. If the Ornas are hollow, then they are not fully ripe, and those that choose to remain hollow finally turn rotten and evil. These have the most to lose if the Sphinx poses his riddle because the hollow and rotten ones never know the answer."

"What happens to them then?" Grant asked.

"When they are devoured, nothing of beauty remains but only the hollowness continues. That hollowness joins with the vast Void of the Nothing at Tree Bottom, the void from which no one ever has or ever shall return. This Void is as black as coal, and it is possible for it to catch fire. If that happens, then it will start to look like molten lava."

"So the hollow ones don't have any treasure inside at all?" Alex inquired.

"No," Kronos replied. "And most of the hollow ones are already rotten on the inside. Those that are rotten become evil creatures that hate Tree King and try their best to get rid of Christmas."

"What about those poor Orna folk the Sphinx ate at the pool?" Grant asked. "We didn't see any treasure fall out of them when they broke. Does that mean they were hollow?"

"Not necessarily," Kronos replied. "The treasure, like the Eagle who carries it into the presence of Tree King, remains invisible to most eyes in Arboria until autumn arrives. Then the treasure is revealed. Tree King, however, makes it visible inside the Star—of that you can be sure!"

"I would love to see that treasure," said Alex. "Will we be able to go inside the Star where Tree King Lives and see it?"

"That, of course, is up to Tree King," replied Kronos. "Some children have been allowed in before. I cannot say whether you will be allowed to enter or not. Tree King will have to be the one who decides."

"What is that thing at Tree Bottom called again?" Alex asked.

"Thing?" Kronos inquired.

"Yeah, that 'nothing' whatever it is," he tried to explain.

"Oh, the 'Void of the Nothing,'" Kronos replied. "It's not a place you would ever want to visit. It is haunted by the emptiest emptiness, the loneliest loneliness, and the saddest sadness you could ever feel in your whole life multiplied thousands of times. It is a dark, sad, hollow, and unhappy place, and it burns with a pitch-black, hungry fire as well."

"What if the Sphinx eats us and we go there?" Alex asked.

"I don't think that will happen to either of you boys," said Kronos. "The secret is always to have your ears open and attentive so you will hear the voice of Tree King whenever he speaks. Only by listening to

Tree King's voice can treasure be formed on the inside of the Orna folk. The Orna folk who choose to remain hollow cannot stand to hear him speak, so they plug their ears and block him out of their minds. No treasure can form inside them because they refuse to listen."

"That's sad," said Grant. "Why don't they want to listen?"

"It's a mystery," answered Kronos. "Just be sure you and your brother keep your ears open and listen, okay?"

"I will!" said Grant.

"Me, too!" Alex added.

"Very good," Kronos said. "Now, it's time for me to open that mailbox door to see if the Sphinx has lost interest in us."

"No!" Alex yelled. "I don't want to go out there!"

"Don't worry," Kronos said. "You won't be going with me. Haven't you noticed the tunnel ahead?" He pointed to the opposite end of the mailbox, but it appeared dark. "Oh, I forgot. Someone must have turned out the lights." He flipped a light switch near the entrance to the mailbox, and the lights came on revealing a tunnel that extended from its other end. "You will be heading that way," he told the boys.

"Where does it go?" Grant asked him.

"Just trust me and follow it. You'll find out soon enough," he answered.

"That Sphinx won't be waiting there, will it?" Alex asked.

"Most likely not," Kronos assured him. "He usually doesn't venture into time-free zones like the one you're in now. At least I've never known him to do so. Now, travel to the other end of this corridor and you will find yourself in the year embroidered on the side of the mailbox. A. D. 2525, I think it said."

"You mean we're going to travel through time into the future?" Grant asked.

"If you choose to go out the other side, yes," he said.

"That is so cool," said Grant. "Don't you think so, Alex?"

"I guess so. As long as we don't get chased by the Sphinx again," he replied.

"Very well," said Kronos. "I must leave you for now. I have two brothers who will help you on your way as you travel into the future and the past, so don't be frightened. Sorry I can't go with you. Since I am 'the Spirit of Christmas Present', my place is here."

"Christmas presents!" Alex blurted. "Are there any here for me?"

"Not 'Christmas presents,'" Kronos corrected him. "*Christmas Present*. I govern that part of the time-line called the 'now.' I have little to do with what happened in the past or what will be in the future. Those domains belong to my two brothers. Do you understand?"

Alex nodded. "I think so."

"Very good," said Kronos. "I must go back to the present now, so have a safe journey." With these words, Pater Kronos cracked the mailbox door and listened. Fortunately, there was no loud roar, so he opened it wide enough to stick his head out and take a look around. "The coast is clear, I think," he told the boys. "I suppose the Sphinx has gone hunting for other Orna folk. Just remember what I told you boys. Keep your ears open and listen for Tree King's voice." He slipped out silently, shutting the mailbox door behind him.

"Okay," Grant said, putting his arm around Alex's shoulder. "Let's explore the tunnel and see where it leads."

—Chapter Five—

FLYING WITH YOUNG NANNY

GRANT AND ALEX QUICKLY realized that the mailbox they were in was not what it appeared to be from the outside. It was, in fact, a doorway to a different dimension, but what kind of dimension? It was not past, present, or future, but a kind of way-station between—or perhaps above—the three. If it is true that time was the fourth dimension, then this might have been a dimension higher still—perhaps the fifth dimension or beyond. This was not, however, a time*less* dimension either, for it was a place where events could take place—just not in the way events normally occurred in ordinary time.

As the boys walked down the corridor that led from the mailbox, they immediately realized they were in what would appear to any reasonable person to be an airport, though a more appropriate name for it might be 'time-port. The corridor walls were lined with posters advertising exotic destinations. None of them, however, were places in the present. One poster read, 'SPEND HANUKKAH IN JERU-SALEM—168 B.C.!' Under these words stood the candelabra with eight branches that the Jewish people called the menorah, and, at the bottom of the poster, the words 'Witness the Menorah Miracle First Hand!' The menorah on the poster was actually burning, and it gave off a warm and enticing light that reflected onto the opposite wall. The boys could make shadow figures with their hands as they once had done with an old movie projector Grampy had found in the attic and had let them play with.

A little further down was a poster about eight feet long. At first glance it looked like an advertisement for the Bahamas. It featured some people in swimsuits running across sandy beaches where palm, olive, and cypress trees grew. Others were lying on chase lounges wrapped in large white 'toga' towels. Others feasted at an enormous table set with every kind of delightful food and dessert imaginable. Children knelt around what appeared to be a Christmas tree and were opening gifts. This poster read: 'WHY SETTLE FOR JUST ANY TIME FOR YOUR DESTINATION? VISIT ROME IN A. D. 350 AND SAMPLE THE SATISFACTION THAT IS SATURNALIA!' A bit further down the corridor was an enormous poster of a Viking wearing a horned helmet and holding a spear in his right hand. Enormous letters above the Viking's head read 'YGGDRASIL', and beneath these, the words, 'See IT and the Midgard Serpent in A. D. 900!' At the bottom of the poster were the words, 'Feel the Terror that is Norse!'

"Do you think we will get to visit the years and places on these posters?" Alex asked.

"Maybe," Grant replied, "but I don't think we can get to them from this corridor. These posters are just advertisements. I think this corridor only goes to the year 2525."

Alex pondered. "I wonder what the year 2525 is like. I don't see any posters advertising it, do you?"

"No," Grant said, "but I would like to know. Whoever put these up probably thinks people going to A. D. 2525 already know what it will be like."

As the boys walked down the corridor, they found more posters advertising other destinations lining the walls. One, featuring a picture of Stonehenge, advertised a Druid Winter Solstice Festival in 1500 B. C. Another, which read, 'Come to Celtic Yuletide, A. D. 125', portrayed what appeared to be Irish river dancers doing some kind of jig in a ring around an oak tree that had its trunk painted red.

"Some of these times look pretty scary," Alex observed, "like that one we saw with the Viking. And this one here—Look how mean those dancers' faces look!"

Grant meanwhile had caught sight of another poster that read 'ROYAL CHRISTMAS CELEBRATION—25 December 800!' Beneath was pictured a glorious royal court filled with all kinds of dignitaries. At the poster's bottom was a Latin inscription '*CAROLUS MAGNUS*', and beneath the inscription were the words 'SEE THE CORONA-TION OF THE HOLY ROMAN EMPEROR CHARLEMAGNE'.

"*Carolus*. That must refer to Christmas Carols," Grant guessed.

"That looks like a pretty neat place to visit," Alex commented. "Why don't we go there?"

But Grant had already found another poster. "Hey, look at this! Do you know who Charles Dickens was? He wrote *A Christmas Carol*. Remember mean old Scrooge?"

"Oh, yeah," Alex answered. "Didn't we see a movie about him that had ghosts in it?"

"Do you see what this poster says?" Grant interrupted. "'Afternoon High Tea with Charles Dickens! Celebrating the Release of his New Book, *A Christmas Carol*, 24 December 1843'. I don't want to miss that, do you?"

"I do if those scary ghosts will be there."

"Oh, don't be silly," said Grant, putting his hands on his hips. "The ghosts were in the book he wrote. How could they be at his tea party if they're not real?"

"Okay, I guess it will be safe to go, then," Alex agreed.

The corridors were lined with so many posters that the boys didn't have time to read them all. Instead, they hurried along, thinking that if they were in an airport, then they would need to run to catch their plane.

Unlike most airports, this one had only a single gate at the end of the corridor. When they arrived at the gate, it was deserted. All they saw was an electronic schedule board that read, 'A. D. flight 2525 now boarding'. Beneath that was a streaming banner that said, "Due to the uncertainty of the future, tickets for all trips to 'what will be' are non-refundable."

"What are we going to do now?" Alex said in a huff. "We don't have tickets?"

"We don't have any money either," Grant reminded him. "I guess we'll just have to go back."

"No! I don't want to go outside the mailbox!" said Alex. "Not if that Sphinx is still there!"

"Maybe we're missing something," said Grant. "Let's check at that counter."

Behind the counter was a station with a computer and a sign beneath it that read 'Self Check-in'. Grant got onto the computer and went through the menu. When it asked for his name, he typed it in and pushed the 'enter' key. A screen came up that said, 'only carry-on baggage allowed with Self Check-in'. Faced with a choice between 'cancel' and 'okay', he pushed 'okay', and immediately a printer was engaged. When the printer stopped, a ticket popped out of a slot beneath the computer.

"That was easy enough," Grant said. "Let me do yours now, Alex."

Grant repeated the process, and soon Alex had his ticket, too. Then Grant said, "Now, I wonder who will take our ticket and let us board." When they approached the gate, they found another computer with a slot that said, 'Insert ticket arrow-first here'. They found the arrow and inserted their tickets. Immediately, the gate turned into the same round portal that resembled the snow globe that they had gone through when they first entered the Tree World.

"Oh, no! Not another roller coaster ride!" Alex exclaimed with a tone of dread.

"Oh, come on, Alex," his brother urged. "Be honest, now. Didn't you really enjoy that ride?"

Alex hesitated for a second, and said, "I guess so."

"Then what are we waiting for?"

Alex held Grant's hand as they started toward the portal, but this time when they stuck their feet through, they were not sucked in at lightning speed. Instead, they calmly walked through. Once on the other side of the gate, they found themselves in the open air. When they looked up at the sky, however, what they saw confused them. The sky was not blue but was the color of turquoise.

"That's weird," Grant remarked. "I wonder why the sky is green looking."

"Beats me," said Alex.

At the gate was a green plane, but it did not look like any plane they had ever seen. In fact, it was a larger version of Nanny's Christmas ornament planes that were hanging on their tree at home, and this meant that the skin of the plane appeared to have been made of the same facing and yarn Nanny had used to make the mailboxes. The plane was a small twin-engine with two white propellers, and the cockpit covering reflected the greenish sky. A set of stairs had been positioned to lead up to a cabin door located directly behind the cockpit. On the side of the plane were embroidered the words, 'The Spirit of Christmas' in white letters.

"How can something like that fly?" Alex asked. It sort of looks like it's made out of carpet?"

The boys climbed up the stairs and before entering the cabin door felt of the side of the plane. To their amazement it was as smooth as silk even though it did look like rough carpeting. Alex ran the palm of his hand quickly across the plane's skin, and as he did, it slightly changed colors from a darker green to a lighter green, much like the way the mood ring he once received from his mom changed colors when it responded to fluctuations in heat. When Grant saw how the skin of the plane behaved, he too tried the experiment. "Wow!" he said. "Okay, Alex. Why don't we go aboard?"

The boys climbed the portable stairs and walked through the cabin door.

"Hello!" Grant yelled.

"Just a minute, and I'll be right with you," came a female voice from the plane's cockpit.

A pretty lady soon appeared at the cockpit door. On her head was a rhinestone tiara, and she wore a forest-green satin dress accessorized with a white pearl necklace, a matching bracelet, and a light green scarf. "Alex, Grant, come on up here. You will be sitting in the cockpit with me."

How did the lady know their names?

"Will we be flying up there with you?" Grant asked her, climbing inside.

"Of course," she said. "Do you think I would make you sit in the cabin?"

Grant and Alex kept looking at the woman's face. She looked vaguely familiar, but they could not exactly remember where or when they had ever met her.

The lady removed a round tin Christmas box from what appeared to be a glove compartment and pried off its lid. Then she reached into the compartment and removed a little stick that had a movable claw on one end and a trigger that could open and close the claw on the other. She used the claw to remove one cookie each for Grant and for Alex.

"These are my special sugar cookies," she said. "I hope you like them."

"Thanks," said the boys who did not waste time devouring them.

"Hey!" Alex exclaimed. "These taste just like Nanny's sugar cookies!"

"And they look exactly like her cookies, too," Grant added. "See the little design from the bottom of the glass that she used to press them down before baking them?"

The lady smiled at them and said, "Surprise!"

The boys immediately recognized that the young lady with the rhinestone tiara was indeed Nanny, but she no longer appeared old.

"Nanny?" Alex ventured.

"Who else?" she replied.

"How come you look so young?" Grant asked her.

"Remember we are in a time-free zone here," she said. "That is why I appear young. So if you want, you can either call me 'Nanny' or 'Young Nanny.'"

"We'll call you 'Young Nanny,'" Grant said. Then he remarked, "How did you get here?"

"Surely you remember that I made all the mailboxes on your tree," she replied. "I put my love into each one. Here love is not invisible—you can see it! That's why you can see me, too!"

"Wow!" Alex exclaimed. "You were really pretty back in the day!"

"Love is pretty no matter where you find it—or in whom," she said. "Remember the saying, 'Beauty is only skin deep, but ugly goes clear to the bone.'"

The boys laughed.

"I like your crown," Grant said. "Where did you get it?"

"Oh, my tiara?" she answered. "I won it in a beauty contest. But I have to admit it wasn't a real beauty contest. It was just a masquerade party I dressed up for once. I thought I would wear it today because it looks Christmassy."

"I love your sugar cookies," Alex said. "Can I have another one?"

"Of course," said Young Nanny, "but don't eat too many. You don't want to spoil your supper." She took out her 'Nanny stick, the apparatus with the claw at one end and the trigger at the other, and used it to serve Alex and Grant another cookie.

"Why are you flying a plane?" Grant asked Young Nanny.

"I'll have you know, boys, that I soloed in an airplane back when I was a young lady. Not very many ladies did that in those days. If I'd been given the opportunity, I would have been another Amelia Earhart, but I met your great-grandfather instead, got married, and had children. I think that was the better choice, don't you? Otherwise I wouldn't be able to fly you boys around now."

"Do you know where we're going?" Grant asked her.

"This is A. D. flight 2525, and everything is green, so I assume we'll be heading into the future."

"Do you know what 2525 is like?" asked Grant.

"Well, future times change just like the weather," Young Nanny replied. "You never know beforehand what it will be like. If it's a pleasant vacation you want, flying to the future is always risky business because everything that *is to be* depends on what has happened and is going to happen up until the exact time you're flying to. That's why we don't advertise future destinations like we do those in the past."

"That explains all the posters we saw, then," said Grant.

"Can I have just one more sugar cookie?" Alex asked.

"All right," said Nanny. "But this will have to be your last one, at least until we land." She again used her stick to give Grant and Alex their cookies. "Okay, boys," she said, "we've got to take off now so we can get you to 2525. Fasten your seatbelts."

The boys did as Young Nanny asked, and soon they were taxiing onto the runway. They watched Young Nanny as she skillfully set the controls and operated all the levers and knobs on the instrument panel. Soon, they were in position to take off.

"Hold on now!" Young Nanny told them.

The plane began to accelerate down the runway, and soon Young Nanny was pulling back on the steering mechanism. The plane gained lift, and in no time they were sailing upward into the green sky. As the plane flew faster, the green color of the sky deepened.

Excitement glowed on the boys' faces. They never knew their Nanny was such an interesting person—much less a pilot. How did she know how to make the world's best sugar cookies and fly a plane, too? When they had reached their cruising altitude, Nanny began to tell them stories.

"In the old days," she said, "Christmas was all about family. We didn't even put up our Christmas trees until the day before Christmas. The decorating was fun, of course, but Christmas was really about getting together with Mother, Father, the sisters, and my only brother."

"What were they like?" Alex asked.

"Mother was a wonderful person and was full of love for her family," she replied. "Father was a bit stern as most men were in those days, but we knew he loved us, too. He always had time for each of us girls. Besides Elizabeth, I had two other sisters, Velma and Arabella Priscilla. My only brother was named Leon, but very few people knew his name because all of us sisters called him by a nickname—'Brother'. Later, when the sisters got married and had their own children, their children called him 'Uncle Brother'. Whenever we got together, we would have the best time telling stories and laughing. We had some wonderful times back then. Did you boys ever hear the story of how your father accidently spelled out my brother's name in their living room window one Christmas?"

The boys smiled and shook their heads.

"Well," Young Nanny continued, "your father had just come home from college. It was his freshman year and not long after his father had passed away—that would be my son and your grandfather. Your dad was already sad because of his father's death, and he had looked forward at least for a month to decorating the Christmas tree. So you can imagine how disappointed he was to find when he arrived home that his mother had already decorated it. Your father, however, who loved to decorate for Christmas, was undeterred and decided he would spell out the word 'noel' in the window. The problem was that he spelled out 'noel' on the inside of the window, so that when the rest of the neighborhood saw it from the outside, it spelled 'LEON', my brother's name. After that, we sometimes acted silly, and, instead of singing 'NOEL, NOEL', we sang, 'LEON, LEON.'"

Alex and Grant sputtered with laugher.

"I'm glad you also think that is a funny story," she said, smiling. "But believe me, it's not the only one. I will have to tell you some others on one of our future flights. But now, we need to make our descent. When we get to the year 2525, do you boys know what to do?"

"No," they replied.

"Just follow the arrows, and they will lead you through the gate to your destination. I hope you boys will have a good time there."

"What will we do about tickets?" Grant asked.

"The ticket you used will be good for all our flights together, so you won't have to bother with them again. The snow-globe portal will recognize you, so you need only walk through it."

"Thanks, that's good to know," Grant said.

"Can't you go with us?" Alex asked.

"No, my dear," replied Young Nanny. "I have mail to deliver."

"Is this an airmail plane?" Grant asked.

"That's right," she answered. "So you boys can go visit 2525 while I take care of the mail. When we have more time, I'll tell you how the 'time-mail' system works." Young Nanny was silent for a moment as she checked the gauges on her instrument panel. "Okay, boys, prepare for landing."

Their great-grandmother made a perfect landing, and after they taxied down the runway, they came to the gate that led to A. D. 2525. When they halted, Young Nanny unbuckled her seatbelt, got up out of her seat, and left the cockpit to open the hatch to the plane's cabin.

"Everything is automated here," she told the boys. "The ramp should pull up to the door in a couple of minutes." She knelt down and gave each of the boys a hug and a kiss. Fortunately, the kiss was not wet like the kisses of Old Nanny, and Young Nanny didn't have whiskers either. "I know what you boys are thinking," she said. "My kisses get sloppier with the years. But don't you forget that those sloppy kisses are filled with just that much more love for you boys as the not-so-sloppy ones."

"Thanks, Young Nanny," said Alex.

"Yeah, thanks for the great plane ride," Grant added. "You're the best."

"The ramp is here now," said Young Nanny. "When you return from 2525, I'll be here to take you back to the present. Remember what I said about return tickets? You need not worry about them. Just promise that you'll be careful in 2525." Then she remembered something. "Why didn't I think to do this before," she said to the boys. "Let me do a quick check on the weather."

Nanny went back to the cockpit and soon returned. "I hate to tell you boys this: The weather in 2525 is not going to be very pleasant. The temperature looks pretty hot, in fact. Oh, well, maybe you won't have to spend too much time there. Whatever you do, don't forget where the mailbox is, okay? You will need to return by that way."

They nodded.

"Oh, I almost forgot," she said. "Here's one more sugar cookie for each of you for the road!" After using her Nanny stick to serve them their last sugar cookie of the flight, Young Nanny and the boys exchanged goodbyes. Then the boys climbed down the portable stairs from the plane and followed the arrows to the gate, eating their sugar cookies as they went. Soon they faced another portal that looked like yet another shaken-up snow globe. They walked through it and found the gate on the other side. Like the gate they had flown out of, it, too, seemed abandoned. They found another corridor, but this time there were no posters lining the walls. Dirty, bleak, and filled with trash, the corridor resembled tunnels that can be found in the subway systems of large metropolitan cities. Some of the florescent lights were burned out, making parts of the corridor dark and foreboding, while others flickered eerily.

"I wish Grampy were here," said Alex. "He would fix those lights and have this place cleaned up in no time."

CHAPTER FIVE

"I hate to think what we'll find at the end of this corridor," said Alex. "I hope this is not a preview of what we will find in 2525."

—Chapter Six—

THE CEMETERY OF THE SCROOGES

WHEN GRANT AND ALEX reached the end of the dirty, dimly lit corridor, they again entered what appeared to be the inside of a green mailbox, but Alex stopped dead in his tracks when he caught sight of the mailbox door. "Grant. Be sure that Sphinx is not out there."

Slowly and carefully, his brother opened the door. When he did, a wave of heat rushed in and he quickly shut it. "Young Nanny was right about the weather here," he said. "It's pretty hot." He opened it far enough to stick out his head and look around. "The coast is clear, I think," he told Alex.

Cautiously, Grant and Alex ventured outside and stood beneath a pitch-black sky inside a cemetery with thousands of tombstones. The tombstones dotted the side of what appeared to be the slope of an immense volcano, but the volcano also looked vaguely like a gigantic Christmas tree whose wood had become petrified into black stone. Instead of a star at the top of this petrified tree, the volcanic cone was belching smoke and spewing lava. The lava crept slowly down the side of the mountain, and the boys knew they would not have much time before it reached them. As they got a closer look at the grave-stones, they noticed something extremely odd. All the markers had last names ending in 'Scrooge'.

"I'm afraid there might be ghosts here!" Alex declared as he looked at the tombstones.

No sooner had he said this than out of one of the graves a ghostly figure emerged. It wore a gray, hooded robe made of coarse material, and instead of a face with eyes peering out from under the hood, the boys could see only empty darkness. Still, despite the absence of eyes, they could almost feel it staring straight through them. Its hands and feet were those of a skeleton, though somehow its gnarled and twisted fingernails had managed to remain attached to its bony fingers. A black rope tied around its waste revealed that only bone lay beneath the garment as well. The ghostly figure grew until it became very tall and towered over them. Alex, trembling, grabbed Grant's arm and whimpered.

"Be brave," Grant urged him. "If it's a ghost, it may sense your fear. It's best not to let it think you're scared." Then Grant shouted at the ghost using the most courageous voice he could muster, "Who are you, and what do you want?"

The strange being said nothing, but slowly and deliberately, turned, lifted his right hand, and pointed its bony index finger with its twisted fingernail at a pedestal with a book on it. Next to the pedestal stood a statue of a hunched over man holding a sickle, like the kind used to cut down weeds.

"We won't go!" Grant exclaimed. "Not until you tell us who you are!"

The being did not speak, but again flung out his arm and pointed his finger in the direction of the pedestal holding the book. The moment he did this, the ground rumbled, and fire belched out of the cone of the volcano.

"Better do what he wants," Alex warned. "Or he might kill us."

"Okay," Grant agreed. "Just be ready to run back in the direction of the mailbox as fast as you can, okay?"

Alex nodded.

The ghostly being led the boys to the pedestal and pointed to the book that rested on it. Next to the book were oven mitts and a steel spatula like the kind Mom used to fry bacon and turn pancakes. The book looked vaguely like a waffle iron. Its binding seemed to be made of cast iron, and on its cover were the words in raised, glowing red letters: 'Read Me If You Dare'. Grant started to open the book, but the hooded figure grabbed his arm and yanked it away before he could touch it. The ghostly being then picked up the oven mitts, handed them to Grant, and signaled for him to put them on.

"The book must be hot," Alex guessed.

"Looks that way," Grant said, slipping on the oven mitts. The second he opened the book to the first page, the boys felt heat flare up against their faces. It was like the heat that escapes when opening an oven door to peek at chocolate chip cookies baking. Only this time, the heat did not carry anything remotely resembling a sweet and enticing aroma. Instead, it carried the odor of central heating when it is first turned on in the autumn. The odor intensified until its stench was like that of burnt toast. Then it got even worse until it smelled like burnt electrical wiring. Grant vigorously flapped his mitt over the open book, trying to get rid of the toxic fumes escaping from it. An inscription on the first page of the book read, 'Ask any question you dare, but stand back!' The letters seemed to be engraved into the page as though they were made by a wood-burning tool. The center parts of them were black, but their edges were brown and a bit raggedy.

"Okay," said Grant, thinking for a moment. "What question should I ask it first?"

Suddenly, fire flared up in his face, slightly singeing his eyebrows. Immediately, he jumped back and patted his face with the oven mitts.

A startled look flashed across his face, and he shouted, "Why did it do that?"

Again, without warning, the book flared like a box of matches set on fire, but this time Grant managed to jump back before the fire burned his eyebrows off. Immediately on the page he noticed the answers to his two questions. To the question, "What question should I ask it first?" the answer appeared, "You just asked it, silly," and to the question, "Why did it do that?" the answer read, "because you asked me a silly question. Ask me a silly question and you will get a silly answer."

"You'd better not ask it any more silly questions," Alex suggested.

Grant frowned. "I didn't mean to ask it a silly question, dummy. What kind of a stupid book is this?"

The book flared again, and when the flame died down, the words appeared, "saying I'm stupid is like the 'pot calling the kettle black'. Look in the mirror."

Alex's face was smug. "Another silly question."

"Thank you smarty," Grant returned. "Now, I've got to be careful and not ask it any questions I don't mean to. From now on, I won't ask anything unless I think about it first."

"Good idea," said Alex.

Grant positioned himself. "Okay, here goes. Who is the scary person in the gray hood standing beside me?"

This time nothing happened.

Grant huffed. "Oh, great. Now the thing is broken."

The scary person in the gray hood picked up the spatula and handed it to Alex.

"And what am I supposed to do with this?" he asked.

At that moment Alex realized he had unintentionally asked another question. He fully expected the fire to flare up from the page, but this time nothing happened.

"I think the scary person wants you to use the spatula to turn the pages," Grant ventured.

Alex followed Grant's suggestion, slid the spatula in under page one, and turned to page two. Then he carefully set the spatula down on the pedestal next to the book.

"Okay, I'll try again," Grant said. "Who is the scary person in the gray hood standing beside me?"

Fire flared out from the book, and when it died down, these words appeared: "Once upon a time, the scary person you see standing before you was the bright and hopeful *Angelus Novum*—which means 'the Angel of the New'. He is the Time Guardian of the future, but now that the future is so bleak and hopeless he grieves in silence, refusing to speak. He has ceased to be a Time Guardian because there is nothing worth guarding here. Time in this place has run out."

Grant patted his chin with the oven mitt as he thought up another question. "Why have these things happened?" he asked.

The fire flared, died down, and left behind these words: "Christmas in the year 2525 is dead, and no memories of any previous Christmases can be found."

"Let me ask it a question," said Alex.

Grant agreed.

"Alright, here comes," said Alex. "If the scary person is an angel, why doesn't he look like an angel anymore?"

Again, the fire flared, died down, and left the answer: "The gray mourning shroud he now wears was once a golden garment called 'the Robe of Joyous Memories', but the moths of forgetfulness long ago ate away its golden hue. Tarnished over time by hopelessness, it now appears drab and gray."

"Now let me," Grant said. "Why is it called a mourning shroud?"

This time, nothing happened.

"Here, let me use the spatula again," Alex said, so he took it off the pedestal and flipped the page. Then Grant asked it the question again. This time, the fire flared from the page, died down, and left the words: "A mourning shroud is worn by a grieving person when a loved one dies. In this case, the scary person you see is grieving."

"But who's he grieving for?" Grant asked again.

The fire from the page flared, died down, and gave the book's answer, "The Ghost of Christmas Future is grieving for the Scrooges."

These words caused fear to flash across Alex's face. "Oh, no! He really is a ghost! And there are Scrooges here, too!"

Grant tried to reassure him. "He is not a bad ghost, Alex. Just look at the pedestal. It is all wet." Alex looked and saw what seemed to be raindrops glistening on the pedestal next to the book. "Don't you see, Alex? He is crying," Grant explained. "We can't see his face, but if you look closely you will see the teardrops falling from that dark, empty place under his hood."

"But I'm scared of Scrooges, too," Alex added. "What about them?"

Suddenly fire flared from the book, and when it died down the words appeared: "Inquiries concerning the Scrooges must be made according to family groupings in the cemetery. Which Scrooge family are you referring to?"

Grant thought a minute. "I've got an idea. Let's get names from some of the tombstones." So they left the book on the pedestal for a moment, walked over to a plot labeled 'A,' and read the names on the graves.

"Okay," said Grant, "Here we have David H. Scrooge, Bertrand R. Scrooge, Alfred J. Scrooge, Madeleine M. Scrooge, Christopher H. Scrooge, R. Dawkins Scrooge, and D. Dennett Scrooge. Let's go ask the book who they are."

They hurried over to it. "Who are the Scrooges in plot 'A'?" Grant asked.

Fire from the page flared and left behind the following words after it died down: "These are the Scrooges who taught that there is no such thing as Tree King, the one who made this Tree World that we call Arboria. Tree King is, among other things, a great artist, but he did not use a 'paint-by-numbers' set to make his Tree World. When the Scrooges in cemetery plot 'A' could not find numbers next to the 'dots' our Tree World is made up of, the Tree World appeared to them like a foreign language. Without the numbers, the Scrooges believed the dots simply could not be connected to reveal any bigger picture that could make sense to them. So they refused to connect the dots even though there was good reason to believe that Tree King wanted them to use their imaginations to do just that and to be surprised by the beauty they would find if they did. They also got very angry with anyone who tried to connect the dots in ways they did not approve of."

There being no more room on the page, Alex turned it with the spatula to a fresh page.

"How did the Scrooges get this way?" Grant asked.

"They all lived in a cave for such a long time they believed their cave was the only thing in the world that was real. Over time, they convinced themselves that the darkness and shadows of their cave were more brilliant than sunshine. Like vampires who shrink from sunlight or turn their faces and hiss when they see a crucifix, these Scrooges turned their faces and hissed whenever they had to look at a nativity scene. They hated the word 'Christmas' so much that they tried to get rid of it in the same way most people try to exterminate roaches and rats."

More tear drops fell from the face of the Spirit onto the pedestal.

"Gosh, Alex," Grant remarked, "they really do sound like vampires. Let's look at the names in this other cemetery plot and find out who they are." The boys ran over to another of the plots. "It says 'VW.'" Grant said. The most prominent of the grave markers had the name 'Verbada Widgmud Scrooge'. Other markers had names such as 'Jamie D. Scrooge', 'Glenn M. Scrooge', 'Stephen R. Scrooge', 'Howard L. Scrooge', 'Kenneth H. Scrooge', 'Chris M. Scrooge', 'Bella W. Scrooge', 'David J. Scrooge', 'Neil A. Scrooge', 'Ronald L. S. Scrooge', 'Julian D. Scrooge', and 'Jeffrey N. Scrooge'.

"Come on, Alex. Let's go ask the book who they are," so the boys returned to it. "There's no more room on this page," said Alex. "Time to turn." He picked up the spatula and flipped the page.

"Okay," said Grant, standing back from the book. "Who are the Scrooges in plot 'VW'?"

After the page flared and died down, the answer appeared: "These, like Ebenezer Scrooge, tried to get rid of all references to Christmas in their businesses. Verbada Widgmud, Chief Executive Officer (CEO) of a place called Widgmus World, tried to build her mud empire inside the Christmas tree of two children named Kim and Jason Jeffery. She tried to abolish Christmas and replace it with her own made-up holiday called Widgmus. Her substitute holiday was based purely on greed and selfishness. In the same way, the CEOs whose tombstones appear in plot 'VW' cared nothing for Christmas but were only interested in making money. Though they depended on people who loved Christmas to buy their products, they were afraid their profits would dwindle if they offended people who hated

Christmas—people like the Scrooges buried in plot 'A'—so they deleted the word 'Christmas' from all their advertisements. The lava you see spewing from the volcano is all that is left of their merchandize. Every last bit of it has been either incinerated or melted down."

"We didn't see Ebenezer Scrooge in plot 'VW,'" Alex commented. "Is he buried somewhere else?"

The page flared, died down, and left its answer, but before they could read it the robes of the Spirit of Christmas Future, turning bright and golden, distracted them. A radiant face suddenly appeared in place of the empty darkness, and, remarkably, the Spirit spoke, "At last, I have found my voice because you have reminded me of the one Scrooge who escaped this dreadful realm. Ebenezer! My dear Ebenezer! He was the hope of the Scrooges, but alas, none here ever listened to him. Though they bear his name, he is forgotten!" The Spirit sobbed as he repeated the word "forgotten," and his sobbing trailed off into silence. The robes of the Spirit again became drab and gray, and his face vanished into empty darkness. No further did he speak, for his despair over the fate of the Scrooges drove out all hope, extinguishing every memory of that rare Scrooge who long ago managed to get away. Instead, teardrops again fell from his invisible face onto the surface of the pedestal. The boys' eyes returned to the page— "Death and Burial Record Request—Ebenezer Scrooge—Name not found," it said.

The boys remembered from Charles Dickens's *A Christmas Carol* how Ebenezer Scrooge was spared the horrible fate these other Scrooges were now suffering because he had had a change of heart about Christmas.

Grant asked the next question. "Did we just see the Spirit of Christmas Future the way he looked when he was happy?"

Fire flared from the page, died down, and left the answer: "Yes, you briefly saw him as the *Angelus Novum*—the 'Angel of the New'. You saw something very rare, for he has not appeared that way for at least two hundred years. Christmas has been dead for at least that long, and just like a string of Christmas lights that goes dark because of a blown fuse, all the connections to this place in the future were broken long ago. No Christmas lights shine here, and no memories of Christmas brightness remain. Instead, there is only the glowing lava of anger, selfishness, hatred, and regret."

Grant remembered how he had repaired the fuse on the string of lights. "Hey, Alex," he said. "Do you think we could repair the burned out fuse and restore light to this land?"

Grant did not intend for the book to answer his question, but when it flared, he knew at once that the book had decided to do just that. When the fire died down, the words appeared: "Breaks in time cannot be repaired from the future. They can only be repaired in the present by reconnecting past time to future time."

"That's hard to understand," Alex said. "I'm sure if Grampy were here, he would be able to explain it."

"True," Grant acknowledged. "I guess we'll have to return to the present and see if we can find the loose connection. Maybe the book can help us know where the burned out fuse is." Grant stated his question for the book: "Where are the fuses in the present burned out?"

After the book flared and died down, the answer appeared: "Fuses connecting time are not known in the future. They can only be discovered in the present. You must go back."

Just then, the ground shook, knocking the boys off their feet. Lava exploded from volcano's cone; and red, glowing cracks began to appear everywhere in the enormous graveyard that was spread across the side of the mountain. Suddenly, Alex saw something that made him scream.

"What's the matter?" Grant exclaimed.

"Look in those cracks!" he shouted.

As they watched, they could see hands reaching up from the crevices. The hands were motioning for them to come—beckoning them to join the throng of Scrooges that lay buried in the graves. The Spirit of Christmas Future signaled for the boys to run for their lives, so the boys sprang up from where they had fallen and ran in the direction of the mailbox they had arrived from earlier. When Alex looked back, he saw the Spirit of Christmas Future clutching his chest and falling to the ground.

"Grant look! He is dying!"

The boys paused and watched as the Spirit of Christmas Future fell into a heap and vanished. Just then, some of the hands coming up out of the cracks grabbed them around the ankles, but they managed to shake them off and stomp on them. Grant and Alex quickly found the entrance to the mailbox.

"Thank goodness there are no combination locks on this side," Grant said. He yanked open the door. "Quick, Alex! Get inside!"

Alex jumped into the mailbox, landing on his belly. Grant followed, quickly slamming the door behind them. The boys could hear the hands outside knocking and clawing on the mailbox door. They could also hear the Scrooges moaning, "Come back! Come back!" The next thing they heard was another volcanic blast! The mailbox shook!

"I think the Ghost of Christmas Future really died!" Alex exclaimed.

"Let's hurry back to the time-port, Alex!" Grant shouted. "Let's just hope it's not too late to hitch a ride with Young Nanny!"

—Chapter Seven—

A BLOWN FUSE ON THE TIMELINE

GRANT AND ALEX HURRIED down the dirty, dimly lit corridor toward the terminal to find Young Nanny. When they arrived at the gate, they could see the propellers of her plane twirling, so through the snow-globe portal they jumped. The automatic staircase had already pulled away from the plane, the cabin door was shut, and the plane was preparing for takeoff. The boys ran out onto the runway, waving their hands frantically and hoping that Young Nanny would see them. When the propellers slowed to a halt, they realized their great-grandmother had indeed seen them. Soon, the door to the plane's cabin opened, and they could see the automatic stairs rolling toward the plane. Once the stairs were in place, the boys ran up to join Young Nanny. When they entered the plane, she stooped down and hugged them.

"I'm so glad you boys made it back," she said. "Something terrible has happened outside the time-port, and all traffic is being rerouted to the year 2100. Word is that this time-port and all other destinations since 2100 will be closed for good in less than an hour."

Alex was huffing and puffing. "Young Nanny," he said. "We've just been to an awful place. We saw the cemetery of the Scrooges! There were ghosts there, too! A volcano in the graveyard is erupting! We've got to get out of here right now!"

"There are no Christmas lights in the future either because something's gone wrong in the past!" Grant added. "A fuse has blown, so we've got to get back and repair it before all future Christmases slip into darkness!"

"I was afraid something like this would happen," Young Nanny remarked. "The mail delivery from all past times up to this current time has been rejected. All letters and Christmas cards are either marked 'Return to Sender' or 'Addressee Unknown.'"

"Who were the letters and cards written to?" Grant asked.

"To people who still believe in Christmas," she answered. There weren't very many letters and cards to begin with, and now even the few that I was supposed to deliver here have all been returned."

"That makes sense," Alex said. "None of the Scrooges buried in the cemetery believed in Christmas, and we're pretty sure the Ghost of Christmas Future is dead, too."

Suddenly, the ground shook.

"Quick!" Young Nanny yelled. "We've got to take off now! Fasten your seatbelts! We may be in for a bumpy ride!"

Young Nanny engaged the propellers, and soon the plane was taxiing down the runway. She managed to get the plane airborne after a very bumpy ascent. When they had reached a safe altitude and the turbulence smoothed out, she said, "That was a close call. These trips to the future seem to be getting more and more dangerous. Are you boys still a bit shaken up?"

"Yes," they replied.

"Maybe a bite to eat will help. Are you hungry? I've got some hot meatloaf and baked beans prepared."

"Some more of your sugar cookies would be nice, too," Alex suggested.

"If you eat the meatloaf first, then I'll let you have a few," she said. "If you are going back to the present, you will need your strength. And I don't want you to make yourself sick on cookies before you've eaten a nutritious meal."

The boys always enjoyed Nanny's meatloaf and baked beans, so they did not put up a fuss. Grant opened a picnic basket and removed a couple of paper plates and some plastic utensils. He cut and placed servings of the meatloaf on the paper plates. Then he spooned out a helping of baked beans for Alex and himself. When they had finished eating, Alex asked Young Nanny, "What about the sugar cookies?"

"Have you eaten all the good food?" she asked.

"Yes," Alex said.

"Very well." She pulled the cookie tin from the compartment in the plane's console, removed the lid, and used her Nanny stick to serve the boys two cookies each. The boys wasted no time devouring them.

"These are delicious, Young Nanny," Grant raved. "How did you learn to make them?"

"From my mother," she replied. "I got the recipe from her, and she got it from her mother. For all I know, that cookie recipe's been in the family for hundreds of years. Those cookies are part of a long Christmas tradition, so the recipe has been a closely guarded secret. You know, it only takes one generation for a wonderful recipe like this one to be lost. If just one careless mistake is made in copying down the ingredients or the directions, the secret to a good recipe can be gone forever. The same is true, of course, for all Christmas traditions. They must be passed down from father to son and from mother to daughter, or they will die and be forgotten."

"Hey! I'll bet that's what happened to the Scrooges!" Alex exclaimed.

"What?" Young Nanny asked.

"They forgot the recipe for Christmas!" he added.

"You may very well be right," Young Nanny said. "It could also help explain why they did not receive the letters and cards from the past. These letters and cards carry past Christmas traditions forward into the future. When the future will no longer accept them, then they go to the Dead Letter Office. When this happens, the traditions die and are forgotten."

"Can't the cards and letters be returned to the senders?" Grant asked.

"Unfortunately that is impossible" replied Young Nanny. "You see, time-mail does not work the same way ordinary mail does. Time-mail goes only one way—from the past, through the present, to the future. Time-mail sent from the past to the future cannot be returned to the past because the past is fixed and cannot be changed. This is why people who send mail to the future, or forward mail from the past to the future, never really know for sure if that mail gets through or not. They can only hope it does."

"I don't understand. Why can't it be returned to the past?" Alex asked.

"Because this would break the laws of time set down by Tree King," she answered. "Time's arrow goes in one way only—from the past, through the present, toward the future—but not the other way around. This means changing the past is impossible. Once something has happened, it has happened. It cannot be undone. One can observe the past, of course, but one cannot change it. The future, however, can be changed by changing the present first. To change present time is hard to do though. One reason is that the present appears to most people like a bunch of jumbled up, disconnected dots. Without clues from the past we have a hard time knowing how those dots should be connected. This is why it is best to mine the past for clues before one tries to change present time. Otherwise, the future, which depends on what we do in the present, may end up being very bleak indeed."

"That sounds like what the Spirit of Christmas Future revealed to us about the Scrooges in cemetery plot 'A,'" Grant ventured.

"Scrooges?" Young Nanny inquired.

"Yes," Grant replied. "They refused to believe there is such a thing as Tree King. The Spirit of Christmas Future revealed that they could not connect the dots to see the bigger picture because they refused to use their imaginations in the way Tree King wanted."

"I suspect another problem with those Scrooges is that they suffered from incurable amnesia," Young Nanny suggested. "Remembering the past helps us to see the bigger picture so that we can figure out how the dots that make up that picture are connected. I know this is true because I make mailboxes."

"We know," Alex told her. "We have them all over our Christmas tree at home."

"When I make those mailboxes from yarn, I sometimes have to stand back to see if the dates line up correctly," she explained. "If I'm looking too closely at what I'm doing, I sometimes lose track of the bigger pattern and make mistakes. That's the way time is, too. On numerous occasions, I have made mistakes and have had to pull out the yarn and start over to get the pattern right. It may seem a waste of time, but it has to be done. You see, boys, to make sense out of present time, we have to try to stand back and look at it from a distance. Usually we can only stand back after the present becomes the past. History gives us patterns that help us understand the present in the same way that standing back from a tapestry helps you see when you've made a mistake and have to correct it. But if we know nothing about the past, then we will be unable to figure out the big picture in the present as well. I suspect that your Scrooges in cemetery plot 'A' were looking too closely at the present at the same time that they were completely ignorant of the past. That may be what caused them to miss seeing how the dots connect to form a bigger picture. As the old saying goes, 'they could not see the forest for the trees.'"

"They were ignorant about Christmas trees and everything else having to do with Christmas," said Grant. "That's for sure."

"Well, there you have it," Young Nanny commented. "If they were ignorant of something as well-known as Christmas, then most likely they were ignorant of many other things as well. When these Scrooges got Christmas recipes from the past, I'm sure they simply threw them in the trash. Surely if they knew that Christmas traditions can be as tasty as my sugar cookies, they would have thought twice. There must be other reasons why they hate Christmas. It simply doesn't make sense."

"I know!" Alex blurted. "They are vampires! The book told us!"

"Book? What book?" Young Nanny asked.

The boys proceeded to tell her about the strange book that the Ghost of Christmas Future had led them to. Young Nanny listened intently as they told her of the book's strange behavior. She was particularly curious about the fact that the book behaved in some ways like an oven.

"I used to have an oven just like that book," she said. "I swear that it would talk back to me! Whenever I would light it, the fire would flare up, and I would have to jump back to keep from getting my face burned. Still, whenever I would make my sugar cookies, that oven would smell just glorious."

"But the heat from the book didn't smell glorious at all," Grant said. "It stunk like burnt rubber."

"That makes perfect sense," said Young Nanny. "If it told you boys that the Scrooges in plot 'A' were like vampires that hiss and turn their faces whenever they are made to look at a nativity scene, I can understand exactly why that book smelled the way it did. If Christmas traditions resemble the sweet aroma of sugar cookies baking, then the place where those traditions are dead and forgotten must smell like skunks-a-roasting."

"I can't get that smell out of my head," Alex said. "Nanny, I really need another one of your sugar cookies to get rid of it, and I need it bad."

Nanny smiled. "After what you boys have been through, I totally understand." She opened the tin, reached in with her Nanny stick, and served them each another cookie. "Just try to remember my cookies if you ever end up in a place like the Scrooge cemetery again, okay?"

The boys nodded.

The droning of the propellers made Alex and Grant feel sleepy, and soon they were napping. A little while later, they were awakened by a 'bump'. The boys yawned and stretched. "Are we landing?" Alex asked.

"Yes," Young Nanny replied. "We're in the present again." They taxied down the runway and soon were at the gate. The automatic stairs then attached themselves to the side of the plane, and the boys made ready to exit.

"Before you boys leave the time-port, would you mind taking these letters to the Dead Letter Office for me? It's located inside the time-port terminal. Here are the directions. If you just follow the signs, you should be able to find it fairly easily."

The boys agreed, hugged Young Nanny 'bye', and trotted down the stairs with the bag of letters. They followed Young Nanny's directions and the time-port signs and soon found the Dead Letter Office. When they arrived there, they were surprised to find Pater Kronos waiting for them, so they greeted him with a "Hi!"

"Hello, boys," he returned. "I see you've made it back safely from 2525. How is my brother?"

"Your brother?" Grant asked.

"Yes, the *Angelus Novum*, the Time Guardian of what is to come, the Ghost of Christmas Future."

"I was afraid of him when I found out he was a ghost," Alex stated.

"I am a ghost, too," Kronos informed him, "and you weren't scared of me."

Alex looked shocked. "I didn't know you were a ghost! If I had, I would have been afraid!"

"Didn't I tell you I was a spirit?" Kronos asked,

"Yes," Alex replied. "But I didn't know a spirit was the same thing as a ghost."

Grant rolled his eyes.

"I suppose I understand your confusion," Kronos said, "After all, we are not ordinary ghosts—at least not like ghosts that are the spirits of dead people." Kronos posed his original question again, "So are you going to tell me how my brother is doing or not?"

The boys sadly hung their heads.

"What is wrong?" Kronos asked.

"He is dead," Alex informed him.

"We saw him clutch his chest and fall to the ground," Grant added.

Kronos's eyes filled with tears, and they ran down his cheek. He quickly wiped them away. "Every year it seems his time is getting shorter and shorter. Do you know where the air traffic to the future has been rerouted?" he asked.

"Yes. Young Nanny told us it was rerouted to 2100," Grant replied.

A wave of shock overpowered Kronos's face. "You mean he's lost four hundred and twenty-five years? Surely that can't be true!"

"I don't understand," said Grant. "Isn't he dead?"

"Yes, in the year 2525," Kronos replied. "You saw him die in that year, but that doesn't mean he's dead tomorrow, or the next day, or even the day after that. But this new date, 2100, has me scared. If that is the new 'terminus' for the future, then all of us have less than one hundred years to live."

"What is a 'terminus'?" Alex asked.

"A 'terminus' is an 'end,'" Kronos replied. "This means that history will end in 2100 unless something is done and done quickly to alter the chain of events. This also explains why the Sphinx has been so active lately. Time is growing short. I should have guessed it."

"Young Nanny asked us to bring these letters to the Dead Letter Office," Grant told Kronos. "Is this it?"

"Yes, how many are there?" he asked.

"The same number that Young Nanny carried to 2525," Grant replied. "None of them could be delivered because there were no people to receive them."

"Do you mean that Christmas is dead and forgotten in 2525?" Kronos cried.

"Yes," Grant answered.

"We saw the cemetery of the Scrooges," Alex added. "It was awful."

"This is very bad news," said Kronos. "And the new date of 2100 means that thousands more of these dead letters will be coming here very soon. Follow me, and I will show you where the undeliverable letters are kept."

Pater Kronos led the boys into an enormous vault with rows upon rows of shelves stretching as far into the distance as the eye could see. The shelves were stacked with containers filled with dead letters returned from the future.

"The more these letters mount, the less hope there is for the future of Christmas," Kronos informed them. "Now that 2100 is the new terminus, I suspect that the Dead Letter Office will have to be expanded to at least twice the size it is now."

"Why is there less hope now for the future of Christmas?" asked Alex.

"The period of time from 2100 to 2525 has gone dark," Kronos replied. "The Christmas traditions are not getting through. Most likely, a fuse on the timeline has been blown. We have never lost 425 years so quickly before! It may already be too late to save Christmas future."

"We know how to repair fuses," Grant told him. "Just show us where the fuse is blown, and we will replace it."

"Not so quick," said Kronos. "You may know how to repair fuses on regular Christmas tree lights, but repairing time-fuses is another matter entirely. If you cannot identify the wires running through the present from Christmas past, how will you ever know the way to connect them to those running from Christmas present to Christmas future?"

"That's easy," Alex told him. "Grampy taught us that all we need to do is match the colors of the wires."

"Young man, Grampy is right about ordinary wires, but time is not wired with ordinary wires, don't you know? You obviously don't understand how time is wired any more than you understand that answering the riddle of the Sphinx cannot simply be done by repeating a word. Before you go messing with time, you've got to know what you are up against. Follow me, and you will see what I mean."

The boys followed Pater Kronos from the Dead Letter Office down the corridor with the advertisements that they had come down earlier. Again, they saw the posters advertising 'Saturnalia in Rome in 350 A. D', 'Hanukkah in 168 B. C.', the 'Coronation of Charlemagne in 800, the 'Terror that is Norse in 900 A. D'. The boys passed poster after poster until they came to the door of the mailbox and halted.

"I must warn you," Kronos said. "The Sphinx remains on the loose, and he is still hungry. Until you are able to solve his riddle, there is a secret password you must use to make him back off—at least for a little while. Whatever you do, you must use this password sparingly, and you must know what it means when you speak it. Repeat after me, 'memento mori.'"

Together, the boys repeated the words, "memento mori."

"Now say it again," said Kronos.

Again, the boys repeated it: "Memento mori."

"What does it mean?" Alex asked.

"It means 'remember death,'" Kronos replied. "But you must understand that it means far more than what it says on the surface. When you say it to the Sphinx, in your mind you must acknowledge that you are remembering that your own life is short and that you, too, will one day die. This is hard for young people to accept, because they believe that their own death is far away and that they have a very long time to live. However, if you remember when you are young that one day you will die—if you remember Tree King when you are young—then you will have the wisdom not to waste the time you have been allotted and your death will not be accompanied with regret over a misspent life like the dead Scrooges you saw. It is the

Sphinx's job to remind us that time is short, so if you can convince him that you understand this, he will be more likely to leave you alone. Still, he may question you and probe you, and this ordeal can be terrifying. Whatever you do, you must show courage when you face him. That courage will best be demonstrated as the courage to live life to the fullest and to do so in the service of your fellow human beings. Do you understand what I'm telling you?"

"I think so, but I'm still afraid," Alex told him. "What if the Sphinx is not convinced?"

"If you fail to convince him, then I'm sorry to say he may eat you," Kronos told him.

"Then I don't want to go outside that mailbox door," said Alex. "I want to stay here."

"It will take both of you to find that burned out fuse," Kronos said, "and you must prepare for the possibility that not just one, but many, fuses are burned out. You can't expect your brother to find the problem by himself. You love your brother, don't you?"

Alex sheepishly nodded.

"Then let brotherly love inspire your courage. Once you have exercised that courage even a little, you will be surprised at how much it will grow. But if you stay here, then we can all expect Christmas to die. If that happens, then you may be no better off than the Scrooges you saw."

The Time Guardian's harsh words caused tears to form in Alex's eyes. "Don't worry, Alex," Grant said. "I'll be with you every step of the way. If worse comes to worse, I'll convince the Sphinx to eat me first. That will give you a head start back to one of the mailboxes, okay?"

Alex nodded his head.

"We're ready, then," Grant said.

Pater Kronos unlatched the mailbox door, and Grant peeked out to see if there was any sign of the Sphinx.

"The coast is clear," he said, grabbing Alex's hand, and together they ventured out of the mailbox back into the present. When they walked away from the mailbox and looked back toward it, they saw Kronos following them from a distance. He had stopped to be sure the door to the mailbox was latched and locked so that no unauthorized persons could enter. The boys also noticed that the date on the side of the mailbox had mysteriously changed. It no longer read '2525' but instead read '2100'. They immediately realized that many of the Christmases yet to be were being eaten away, and they knew that it was now their job to reconnect the lights of Christmas past to a dark and uncertain future.

—Chapter Eight—

TIME-DREIDELS AND MATZO-BALL TRADITIONS

G rant and Alex gazed at the landscape. Across the sky, luminous curtains of green, red, blue, and yellow scattered waves of colored light upon the green, silvery, and golden grass. At times, when the aurora of colors from the sky would mix, the light would become white like sunlight. The effect across the landscape was not unlike the shadows cast by clouds on a sunny day. In this case, however, the shadows were like bands and patches of color separated by bands and patches of what looked like sunlight. After the boys had traveled a little distance from the mailbox, they began searching for strings of Christmas lights so that they could reconnect Christmas past through Christmas present to Christmas future and restore hope to that bleak world yet to be, for it was slowly being eaten away by dark hopelessness.

Grant and Alex had found two sticks and were thrashing about in the evergreen bushes, trying to locate the wiring for the lights. When Pater Kronos caught up with them, he asked them what they were doing.

"Looking for strings of Christmas lights," Grant replied. "Do you know where they are?"

"This road you're traveling down is one of the light strings," Kronos replied. "If you keep traveling, you will soon come to one of the angel stars. In your world, those are the Christmas tree lights."

"Oh," said Grant. "I guess we thought the lights looked the same here as on our tree. When we find an angel star and it is burned out, how do we repair it?"

"I'm not sure I can explain how to do that," Kronos answered. "The angel stars are more complicated than ordinary Christmas tree lights. For one thing, they guide the Orna folk here in Arboria to the Star at Tree Top where Tree King dwells. They are also good at helping people with their questions, however. Maybe you need to ask the first one you come to what you need to do."

"Will you go with us?" Alex asked.

"I'm sorry, but I have business elsewhere," Kronos replied. "Just remember what I told you about the Sphinx. Do you remember what you need to tell him if you see him?"

"Yes," Grant replied. "*Memento mori.*"

Kronos then stared at Alex, who repeated the words, "*Memento mori.*"

"Good," said Kronos, "and just be sure you *mean* the words when you say them. Can you do that?"

The boys nodded.

"Goodbye then, young fellows. I'm sure we will be meeting again soon. Just travel down this road and ask the first angel star you come to how to repair the connection. Good luck."

"Thanks," the boys said, and they told Kronos goodbye.

As the boys traveled down the road they saw hills and valleys. At times, the roads were spanned by bridges that crossed great gorges. After crossing one of these bridges, they came to what appeared to be a village. It was comprised of all shapes and sizes of quaint houses and buildings, made of honey-colored limestone, and having slate roofs. Around these houses grew gardens with holly bushes and Christmas flowers such as poinsettias.

From the road the boys were on, they could see white light shining above the housetops. It shone from some source they had not yet discovered, but as they continued onward, they eventually found it at the center of what appeared to be a town square. They realized at once that this had to be one of the angel stars. At first glance, it did look to them like a star, but as they continued to gaze at it, they began to see the form of an angel inside. The angel, in fact, was like a filament that glowed brilliantly inside a star-shaped globe. The angel star's feet were submerged well beneath the cobblestone pavement of the square much in the same way the greater part of an iceberg lies hidden beneath the ocean.

About fifteen Orna folk, arrayed in beautiful Christmas apparel, were standing around the angel star, and in its presence, they sparkled and glistened. The skin of some Ornas reflected its image and projected many-colored spangles across the square onto the buildings surrounding it. Other Ornas acted as prisms, which divided the angel star's light into all the colors of the rainbow.

As the boys watched, they figured out that the angel star was not only the Orna folks' teacher; it also seemed to be their judge. Whenever some of the Ornas would successfully answer the questions it posed, they would become more beautifully adorned. Some were allowed to continue traveling on to the next village. However, others of the Ornas, who obviously had not studied for their examinations, were turned away and told to study more. Some of those who had been turned back were grumbling. Grant and Alex recognized a couple of them from the swimming pool they landed in when they first entered the Christmas Tree World. These Ornas were loitering and griping that the angel star had treated them unfairly. Alex and Grant paused in the square for a while to listen in on their conversation.

"What does that ridiculous angel star expect us to do?" one of them asked. He was of a metallic red color, and when he spoke an echo reverberated inside him.

"Aren't you one to complain?" replied a second, who was lime green with pink stripes. "You shouldn't have tried to cheat the way you did." This Orna also echoed when it talked.

"How do you know I cheated?" the red one asked.

"I heard about it at the swimming pool," replied the green and pink one. "You should know that you can't keep that sort of thing a secret there. Anyway, when the angel star asked the questions in a different order from the way you expected, it really messed you up. You don't have any excuses. But me? That is another matter. I do have an excuse. I had a headache."

"Yeah, the one hundredth one this year," the red one scolded. "How likely is that? I expect you will die any day now."

"Shut your mouth!" the pink and green one returned. "Don't you know it is bad luck to talk about dying? The Sphinx may hear you!"

"Oh, blast that silly Sphinx!" the red Orna said. "I wish I knew of a good dentist who could pull every last one of that old creature's teeth and take the twinkle out of his smile once and for all. Anyway, if I see him, I won't try to pull his teeth, but I will try to pull the wool over his eyes with that '*memento mori*' trick."

"Excuse us," Grant said, interrupting their conversation. "Do you know if the angel star is busy? We need to ask him a few questions."

The red Orna laughed, and the echo of the laughter in its belly made him sound wicked. "The angel stars are always busy," he said. "I hope you know the answers to its questions. If you don't, then you'll be sent down like the rest of us."

"We'll be sure to say 'please' and 'thank-you,'" Alex assured him.

The Ornas laughed, and the hollowness inside them again made their laughter sound evil.

The boys left the hollow sounding Ornas and soon joined the others standing in front of the angel star. Grant asked a beautiful Orna who was crimson and purple and decorated with golden brocade, "Do you know how long it will be before we can ask the angel star a few questions? It is really important."

"What do you want to ask it?" the beautiful Orna inquired. The voice of this Orna did not echo, but sounded clear and solid.

"We are trying to save Christmas future," Grant told him. "All the lights have burned out there. We found out when we traveled through one of the mailboxes to the year 2525 and found the cemetery of the Scrooges. Christmas future has now been cut short to the year 2100."

The gilded crimson and purple Orna bowed and said, "Then you are obviously outlanders, for only outlanders are allowed into the mailboxes. You have been sent from the other world to help us then?"

"I guess so," Grant said. "There are no Christmas lights in 2525, and that means there are no angel stars either. Something has to be done fast, or Christmas will be dead in only one hundred years."

"What grievous news!" the beautiful Orna remarked. "Of course, you, being outlanders, will go to the front of the class. Your task is more urgent than ours. Let me assist you."

The beautiful Orna shouted, "Clear the way, people of Arboria! We have outlanders in our midst!" The Ornas parted to allow Grant and Alex to pass. As the boys walked through their midst, the Ornas gazed at them with astonishment. The boys could hear them whispering to one another, "outlanders," "how wondrous," and "has any-one known of such a thing in our time?" The boys approached the angel star and knelt.

"Do not!" the angel star commanded. "Kneel only to Tree King and him alone. He is Arboria's beginning and end."

The boys quickly rose up and looked upon the angel star with frightened faces.

"State your purpose," the angel star commanded.

"We have just returned from Christmas future," Grant began.

"Stop!" the angel star interrupted. "Why does the younger outlander not speak? I want to hear from him!"

Alex's knees suddenly buckled, and he started stammering. "I...we...the future...the Scrooges...Things are not too good in the future."

"Courage, young outlander," the angel star said. "Take your time and explain. This is part of your test, and I am confident that you can pass it."

Alex tried again, and when he did, the most extraordinary words flowed from his tongue. "On an ordinary summer day, having escaped the Sphinx's fatal jaws, my brother and I were guided by Pater Kronos through a mailbox to the future year A. D. 2525 where we witnessed firsthand a horrendous devastation brought on by the death of Christmas future. With the help of a super-heated magic book, we learned that a time-fuse had blown out in the present, and that it was our destiny to find it and to repair it. For this cause, we have come to inquire of you, most Blessed Angel, how we may accomplish our task quickly and well."

Grant, who was listening to Alex, stood there with his mouth hanging open, and as soon as Alex finished his speech, the Orna folk broke into applause. By now Alex's mouth was hanging open, too, and he asked the angel star, "How did I do that?"

"You did it with the help of Tree King," the angel star told him. "Now, are you ready for my answer?"

"Yes," Alex replied. "Just tell us what we need to do."

"Very well," said the angel star. "You will have to travel to the past to find the key to the time-wiring plans. To keep them safe from the enemy, they are scattered across the years like pieces of a puzzle. You will need to travel to past years to gather up these pieces. Once the pieces are gathered, the task will fall to you and the Orna folk to solve the puzzle."

"Is the Sphinx the enemy?" Grant asked.

"No," replied the angel star. "He is a guardian of the throne of Tree King. His weapon against those who are lazy and forgetful is time. Indeed, his jaws are the jaws of time, and with those jaws, he crushes and eats away all that is false, deceptive, and temporary. But his roar is also the roar of time, and that roar spurs on all who dwell in Arboria, encouraging them to make the most of every precious moment they are given. If you are industrious and work hard, you need not fear him. If your hearts are pure, then his roar will only increase your courage. However, hearts filled with hatred and selfishness can be easily shattered by his roar. These are the hollow Ornas. You can know them by their speech, for when they do speak, you can hear their words echo through their empty souls."

"That explains the echo we heard from the two Ornas we met earlier," Grant remarked. "They sounded very strange when they spoke, and their laughter was scary."

"They have failed my test yet again," the angel star told them, "and they are dangerously close to being devoured by the Sphinx."

"I don't understand," said Alex. "Why do the Ornas who live in this village have to pass tests?"

"First of all, this is not exactly a village," replied the angel star. "Villages in our world are in fact schools, colleges, and universities. People are allowed to live here as long as they are doing well with their studies. Those who do not are sent down to the lower levels of the Tree World. Those who succeed are promoted."

Grant remarked, "The red Orna we saw said that he would use the *'memento mori'* to pull the wool over the Sphinx's eyes."

"That is called presumption," the angel star said. "Do you know what 'presumption' is?"

"No," Alex answered.

"'Presumption' is the false belief that one is in good standing with Tree King and has all the time in the world when one in fact is not in good standing and is fast running out of time. The red Orna you saw is the victim of a dreadful lie spun in the depths of his own hollow soul. I doubt he will last the week."

Suddenly, the boys heard the Sphinx roaring somewhere in the village.

"The Sphinx is coming to reap," said the angel star. "You must find one of the red mailboxes. There you will be safe. I suggest you duck into the first red mailbox you see!"

"Will all the Ornas here be eaten?" Alex asked.

"No," replied the angel star. "Only those to whom he presents his riddle need fear him. Those who know the answer will be spared, and those who know it not will be eaten. Run now, boys, so that you will be safe."

Grant and Alex started running and soon came to the edge of the village. As they did, the Sphinx's roar grew louder and louder. When they looked behind them, they could see its brilliant golden light shining brightly from a street they had just run down.

"Look!" Grant shouted. "There's a red mailbox! It says 168 B. C.! Let's see where it takes us!"

* * *

Grant opened the lock on the red mailbox door by using the combination '861', and soon the boys were running down the corridor past posters like the ones they had seen before. This time, however, they did not stop to look at them because they knew future time was growing ever shorter. When they arrived at the gate, they made their way through the snow-globe portal onto the tarmac. Young Nanny must have been expecting them, for she was standing, looking out from the cabin door of her plane. This time her plane was red, though in every other respect the plane was the same. Its skin, like one of those mood rings, had merely shifted in color. The color of the sky had also changed from turquoise to pink. In a hurry, the boys climbed the automatic stairs to the door. There they found Young Nanny dressed in a grey robe like a biblical character would wear, but this time, the scarf, which she usually wore around her neck, was made of black silk, was much larger, and was covering her head. Young Nanny greeted them with the word, "Shalom!"

The boys gave her a strange look.

"That is the Hebrew word meaning 'peace,'" she explained. "Quick, boys, we've got to leave, so buckle up and help yourself to some of my special chicken soup."

"Won't it slosh all over us?" Alex asked her.

"No," Young Nanny replied. "I've got it in thermos bottles for you, so you can drink it, but you will have to spear the matzo balls with a fork."

"What are those?" Grant asked.

"They are like dumplings made from unleavened bread and eggs," she answered. "Matzo-ball soup is Jewish. I think you will like it, especially since we're on our way to ancient Israel to celebrate a Jewish holiday."

"Wow! That sounds like fun!" Alex exclaimed. Then he asked, "Can we have sugar cookies, too?"

"Of course," Young Nanny said, smiling. "But first eat your matzo-ball soup. The weather is going to be a bit chilly where you're going."

Young Nanny engaged the propellers, and soon the plane was taxiing down the runway. As they became airborne, the boys noticed that the pink sky deepened to a light red, so they asked Young Nanny why this was happening.

"Because we are headed to the past now," she said. "We are going to Israel in the year 168 B. C., to celebrate the first Hanukkah. That is the Jewish holiday I was telling you about."

"What is Hanukkah?" Alex asked.

"It's called the Feast of Lights or the Feast of Dedication, and it is one of the Hebrew traditions that celebrated the Tree World of Tree King before there was a Christmas. You will learn all about it once you get there, so finish your matzo-ball soup while I tell you a story about my sister Arabella Priscilla."

As they ate their soup, Young Nanny started her story. "Arabella Priscilla was my littlest sister—the baby of our family—and when she grew up she married a Jewish man that everyone in the family called Uncle Karl. He had a wonderful sense of humor and was very loving and generous. In fact, he was the very opposite of any Scrooge you might meet anywhere in time past, present, or future. Your daddy loved Uncle Karl so much that he wanted to learn everything he could about the ancient Jewish feasts like Passover and Hanukkah. He learned from Uncle Karl all about dreidels, the special spinning toy that Jewish children play with during Hanukkah."

"I remember those," Grant said. "Daddy bought us some a couple of years ago."

"Dreidels are neat to think about," said Young Nanny, "because they spin along like time spins along. And like time, they wind down and finally stop spinning. I don't know if you will see any dreidels at the first Hanukkah because usually traditions are added over the years. Traditions are like snowballs, you see. They usually start off small, but as time rolls along, they accumulate more and more snow and become so large you can make a snowman out of them. When dealing with snow, of course, you can't usually tell where one layer begins and another ends. They all become part of the one big snow-ball. So it is with traditions."

"I think I see what you mean," Alex said. "Traditions are like these matzo balls, too. They are made out of cracker crumbs, but when all the crumbs get rolled together, the matzo ball is almost as solid as a golf ball."

"Well," said Young Nanny. "I hope my matzo balls are not as hard as golf balls! They wouldn't be very digestible then, would they?"

Grant and Alex giggled. "They enjoyed spearing the matzo balls in Young Nanny's soup, and though the soup was somewhat bland, it was warm and very filling. They were glad of this, because as they traveled into the past, the air became quite nippy.

"My, it's getting chilly," Young Nanny commented. "I think it's time I gave you some special presents I crocheted for you." She removed a plastic shopping bag from under her seat, took out of it two scarves and two special toboggans, and handed them to the boys. "These will keep you warm, but they will also double as prayer shawls and yarmulkes," she explained.

"What are *they*?" Grant asked.

"The prayer shawls or the yarmulkes?" she questioned.

"Both," Grant stated.

"The prayer shawls have tassels on them, and they help you keep track of your prayers," she explained. "The yarmulke is also called a skull cap. Jewish males wear them as a sign of respect when they worship."

"Oh," Grant said. "Thanks so much, Young Nanny."

"Yeah, thanks Young Nanny," Alex added.

Soon, they were beginning their descent to ancient Israel in the year 168 B. C.

"What about the sugar cookies?" Alex reminded her.

"Dear, dear, how could I have forgotten those?" She took the tin from the compartment in the console, removed the lid, and used her Nanny stick to serve the boys two sugar cookies each.

"We might need one more for good measure," Alex suggested.

"Okay, just one more," Young Nanny agreed.

Soon, the plane touched down and they were taxiing down the runway. When the plane came to a halt, Young Nanny opened the cabin door, hugged them goodbye, and gave them her final directions. "Remember. When you greet people here, the proper word to say is 'shalom'. Can you say that?"

"Shalom," said Grant.

"Shalom," Alex repeated.

—Chapter Nine—

THE BEAST, THE PIG, AND THE CANDLES

AFTER GRANT AND ALEX entered the time-port terminal, they made their way down the corridor that exited to ancient Israel in the year 168 B. C. The corridor walls in this terminal were made of rough-hewn stone, and in the cracks of the walls grew a compact little plant with small oval leaves and little white flowers. Alex tore off a snippet and took a whiff. "Hey, this smells kind of like mint," he said, holding it up to Grant's nose.

Grant sniffed. "It smells good, I wonder what it is? Let's pick some more and put it in our pockets in case we have to smell another one of those awful cemetery books."

"Good idea," Alex said, so they picked several springs and stuffed them into their pockets. Soon, they came to the mailbox door and were about to open it when without warning it swung open from the outside. When it did, cold air rushed in, and Grant and Alex were glad they had the prayer scarves and yarmulkes Young Nanny had crocheted for them. Before them stood a tall man with long gray hair and a gray beard. On his head a single candle burned brightly. He was dressed in a golden robe and had a white silk sash tied around his waist. He looked a bit like Pater Kronos, but he was not as muscular. He was quite slender, in fact, and his face was not round but oval.

"Shalom," Alex and Grant both said.

"I see you know the proper greeting," the man said. "Shalom to you, too, and welcome to the events leading up to the Festival of Hanukkah. My name is *Adelphos Mneme*. I am the Guardian of Time Past. Since my name is hard to say, you may call me 'Brother Memory'. That is what my name means."

"How did you know we were coming?" Grant asked.

"I received word from my brother through a vision granted me by Tree King that I was to meet you today," he told the boys. "My brother is Pater Kronos."

"We know him!" Alex exclaimed. "He's the Time Guardian of the Present!"

"Correct," Brother Memory confirmed. "In my dream, he told me everything about your adventure thus far, of how you traveled to the year 2525 and found the cemetery of the Scrooges. I know that Christmas future is in danger of being extinguished unless the fuse is repaired, so I am here to help you find the pieces to the puzzle that will help you repair the time-wiring connecting past time to present and future time. You will need to memorize the puzzle pieces when you find them, because nothing can be removed from any past times and places."

"Are you also the Ghost of Christmas Past?" Alex asked.

"Not quite yet," Brother Memory replied. "We are still in the time before the first Christmas, but in less than two centuries I shall indeed take on myself the further name, 'Ghost of Christmas Past', as you have already correctly guessed."

"I used to be afraid of ghosts like you, but not anymore," Alex told him. "Now I have courage because I met an angel star."

"That's a good thing, but try not to boast too soon," Brother Memory remarked. "You will need even more courage where I am taking you."

Brother Memory extended his right arm in the direction of a path that led from the mailbox and said, "Enter." The boys walked past him and stood on a cobblestone path. Ahead, they could see an ancient city. All its buildings were made of the same kind of stone that they had seen in the wall inside the mailbox corridor.

"That looks like the city of Bethlehem," Grant remarked. "Remember the pictures on our Christmas cards, Alex?"

He nodded.

"This is not Bethlehem, but you are close," Brother Memory said. "This is Jerusalem in the year 168 B. C. Walk with me to the city, and I shall tell you what you need to know about this place and time."

As Grant and Alex walked with Brother Memory, he began his explanation. "First, you need to understand that nothing you see in this place and time can be changed," he told them. "All that is here has already happened, so you will not be able to change things here no matter how hard you try. *You*, however, can be changed by what you see here, and you can be changed either for the better or the worse. Dark spells lurk about in past worlds like the one you are going to view, so you must be careful not to fall under their influence. If they infect your soul, then you could end up like the Scrooges you saw in the graveyard of the future. This is why you must be on guard against the most notorious enemies from these past worlds. One is the enemy of ignorance, a second is the enemy of forgetfulness, and a third is the enemy of the lie. You will need to do all you can to battle these enemies. If they are victorious over you, then Christmas future will surely die. Are you ready to enter this world?"

The boys nodded with some hesitation because of what Brother Memory had said about the dark spells.

"Courage, boys," Brother Memory urged.

Alex pulled out a spring of the plant he had plucked from the wall, held it up to his nose, and took a deep whiff as Brother Memory watched. "I see you have found some hyssop," he said as they continued down the path. "That will help protect you. Hyssop, like the herb rosemary, aids memory and guards against ignorance, forgetfulness, and deception. The people of ancient Israel used hyssop to sprinkle lamb's blood on the entrances to their houses during Passover so that the plague of the death of the firstborn of Egypt would not touch them. Hyssop not only keeps the Angel of Death at bay, but its scent also helps keep past memories alive—especially memories of miracles. The scent of hyssop in this way is like the scent of evergreen trees like cedar, pine, and fir—the trees of Christmas. The leaves and the scent of evergreens do not die or fade like trees whose foliage winter strips away. Their branches are ever true. This is an important lesson to remember."

"We thought we could smell this plant if we ever came across one of those hot, smelly books like the one we found in the cemetery of the Scrooges," Grant remarked.

"What you smelled from that book could have very easily been vampire perfume," Brother Memory remarked. "Just hope that you never grow to love the smell of it. Just keep smelling the hyssop, and you should be fine."

"Are there vampires here?" Grant asked.

"In ancient times, before there was an Israel, the vampire was the serpent who crept into the Garden of Paradise and worked his evil spell on the parents of the human race. Before he introduced his foul smell into that Garden, the fragrance there was sweeter than this hyssop. However, the serpent's perfume, like the odor from that cemetery book you read, is the perfume of regret. It may smell sweet at first—even like the aroma of fresh baked cookies—but as time passes its stench grows ever fouler until it smells like brimstone."

"What's that?" Alex inquired.

"Brimstone?" asked Brother Memory. "It's the same thing as sulfur. It smells kind of like burnt electrical wiring, burnt toast, and roasting skunks all mixed together."

"Hey!" Grant exclaimed. "That's exactly what we smelled coming from that book! So what we smelled was vampire perfume?"

"I would say so," Brother Memory answered, "and I'm certain you will smell it again before your visit here is over."

Brother Memory led the boys to one of the immense gates of the city of Jerusalem and halted. "This is Jerusalem's Eastern Gate, and beyond it is the Hebrew Temple. When we enter, you must stay close to me until we are safe inside the Temple. Do you understand?"

The boys nodded.

"Very well, then, let us go in."

The boys walked through the gates with Brother Memory, but inside a throng of people were rioting. The fighting and shouting continued all the way into the courts of the Temple. In the Temple's Outer Court, a battalion of soldiers were poised with spears and were pushing back a crowd that seemed to be trying to get to the great altar of Burnt Offering that stood in the Outer Court before the doorway of the Temple.

"What's happening?" Grant yelled at Brother Memory.

"The Beast is coming," he answered gravely. "He will be here in less than an hour, so we must hurry!"

Alex was frightened. "Beast? What beast? Is the Sphinx on the loose again?"

"Not a Sphinx, but something far worse," Brother Memory replied. "You will see him by day's end. But now, we must hurry to the scriptorium. It should be safe there for now."

"What is a scrip...?" Alex could not pronounce the word.

"Scriptorium," Brother Memory repeated. "That is where the sacred scrolls are being copied. There is little time now because the Beast will destroy the scrolls if he finds them."

By now, Alex, who had boasted of his courage, was trembling. He wondered if the Beast was a vampire. Alex feared vampires even more than ghosts because vampires could bite!

Brother Memory led the boys through double doors into the scriptorium of the Temple. Rows of scribes sat there copying sacred scrolls. The scribes were hurriedly writing. Suddenly, one scribe rose from where he was sitting, tore his robes, and wailed. Some of the scribes ran over to him and looked at the manuscript he had been working on.

"*Melek ha Olam* understands, brother," an old scribe said, trying to comfort him. "We must not grieve over our mistakes. Have courage. The word of *Melek ha Olam* is not a light that can be snuffed out."

"Who is he talking about?" Grant asked. "Who is Mel Olam?"

"*Melek ha Olam* is Hebrew for 'King of the Universe,'" Brother Memory replied. "In the Christmas Tree World, he is known as Tree King. Do you know of Tree King?"

"Yes," Grant replied. "He is the Lord of Time."

"Why is the scribe weeping?" Alex asked.

"He made a mistake copying the scroll," Brother Memory answered. "He was almost finished with it when he made the error. This means the scribes will have to bury this scroll, and he will have to start over from the very beginning on a fresh one."

"Can't he use an eraser?" Alex asked.

"No," said Brother Memory. "To erase something from a sacred scroll profanes it and makes it un-kosher. That means the scroll is considered unclean. Any scribe who makes a mistake must start again from scratch. This is why the scribe you see is so frustrated and sad."

The boys watched as the scribe who made the mistake brought his crying under control, opened a fresh scroll, and courageously began copying again from the very beginning. Then the scribes who had run over to comfort him quickly returned to their copying.

"These scribes are under terrible pressure to copy as many scrolls as they can," Brother Memory told the boys. "They are in a race against time because they know that the Beast who is coming will destroy every scroll he can find. These scrolls will have to be hidden soon, or all the work these scribes have done will be for naught."

Just then, they heard shouting coming from the hallway outside the scriptorium. "In here!" sounded a harsh voice. Quickly, the scribes hid their scrolls in secret compartments inside their desks, pulled out coin pouches, poured money on their desks, and gathered around the desks in small groups. The next thing the boys heard was the sound of spinning tops and laughter.

"Look," Alex said. "They are playing with dreidels!"

"The scribes are hoping to fool the Greek soldiers," Brother Memory explained. "Copying sacred scrolls is punishable by death. The scribes are trying to make the Greek soldiers think they are gambling. You see, the Beast approves of gambling, but he severely punishes anyone caught copying a sacred scroll."

The soldiers came in, rounded up the scribes, and began tearing their desks apart piece by piece.

"You think you can fool us?" the commander of the troops roared.

The soldiers soon found the scrolls in the hidden compartments and started gathering them up.

"Chain them all!" the commander shouted, and the soldiers began putting shackles on the wrists and ankles of the scribes.

"Who's in charge here?" he asked.

The old scribe who had comforted the younger scribe who made a mistake slowly raised his hand.

"You have broken the edict of King Antiochus the Fourth!" he accused. "Now we will make you witness the end of your crazy religion! Take them to that blasted sacrifice altar of theirs!"

The soldiers rounded up the scribes, pushing and shoving them toward the door. Grant, Alex, and Brother Memory followed them until they reached the Outer Court of the Temple. There was now blood covering the ground from where the soldiers had killed the courageous protestors who had been inciting the mob. The Jewish High Priest, who stood next to the altar, was dressed in his priestly regalia and was wearing the breastplate of the precious gems that represented the twelve tribes of Israel.

"This will all be for the best," he said to those assembled. "Our glorious and divine King, Epiphanes, is coming even now to sacrifice on the blessed altar. You will see that accepting his conditions will be the best thing for our people."

"The High Priest may seem like he is on the side of *Melek ha Olam*," Brother Memory told the boys, "but you will soon see that he is a traitor. His name is Menelaus, and he has made a bargain with the one he calls Epiphanes to corrupt the Hebrew religion beyond recognition. 'Epiphanes' is Greek for 'shining of the light', but do not be deceived. Epiphanes is none other than the Beast, King Antiochus the Fourth, and his stock-in-trade is a deep and engulfing darkness that will drown every soul it manages to touch."

Just then, trumpets blasted from the direction of the Eastern Gate. The crowd turned and looked to see who was coming. What they saw was a king, trotting on a white stallion through the midst of the crowd. As he approached, a few voices from the crowd started chanting, "Hail Epiphanes!" The chanting increased in volume and intensity as he approached. Grant and Alex were about to join in, but Brother Memory, realizing that they were getting ready to make a mistake, placed his hands over their mouths.

"Do not join in!" he cautioned. "The one you see is the Beast! If you chant, then his dark spell will infect you."

"But he doesn't look like a beast," Alex remarked.

"Looks are deceiving. Just watch. Then you will understand."

Behind the king who was riding the stallion was a horse pulling a wagon covered with a swath of crimson cloth. The boys could hear grunting sounds coming out from under it.

"Is the Beast hidden under that cloth?" Grant asked.

"Just watch!" Brother Memory replied.

Some men removed the cloth, revealing a cage. Inside was a fat sow—a female pig.

The moment the pig was revealed, a cry of horror arose from the crowd.

"What's the matter?" Alex asked Brother Memory.

"Do you not know that pigs are unclean animals here in Israel?" he replied. "Even to bring a pig into the sacred precincts of the Temple violates Hebrew law. But you haven't seen anything yet. Just keep watching."

The sow was led by a rope to the north side of the Altar of Burnt Offering—the altar of sacrifice. Then the High Priest took his knife and slaughtered it. Again, wails of horror arose from the crowd.

"Why did the priest do that?" Grant asked.

Brother Memory was silent. The boys continued to watch as the pig was placed on the altar and offered there as a burnt offering sacrifice. Now wailing and sobbing filled the Temple courtyard, but the soldiers stood poised with their spears to run anyone through who dared cause trouble. Meanwhile, the King was laughing wickedly as fat from the pig's carcass caused the fire to flare up from the altar. Soon, the stench of burning pig could be smelled throughout the Temple courts.

"Alex, do you know what that smell is?" Grant asked.

"How could I forget," he replied. "It's the same smell that came from the book in the cemetery of the Scrooges." Alex and Grant removed the hyssop from their pockets and smelled it in an attempt to filter out the nauseating odor.

"You're right," Brother Memory said, "and the so-called King who has done this terrible thing to the Hebrew people is the prototype of all Scrooges who will ever live. Do you know what a prototype is?"

"No," the boys replied.

"A prototype is the first in a long line of similar types of people. The Beast is the first of a long line of Scrooges who over the centuries will try to destroy all memories of holidays that celebrate the world of Tree King. What you do not understand yet is the gravity of what he has done. Do you know why this Burnt Offering Altar is so important to the Hebrew people?"

"No," the boys answered.

"Long ago, before this altar was erected, Father Abraham, the ancestor of the Hebrew people, brought his son Isaac here to sacrifice him, but *Melek ha Olam* provided a ram to be sacrificed in Isaac's place. This place is none other than Mt. Moriah, also called the place of provision. This happened during a time when the pagans sacrificed their children on these kinds of altars to false gods who went by the names of Molech and Chemosh. The Beast, Antiochus the Fourth, wants to bring back the sacrifice of children. He is already planning to murder little Jewish boys, tie them to their mother's necks, and throw their mothers over the walls to their deaths. These scribes who have been made to watch the sacrifice of the sow will no doubt be crucified for violating the Beast's edict against copying sacred scripture. Forty thousand Jewish people have been killed thus far in the city of Jerusalem, and another forty thousand have been captured and are being forced into slavery. The people of Israel have indeed met with very dark times."

"When will their suffering end?" Grant asked.

"In approximately three years, a hero named Judas Maccabeus will drive the Beast out. At that time, all the holy vessels that the Beast stole from the Temple will have to be replaced, including the Menorah, the seven-branched candlestick that stands in the Temple's Holy Place. This new Menorah will then be lit, and the first Hanukkah will be celebrated."

Just then, the boys heard the soldiers trying to get the crowd to shout, "Hail Epiphanes!" The crowd this time, however, was unenthusiastic, so a soldier ran his sword through the young scribe who earlier had made the copying mistake. When the boys saw this, they started crying. Then the old scribe shouted to the top of his lungs, "Hail *Epimanes!*" The boys were so shocked, they stopped crying. How could the old scribe stoop to such a low level?

"You think you know what he just shouted," Brother Memory said, "but you don't. Just as the scribes tried to fool the soldiers by spinning the dreidels, the old scribe has figured out an ingenious way to help his people live through the evil times that are coming. When you heard the old scribe, you thought he cried out, 'Hail Epiphanes!' The Beast and his soldiers thought that's what he shouted, too. Those close to him, however, heard him say, 'Hail Epimanes!' The word 'Epimanes' means 'mad one.'"

"That's a good name for him!" Grant said. "I hope the Beast never finds out they are calling him that."

"This is part of an old tradition among the Hebrews," Brother Memory explained. "In the days when the worship of *Melek ha Olam* was threatened by the worship of a false god, who also went by the name of 'Melek' or 'King', the Israelites mispronounced it 'Molech'. The vowels 'o' and 'e' were substituted, because those vowels appeared in the Hebrew word '*bosheth*' which means 'shameful'. 'Molech' was the 'Shameful King' that required people to sacrifice their firstborn children to him. In the same way 'Epimanes' is a suitable name for the Beast."

The chanting of the crowd grew as 'Hail Epimanes!' started to catch on. Fortunately, the Beast and his men seemed too full of themselves and too blinded by their own lies to understand. Most of them rode away, thinking they had destroyed the Jewish spirit. Some of the men, however, stayed behind and started uprooting hyssop from the surrounding walls.

"What are they doing that for?" Alex asked.

"Hyssop is the herb of purification," Brother Memory answered. "They want to get rid of anything that will help the people purify their Temple and remember their religion."

"That is terrible," Grant said. "I don't want to see anymore."

"You're right. We have seen enough here," Brother Memory said. "It's time to show you something more hopeful. But to do that, I need for us to fast-forward our time three years to the first Hanukkah. Are you ready?"

The boys nodded.

"Then hold my hands, and I will take you there."

After joining hands with Brother Memory, they soon were fast-forwarding three years into the future. As they stood in the Temple court, they saw many events pass by in rapid succession. Crosses appeared and disappeared. Weeds sprang up between the stone slabs in the Temple courtyard. Repeatedly, Jews mourning the desecration of their Temple would appear only to be followed by legions of soldiers enacting bloody purges. Through it all, however, the Jews persisted. Then Brother Memory slowed their time travel down for a brief period.

"You need to see what the Beast has done to add insult to injury," he told the boys. "He has erected a statue to the Greek god Zeus in the Temple. This is an even greater insult than the sacrifice of the pig. The Beast thinks he is Zeus on earth, and he has now converted the Temple of *Melek ha Olam* into a temple to Zeus. He has also replaced the scribes we saw earlier with followers of the evil High Priest Menelaus. These corrupt scribes are planning to alter the Hebrew Scriptures that are offensive to the god Zeus, and they don't care if they abandon traditional Jewish beliefs to do it."

As the boys watched, more pigs were sacrificed on the Burnt Offering Altar. Still, Jews wearing sackcloth and ashes continued to congregate in the Outer Court of the Temple to mourn when soldiers were not present. As the time travelers approached the year 165 B. C., Brother Memory again slowed down their rapid journey forward through the remaining months.

"What you see now are Jewish rebels driving out the Greek soldiers," he informed the boys. "They are led by the five sons of a priest named Matthias. One of them, Judas Maccabeus, is their leader. The Maccabees will fight valiantly and will finally rid Israel of the armies of the Beast. Independence Day will then come for the Jewish nation."

Grant and Alex watched as the old Altar of Burnt Offering was disassembled stone by stone and was replaced by a new altar made of rough-unhewn stones.

"We have finally arrived," Brother Memory said. "We shall soon witness the miracle of Hanukkah."

"It's cold," Alex said when they came to a halt. He and Grant pulled their prayer scarves up around their faces. The yarmulkes Young Nanny had crocheted for them were not large enough to pull down over their ears, but they did keep the top of their heads warm.

"It's cold because the day is the 25th day of the Jewish month of Kislev—the time of the winter solstice when the sun is low on the horizon," Brother Memory told them. "The 25th of Kislev is the shortest day of the year, but this day is especially important to the Jews for another reason. On this day, the Beast has finally been driven out of Israel by Judas the Hammer and his brothers. 'Hammer' is literally what the name 'Maccabee' means. Indeed, now that the five Maccabees have managed to hammer out the invaders, their Temple is ready to be rededicated. This must start today because it is midwinter. The Menorah in the Temple must be lit, but there is a problem as you will soon find out. Follow me."

The boys followed Brother Memory to a storage room where the oil was kept for the Temple Menorah. A group of priests were frantic because something was wrong with the oil.

"It is unclean, I tell you!" the priest in charge was saying to the High Priest. "Epimanes and his men contaminated it! Only one flask of oil is still kosher! All the other flasks have been polluted!"

"What shall we do?" the High Priest asked. "There is only enough oil in this flask for the Menorah to burn for one day. How much time will it take to prepare more holy oil for the lamps?"

"Eight days," the priest replied.

"Eight days?" the High Priest exclaimed with a look of conster-nation. "There will not be enough oil for the Menorah to burn for eight days! Go at once and begin preparations to replenish our supply so that it is clean and kosher. Meanwhile, we shall just have to use what we have and hope the Menorah will not go out. Go now and fill the lamps of the Menorah. The first day of purification must begin this evening."

"As you wish, master," the oil priest said, and he proceeded into the Holy Place of the Temple where the Menorah stood. Grant, Alex, and Brother Memory followed and watched him as he very carefully filled its reservoirs, being careful not to allow even one precious drop to splatter on the floor and be wasted. When the priest had finished filling the lamp, he went and informed the High Priest that his order had been obeyed. The High Priest then gathered together all the priesthood in the Temple's Holy Place. A ladder was brought in and placed before the Temple veil that separated the most sacred pre-cincts of the Temple—the Holy of Holies—from the Holy Place where the priests were gathered. Burning in front of the Holy of Holies was a lamp. Two priests carried the ladder and placed it be-neath the lamp.

"What is the lamp up there for?" Alex asked Brother Memory.

"It is called the '*ner tamid*' or the 'Everlasting Light,'" he replied. "It symbolizes the uncreated light of *Melek ha Olam*. His light is an eternal light that will never dim. In this Tree World called Arboria, the never-ending light is represented by the Star at Tree Top. It is also found in the Star of Bethlehem that pointed the Wise Men to the Christ Child. Remember the verse of the Christmas Carol, 'O Little Town of Bethlehem', that reads, 'for in thy dark street shineth the Everlasting Light, the hopes and fears of all the years are met in thee tonight'? The *ner tamid* is a symbol of that Everlasting Light."

The High Priest stood at the foot of the ladder as another priest, carrying a taper, climbed up it, lit the taper from the *ner tamid*, and then carefully climbed down. When he reached the floor, he handed the burning taper to the High Priest. Joined by the other priests, the High Priest proceeded to the Menorah and started lighting its lamps. As he lit each one, he recited a blessing in Hebrew. When all the lamps were lit, a scribe recited a passage from the Hebrew Scriptures. Then the High Priest, joined by all the other priests, exited the Temple into the courtyard. Thousands were gathered, holding candles and shouting the word 'hosanna'. The High Priest raised his hands and cried with a loud voice, "It is done!" The throng immediately burst into cheers, and celebration and dancing commenced in the courtyard.

"I'm so glad they are happy now," Alex said, "but what will happen if the Menorah burns out again? There's only enough oil for one day, remember?"

"We are getting ready to be on Hanukkah watch," Brother Memory replied. "Follow me into the Holy Place of the Temple again, and we shall observe what will happen over the next eight days."

Brother Memory led the boys back to the Holy Place. "I shall speed forward one day at a time so that you can see the Hanukkah miracle unfold," he said. They sped forward one day. When they arrived at the evening that began the second day of Hanukkah, nervous priests were gathered around the Menorah waiting for the lamps to go out. The lamp had burned from the evening before and all through the next day, since the Hebrews reckoned days from one evening to the next instead of from morning to evening.

"Are you sure there is no more oil?" the High Priest asked the priest in charge of it.

"No, master. Word has gone out through all of Israel, and there is not a drop of holy oil to be found anywhere in the land."

"What of the contaminated oil?" the High Priest asked. "Has it been destroyed?"

"Indeed it has, master. It has been burned outside the camp as you ordered."

"Good," the High Priest replied. "Now we can only hope that *Melek ha Olam*, whose bush in the days of Moses burned but was not consumed, will repeat that miracle here."

"Time to fast-forward to day three," Brother Memory told the boys, so they joined hands and soon reached the evening that began the third day. The priests were still keeping vigil near the lamp.

"Any word on the new supply of oil?" the High Priest inquired again of the priest in charge.

"As you know, master, the process cannot be hurried."

"On the third day, the prophet Jonah emerged from the darkness of the great fish's belly into the light of day," said the High Priest. "May Israel also emerge from the Beast's dark belly to behold the light of *Melek ha Olam*."

"Now," said Brother Memory, holding the boys hands, "on to the next day."

"This evening begins the fourth day," the High Priest said. "On the fourth day of creation, *Melek ha Olam* created the sun, the moon, and the stars. Is it too much to ask Him who created such great lights through the mere utterance of a word to create light for our Menorah, too? What a small feat it would be for him."

The boys and Brother Memory again zoomed forward and reached the evening that started the fifth day. The boys were amazed when they saw the Menorah still burning. Some priests were rejoicing that the Menorah had not yet burned out. The High Priest was optimistic but remained cautious.

"Is it really a miracle?" one priest asked.

"It still may be too soon to say," the High Priest answered. "*Melek ha Olam* told Moses to fashion this Menorah like an almond tree. As you know, the almond is the first tree to blossom in spring after the dead of winter is passed. May this lamp that is a tree now be like the Tree of Life in Paradise!"

"I didn't know the Menorah was a tree," Grant remarked. "Does that mean it is like a Christmas tree?"

"It is one of the traditions behind the Christmas tree, yes." Brother Memory replied. "The tree that is ever green is also a tree of lights. Still, the miracle of Hanukkah is not complete. We must fast-forward to day six."

Brother Memory joined hands with the boys, and they sped on to the evening that began the sixth day of Hanukkah.

"Blessed be *Melek ha Olam*, the Light of Israel, who has kept our Menorah burning yet another day," the High Priest said the moment the sun had set. "We must remember that on the sixth day *Melek ha Olam* created man and woman in his image to reflect the light of Torah into the souls of their children. May he who guided Israel through the wilderness of Sinai with the pillar of fire by night and the pillar of cloud by day, lead the children of Israel through one more night and one more day! May we live to pass the torch of Everlasting Light to our children and our children's children! May the fires that light these days of Hanukkah ever remind us that *Melek ha Olam* is the King of All." The priests who were there listening said, 'amen,' which is the Hebrew word that means 'may it be so!'

"It's on to day seven, then." Brother Memory told the boys, so they held his hands and soon arrived on the evening that began that day.

"It is the seventh day, the day of Sabbath," they heard the High Priest saying. "On this day, our mothers light the Sabbath candles. Go out at once to the Outer Court," he commanded the priests. "Send word for the mothers of Israel to pray. As they light the Sabbath candles, let them keep this Menorah burning with their prayers." The priests ran from the Holy Place into the Outer Court and spread the word. When they returned, they assured the High Priest that his orders had been carried out.

"How much longer before the oil is ready?" the High Priest asked the keeper of the oil.

"One day," he replied.

"One day," the High Priest repeated. "Let us pray that the lamps do not dim."

"And now," Brother Memory said to the boys. "We must go to the evening that begins the eighth day."

When they arrived at the eighth day of Hanukkah, the Menorah still miraculously burned. A spirit of hopefulness was everywhere in the Temple. The priests were rejoicing, and the High Priest had begun making up songs for children to sing. In the Outer Court many people had gathered. By now, all Israel had heard of the ongoing miracle of Hanukkah. The Outer Court remained full of people throughout the night, and many had refused to sleep. In the streets of Jerusalem, much celebration could be seen and heard. Already, merchants were selling little menorahs for people to place in their windows. Everyone now knew that faith and faith alone was the only thing allowing their Temple Menorah to burn, for it could be explained in no other way. Throughout the next day, Brother Memory led the boys through Jerusalem to show them how the horrible memories of the times of darkness that the Jewish people had endured were being scattered by the light of liberation.

"Keep this in mind," Brother Memory told Alex and Grant, "because what you are seeing will help you know how to restore the lights to Christmas future."

By day's end, an announcement was made at the Temple. "Good news! The new oil for the Menorah is here! It is being filled at this moment! The miracle of Hanukkah is complete! The lights have burned for eight days, when there was only enough oil for one!"

The throng that was gathered in the Outer Court of the Temple shouted for joy. In the streets, children were spinning dreidels, and vendors were serving all kinds of fried foods and pastries to the crowds.

"They are eating food fried in olive oil to commemorate the miracle of the oil," Brother Memory told the boys.

"Those doughnuts look as good as Nanny's sugar cookies," Alex remarked. "Can we have one?"

"Unfortunately you cannot eat anything from the past," Brother Memory replied. "You might try tasting them with your imagination, though you might not find doing that too satisfying. Maybe you will have a chance to eat some Hanukkah food on your flight back to the present.

"I shall be taking you back to the mailbox soon," he continued, "but I have one more important thing to show you. Follow me."

The boys followed Brother Memory as he led them to the scriptorium they had arrived at earlier. "There is a special scroll here I want you to see. It is important that you remember it if you hope to put the puzzle pieces of the time-wiring-diagram together when you return to the present. Come and gaze into this scroll. It is a magic scroll that will show you the deeper meaning of what you have seen here."

The boys looked on as Brother Memory placed the scroll before them. "I want you to notice first of all the seal on this scroll. Do you know what it is?"

"A star?" Alex asked.

"Yes, but not just any star. It is the Star of David. Notice that two equilateral triangles of equal size are turned in opposite ways and laid over each other so as to complete the star. Now look carefully at the right and left sides of the star and see if you can find two 'M's' turned sideways."

"I can't see them," Grant said.

"Then let me trace them out with my finger." Brother Memory first traced the 'M' on the left. Then he traced the one on the right.

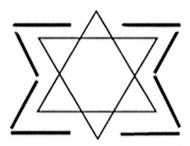

"Oh, I see now!" Grant exclaimed. "The 'M' on the right is a mirror image of the 'M' on the left."

"Exactly," Brother Memory said. "These two 'M's' stand for two important things you have learned thus far. One 'M' stands for 'Memory', and the other stands for 'Miracle'—the miracle of Hanukkah to be exact. The two 'M's' are united in the symbol of the Star which represents *Melek ha Olam*. The Star can represent the Star at Tree Top as well. Remember, too, that the Tree World is shaped like a triangle, so it is a reflection of the two triangles that make up the Star of David. However, since the Tree World is shaped like only one triangle, it must be viewed as an incomplete reflection of the Star. The Star contains within it an eternal world. The Tree World is not eternal. The star-shaped seal is also like the Star at Tree Top because both hide a revelation that has yet to unfold. The star-shaped seal on this scroll hides the revelation in the scroll. In a similar way, the Star at Tree Top is like an unbroken seal that hides what is yet to be revealed in the Tree World below it."

The boys watched as Brother Memory broke the seal on the scroll and unrolled it. "Now, boys," he said, "watch the mystery inside this scroll unfold before your very eyes."

The scroll was blank when they first peered into it, but soon a red, horned serpent slithered across the page, shot open its fanged mouth, and, with a hiss, tried to strike them. Shocked, Grant and Alex almost fell over backwards. Though the serpent had tried to escape from the paper, the scroll held it in its prison, and they remained unharmed.

They watched until the serpent turned first into a flood and then into a violent, dark sea. As they watched the sea churn, a hideous beast rose up out of it. Then above the sea, the figure of a Heavenly Man riding on white clouds appeared. This Heavenly Man got off his clouds and walked up to another Heavenly Being sitting on a throne. The eyes of the one sitting on the throne were like coals of fire, and he had long white hair and a white beard. From his glorious throne flowed a river of golden fire. They continued to watch as the Heavenly Man received something from the Being who sat on the throne. Then they saw the Heavenly Man get back on his clouds, ride down from heaven, and drive the beast back into the sea. Soon the sea burst into flames and the beast that had come out of it was destroyed. Finally, the sea disappeared, and the Heavenly Man became king of a vast kingdom that covered the entire earth.

When the pictures on the magic scroll disappeared, Alex said, "I don't understand what they mean."

"Me neither," Grant echoed.

"I didn't expect you would, because the pictures you have seen are in code," said Brother Memory. "They were deliberately put in code to keep the enemy from figuring out pieces to the time-wiring-diagram puzzle. We don't want the enemy messing with the wiring, now, do we?"

The boys shook their heads.

"Then I will explain the code, but do not let it fall into enemy hands. Is that clear?"

"Yes," they replied.

"Very well, then. The serpent you saw is the one who crept through the Garden of Paradise and brought misery upon the entire human race. He is the original vampire who eats away at the Tree World until he gains enough power to transform himself into flood waters and drown the world. The flood waters eventually become a sea, but this sea is in no way ordinary. It represents in an extraordinary way the throngs of people whom the vampire has bitten and infected with his poisonous lies. These become the enemies of *Melek ha Olam*. From this sea, the horrible Beast arises. This Beast, who is also a vampire like the serpent that gives him birth, is also the first Scrooge. He is none other than Antiochus the Fourth, the persecutor of the Jewish people in the days before the victory of Hanukkah. He is one of many beasts and Scrooges who will come throughout time. The Heavenly Man, you saw, brings in a kingdom that comes from above. That is why he rides on the clouds. The Heavenly Figure sitting on the throne who receives the Heavenly Man is *Melek ha Olam* himself, the one who in Arboria is known as Tree King. From *Melek ha Olam*, the Heavenly Man receives an everlasting kingdom that will never pass away. It is the Heavenly Man who made possible the miracle of Hanukkah, but not everyone understands who he is. Some think this Heavenly Man was Judas Maccabeus—the Hammer who drove out Antiochus the Fourth. But I will now try to explain to you why the one they call 'the Hammer' cannot really be the Heavenly Man. While the Heavenly Man will bring in a kingdom that is as everlasting as the light of the *ner tamid*, the kingdom brought about by Judas the Hammer is still only temporary. In fact, his kingdom will last about one hundred years, and that is all. Then another beast will rise up out of that sea, and the suffering of the Jewish people will start up all over again. This means that the Heavenly Man is not Judas Maccabeus but another who is yet to come. This one yet to come will not be called 'the Hammer', though a *hammer* will nail his hands and feet to a cross. The failure of Judas Maccabeus to bring in the everlasting kingdom also explains why Hanukkah is only one piece of the jigsaw puzzle that needs to be solved. You will need to gather the other pieces and figure out how to fit them together before you will have full knowledge of how to rescue Christmas future from oblivion. Do you understand?"

"I think so," Grant replied, and Alex nodded his head.

"What the scroll reveals is that the oil of Hanukkah is more than just ordinary olive oil," Brother Memory continued. "That oil is also the oil of faith in *Melek ha Olam*, who is the true source of light and the one represented by the symbol of the *ner tamid* that burns before the Holy of Holies in the Temple. You will need his light to battle the Scrooges. For now, that light is the light of 'Miracle' and 'Memory' that stamps out lies and forgetfulness. There is, however, much more to this light, and you will have to visit other times to learn its fuller meaning. Just as the lamps of the Menorah are eight in number, the light of *Melek ha Olam* has multiple meanings as it shines into the world. Now," Brother Memory said. "The time has come for you to return to the mailbox you arrived from. You will need briefly to go forward to Christmas present before you visit the past again. Are you ready?"

The boys nodded, and Brother Memory walked with them until they reached the mailbox. "Shalom," he said. "If you think you are forgetting what you have learned here, sniff the hyssop. That should refresh your memory and help you recall the Hanukkah miracle."

"I thought you said we couldn't take anything back with us?" Grant asked.

"You gathered the hyssop on the other side of the gate, so it does not count," he replied. "Anyway, you are allowed to take back the memories of this place. The hyssop will only help you do that."

The boys thanked Brother Memory and wished him 'shalom'. After they exchanged their final farewells, the boys entered the mailbox, and Brother Memory shut its door behind them.

"We had better pick some more hyssop," said Alex as he walked along the wall. "We need to be sure we don't run out."

"True," Grant agreed, and joined Alex in gathering the hyssop that grew from the wall. When they had finished, Grant said, "Time now to go find Young Nanny," so they headed back down the corridor in the direction of the time-port terminal.

—Chapter Ten—

SATURN ALIENS?

GRANT AND ALEX HURRIED down the corridor to the gate and found Young Nanny's plane after jumping through the snow-globe portal. The automatic stairs were already set up and the door to the cabin was open. The boys ran up the stairs and found her stacking bags of mail.

"Hi, Young Nanny!" Grant said upon entering the plane.

"Oh, there you boys are!" she returned. They ran over to her, and she stooped down and hugged and kissed them. She now wore a red satin dress styled exactly like the green one. Her tiara was again perched on her head.

"Where's all the mail from?" Alex asked.

"There's lots of mail that comes from the past to the present," Young Nanny told them. "Remember that no mail comes here from the future because past times cannot be changed. They are what they are. However, mail can be brought from here to all future times. This mail contains Hanukkah traditions like the ones you saw in ancient Israel in 168 B. C. We can only hope these letters do not end up in the Dead Letter Office. As you know, the Dead Letter Office is filling up with undelivered mail because Christmas future is in danger. We have little time, in fact, because Christmas present is also showing signs of stress. Quick, boys! Go to the cockpit and buckle up, and I'll be there in a minute."

Grant and Alex went to the cockpit, sat in their seats, and fastened their seatbelts. Soon, Young Nanny climbed into the pilot's seat, engaged the propellers, and started taxiing for takeoff. When they were airborne, Young Nanny took her cookie tin from the compartment in the console.

"Oh, boy!" Alex exclaimed. "Sugar cookies!"

"Not so fast," Young Nanny said. "I've got a special surprise for you." She opened the lid, revealing pastries that looked like piping hot doughnuts.

"Those look like the doughnuts we saw in Jerusalem!" Alex exclaimed.

"They are called *sufganiot*," she informed them. "They're filled with strawberry jelly and deep fried in olive oil." With her Nanny stick, she served the boys one each.

"These are delicious!" Grant exclaimed.

"Yum, yum!" Alex added. "They're as good as sugar cookies, but in another way."

"I'm glad you like them," said Young Nanny. "They are fried in olive oil to remind people of the miracle of the oil at Hanukkah. Eating them will help you remember what you saw on your trip."

"We've got something else to help us remember, too," Alex told Young Nanny. He pulled a spring of hyssop from his pocket and handed it to her. "Here, smell it."

Young Nanny took a whiff. "That would make good potpourri, wouldn't it?" she said. "Do you remember the special box of potpourri I gave your mother for Christmas? It had cinnamon, cloves, and dried orange peel in it, among other things."

"Yeah," Alex replied. "That smelled really good."

"The plant's called hyssop," Grant told Young Nanny. "That's what the Hebrew people used to sprinkle the lamb's blood on the door at Passover."

"I see," Young Nanny replied. "I've never smelled hyssop before. I love its fragrance."

"It also helps people remember," Alex added.

"Smells can be memorable alright," Young Nanny said. "For me, the smells of Christmas always bring back memories that flood my heart with joy. There's nothing like the smell of fir trees, scented candles, goodies baking, and candy cooking to put one in the Christmas spirit."

The boys were silent for a time as they thought of the many scents of Christmas. As the plane zoomed along, the droning of the propellers made them sleepy. Because they were both very tired from their Hanukkah adventure, they were soon napping. Young Nanny didn't bother them because she knew they needed their rest. However, when the plane touched down, they both were startled.

"The sleepy heads are awake," Young Nanny remarked, bringing the plane to a stop.

The boys stretched and yawned. "Are we in the present again?" Grant asked.

"Yes," Young Nanny replied. "You boys can run along because I have mail to deliver. I'll see you soon!"

When the automatic stairs had pulled up to the plane, the boys hugged Young Nanny, exchanged goodbyes, and climbed down to the runway. They now were used to the mailbox terminals, so they ran quickly through the gate and down the corridor until they reached the mailbox door.

"Remember we're back in the present," Alex told Grant. "Don't forget to check for the Sphinx."

"Right," he replied, and he opened the door and peered outside. "The coast is clear. Let's see if we can find Pater Kronos."

When they walked outside, the summertime breeze carried the smell of rotting garbage into their nostrils.

"There's that smell again," Alex remarked. "It has to be vampire perfume."

"You're right," Grant chimed in. "It smells just like the cemetery book and the pig burning on that altar."

The atmosphere was hot and humid, and the sun was baking the earth. Trash was strewn all over the ground—empty chip bags, partially eaten fruit, spilt soda cans, bread crust, chicken bones, half-eaten pieces of lunch meat, pieces of cookies, pastries, and pies. Some Orna folk were lying on quilts, drinking from bottles, and gorging themselves with every kind of junk food imaginable. Then the boys caught sight of some Orna folk with bloated bellies sauntering down one of the paths, but they were not headed in the direction of the Star at Tree Top. In fact, they were going the opposite way.

"They must have been turned away by the angel star," Grant ventured to guess.

"They seem to be having a hard time walking," Alex said. "I wonder what could be wrong with them."

Then they heard a voice from behind and realized at once it was Pater Kronos. "There you are, boys. As you can see, we've got a mess here. Garbage has been mounting up since you left. There was a wild celebration here last night that made matters even worse. The Ornas have just about eaten and drunk themselves into a coma. Look over there for instance."

The boys saw Orna children shaking their sleeping parents, trying to wake them up. The children were crying and looked very hungry. Then the boys caught sight of a strange-looking character with stringy oily hair and a straggly beard. He was wearing a sandwich sign that read 'Saturn Aliens Invade Tree Earth! The End of Days Is at Hand!' The strange-looking character was shouting, "Follow me, or Saturn Aliens may abduct you!" Some of the children whose parents seemed to be in a coma gathered around the strange man. Their eyes were glassed over, and they seemed to be under his spell. As he walked, they started following him.

"Who is he?" Grant asked.

"He is a crackpot," Kronos replied. "He is hoping beyond hope that the end of the Tree World will come tomorrow, but he only wants it to happen because he enjoys seeing disasters. He really does not care for the Orna folk or for their children who are now following him. What he wants to do is brainwash the children so that they will become his prisoners. If he succeeds, then they will become his slaves forever. Stay away from people like him, understand?"

The boys nodded.

"Are there really Saturn Aliens?" Grant asked.

"Not exactly," Kronos replied. "At least, there has not been an alien invasion from the planet Saturn if that's what you mean. The old crank misunderstood that the invasion was by evil spirits from the past known as the 'Saturnalians.'"

"What are they?" inquired Alex.

"You will need to travel back in time again to find out," Kronos told the boys, "and it will be up to you to help stop them. But before you return to the past, I want you to get a good look at what is happening here, because the problems the Ornas now face can be traced to the past. Follow me, and I will show you."

Pater Kronos led the boys down a road to a town. As they traveled, they saw more trash everywhere. Black plastic garbage bags filled with torn Christmas wrapping paper, ribbons, bows, and torn up boxes lined the streets. Large crowds of Orna folk stood in front of department stores, waiting for the doors to open, and when they did open, the Orna rushed in, not caring whom they trampled. Shop-keepers with brooms would simply sweep up into large dustpans the pieces of the Orna folk who had been shattered by the others and dump the pieces into more of the large black plastic bags. In front of the department store, black bags filled with trash towered like moun-tains. Then the boys noticed that all the department stores had simi-lar names, all ending in the name 'Scrooge's'. There was 'V. W. Scroo-ge's', 'G. P. Scrooge's', 'O. N. Scrooge's', 'F. L. Scrooge's', 'C. M. Scroo-ge's', and many others.

"Are these stores owned by the same Scrooges we saw in the 'VW' plot at the Scrooge cemetery?"

"Some of them are," replied Kronos, "But others here are their an-cestors. The Scrooge stores are churning out lots and lots of inferior merchandise, and the Ornas cannot help buying it. Some of it is junk, but they are addicted to buying it regardless of how low the quality of the merchandise is."

Suddenly, they heard shouting, and they caught sight of another group of Ornas marching down one of the streets and carrying signs that read, 'Death to the Scrooges!' and 'Forgive Our Debts!' They were chanting the same words.

"Who are they?" Alex asked.

"Most of the Ornas you see spent way more money than they made, so now they expect everybody else to chip in and bail them out. They all believe they have been treated unfairly. The truth is that some in their group *have* been treated unfairly. However, the real vic-tims of the Scrooges corporate greed are not the ones likely to be heard. The greedy, undeserving Ornas who themselves are to blame for their dire circumstances will see to that. The greedy Ornas are merely using the real victims as pawns to increase the size of their crowds. The message of those who have legitimate needs soon will be drowned out by the others."

"Will there be a riot?" Grant asked. "We saw a terrible one in Jerusalem when we were there. Many people got killed."

"The Scrooges are figuring out a way to avoid riots by giving the disgruntled Ornas occasional tax holidays," Kronos said. "Unfortunately, the Scrooges' policy is all a big sham. Their policy just postpones solving the problem. As time passes the problem will only grow bigger. When it reaches the critical 'point of no return', then the result will be the Scrooge graveyard you saw in the future. Unfortunately, it looks like that graveyard has moved from A. D. 2525 to the year A. D. 2100. What you see now is part of the problem that has caused the fuse to blow and make the lights go out in Christmas future."

"How has it made the fuse blow?" Alex asked.

"The greed, selfishness, and overindulgence here caused a power surge that made it blow. Like electricity, human desires and wants must be regulated. If they are not, then the fuses will not be able to handle the load and the result will be a blown fuse and a blackout."

"How can we stop the invasion of the Saturnalians?" Grant asked.

"You will need to go back to ancient Rome in the year A. D. 350," Kronos told them. Suddenly, they heard an almost deafening roar. It was coming from the Sphinx! He was again on the prowl! Frightened Orna folk began to run for their lives in every direction!

"Time grows short," said Kronos. "Quick, follow me, and I will guide you to the proper mailbox."

As they traveled down the road to the mailbox, Alex noticed for the first time that all the black trash bags had dark logos stamped on them. "Look," he pointed. "What are those logos stamped on the bags?" The boys went up and examined them. They had not seen what they were before, but now they clearly saw the bags were all stamped with dark gray skull-and-crossbones symbols.

"Do you know what those are?" Kronos asked.

The boys shook their heads.

"They are *memento mori*," replied Kronos. "What you have seen here is the aftermath of the banquet of life. Soon, the banquet of life here in Christmas present will be finished. When that happens, death will follow quickly. Soon these bags will be thrown into the incinerator. That will be the beginning of the lava that spews from the volcano you saw atop the Scrooge cemetery."

Suddenly, without warning, the Sphinx jumped out in front of them and cornered them. The boys' hearts jumped into their throats. They went weak in their knees, and their legs trembled. The Sphinx opened its immense mouth and roared.

"Remember what I told you," whispered Kronos.

Alex quickly recited the words, "*memento mori*," and Grant repeated them, too, in quick succession. The moment the boys had spoken the words, they felt courage rise up in their hearts. As the Sphinx stared at them, its face seemed more human than like that of a lion. The boys could have sworn that it was smiling at them, so they smiled back at him. Still, they couldn't quite tell whether the creature was really smiling. Soon, it turned and walked off, leapt into the air, and took flight in search of other prey.

"That was a close call," Kronos remarked. "Good work, boys! You must have convinced him! Now, it's time for you to journey to the past again."

The boys followed Pater Kronos, and they soon came to another red mailbox that had the date A. D. 350 embroidered on its side. Grant again managed to open the combination lock, and inside they went. When they had exchanged goodbyes with Pater Kronos, he gently shut the door behind them. The boys were now on their way down yet another corridor.

On the way to the gate, they again saw the poster that said, 'Celebrate Hanukkah in the year 168 B. C.' The light projecting from the Menorah onto the opposite wall brought back memories of the victory of the light over the darkness of the Beast. They paused for a moment to remember their trip, and then continued on to the gate. When they arrived, they jumped through the snow-globe portal and found Young Nanny's plane preparing for takeoff. They climbed the automatic stairs, entered the cabin door, and found young Nanny stacking empty mail bags. She still had on her red satin dress and was wearing her tiara.

"We're back, Young Nanny!" Alex shouted.

"Hello, boys," she said. "You've come just at the right time. I've finished delivering the mail, and the empty bags are folded and stacked. Are you ready to travel to the Roman Empire in the year A. D. 350?"

The boys nodded.

"Good. Then go buckle up, and I'll be with you shortly."

The boys found their seats and got buckled in. Young Nanny soon entered the cockpit, sat in the pilot's seat, and engaged the propellers. After taxiing down the runway, the plane took off and was soon airborne.

"Do you have any more sugar cookies, Young Nanny?" Alex inquired.

"No," she replied.

Alex's face fell. "What about some of those jam-filled doughnuts?" he asked.

"I don't have any of those either," she answered.

The boys were disappointed. They couldn't understand why Young Nanny had not baked any more cookies.

"Didn't you have time to bake them?" Alex asked.

"I have something else for you." She took the tin from the compartment and pulled off the lid. When the boys saw what was inside, they shouted, "Sugar cookies!" Then Grant asked, "Why were you teasing us Young Nanny?" She did not smile. With a somber face, she took her Nanny stick and served the boys. When they bit into the 'cookies' they were again disappointed.

"Young Nanny!" Alex exclaimed. "You accidentally left out the sugar!"

"Not accidentally," said Young Nanny. "I did it on purpose. I left out the baking soda, too. Those are wafers of unleavened bread you are eating—the same stuff I made the matzo-ball soup from."

"Did you have extra matzo you needed to get rid of?" Grant asked.

"No," she replied. "I made them especially for this occasion. What you are eating are communion wafers. I wanted you to be protected from the evil spirits that lurk about in the place we're going."

"Evil spirits?" Alex exclaimed. "Are there more Scrooges, ghosts, and vampires there?"

"Yes, and other evils things that may look beautiful upon first sight," Young Nanny replied. "You must be on your guard when you arrive in Rome, because the feast they will be celebrating there will remind you of the way most people celebrate Christmas in the present. I caution you not to fall under the spell that works in the place you're going. The lessons you learned from Hanukkah should help."

"How?" Grant questioned.

"What lessons did you learn from Hanukkah?" she asked.

"To remember and not forget?" he replied.

"Yes, and what else?" She looked at Alex.

"To avoid being ignorant?" Alex replied.

"To avoid ignorance and forgetfulness are two important lessons of Hanukkah, but where you are going, these will be difficult to practice. Do you remember the Beast and his vampire perfume?"

The boys nodded. "It really stinks," Alex remarked.

"It starts to stink after a while," Young Nanny said, "but at first it can smell as sweet as my sugar cookies. You may not realize what it is when you smell it at first, and this means you may give in to it. Vampire perfume is intoxicating, and the one thing it always does is to make the mind forget so that lies can take root there. Be careful that you avoid it."

"Can I have another communion wafer?" Alex asked.

"Yes," Young Nanny said. "Eat them in remembrance of the one who sacrificed himself to uncover and bring to light the lies of the evil spirits of Saturnalia."

The boys ate several more of the wafers. As they did, they remembered how the Orna folk in Christmas present had gorged themselves with junk food. They also recalled the sad sight of the hungry and neglected children whose parents had fallen into a coma.

"I have something else for you," Young Nanny told them after a few minutes. She removed a mailbag from beside her seat, opened it, and pulled out two very strange looking flashlights. The flashlights each had a central cylinder with one main light. Four other cylinders, equally spaced, branched out from the central cylinder. These had lights pointing in the same direction as the central light. The way the flashlights had branches reminded them vaguely of the Hanukkah Menorah they'd seen in the Hebrew Temple, only the flashlights had fewer branches. Young Nanny handed each of the boys one of the strange-looking apparatuses.

"Go ahead and try them out," she said.

When they flipped the switches, the smaller flashlights on the branches lit up one after the other in rapid succession. Last of all, the central lights of the two flashlights came on. When they did, an almost blinding light filled the whole cockpit.

"Okay," said Young Nanny, shielding her eyes. "You know how they work, so you can turn them off now. You will need those where you are going. When you shine the light on something you suspect is evil, you will be able to see it for what it is."

"What kind of flashlights are these?" Grant asked.

"They are special 'Advent' flashlights," Young Nanny replied. "Have you ever seen Advent candles being lit during the four weeks leading up to Christmas?"

"Yes," Grant said. "Each candle has a meaning, but I don't remember now what they stand for."

"That's alright," Young Nanny assured him. "Where you are going, you will see why those who celebrated the birth of the Christ Child started using those Advent candles to help them avoid the attraction of Saturnalia. I urge you to use those Advent flashlights whenever you suspect the evil spirits of Saturnalia are afoot. Will you promise me you will do that?"

"Yes," the boys replied.

They soon began their descent, and Young Nanny made a smooth landing. They taxied down the runway and came to a halt.

"Can't you come with us this time Young Nanny?" Alex asked.

"I wish I could, but I've got to take all those bags and get them filled with mail to send to the future," she replied. "Remember the saying, 'Neither snow nor rain nor heat nor gloom of night stays these couriers from the swift completion of their appointed rounds!' By the time you return, I should have the plane loaded again. We can only hope that people in the future will not throw this precious mail away before they read it. More and more, people in the present are throwing away traditions just like they do junk mail. They don't even bother to open the mail I deliver anymore. But I can't let that discourage me. I keep hoping that someone will open one of these letters and spread the news of what's inside. It's just terrible when people throw away letters and cards that may be more precious than gold." Young Nanny stood silent for a short time, hoping that the boys would understand what she had just told them. "Now, boys," she finally said. "You need to be on your way."

The boys hugged her, climbed down the automatic stairs, made their way through the snow-globe gate and the corridor, and soon arrived at the mailbox door.

"Be sure to keep track of your flashlight, Alex, okay?" Grant told him, and Alex nodded. Grant then turned his flashlight on and the inside of the red mailbox became filled with brilliant light. Then Grant slowly opened the door and shined the flashlight to see outside.

"Right in my face!" came a voice from the other side of the door. Grant turned the flashlight off and saw Brother Memory standing there rubbing his eyes.

"Sorry about that," Grant apologized.

"Oh, don't worry about it," Brother Memory said, trying to get his eyes to adjust. "We are on a special mission now boys," he told them. He widened his eyes and flapped his hands in front of his face, still trying to shoo away the after-image spots the bright light had imprinted on his retinas. "What you learn here will help you understand what has gone wrong with Christmas. You will need to pay attention to be sure you find the piece of the time-wiring puzzle that is hidden here. Follow me."

—Chapter Eleven—

ADVENT CONQUERS SATURNALIA

OWN A STONE-PAVED ROAD, fifteen feet wide from curb to curb and lined on either side by cypress trees, Grant, Alex, and Brother Memory traveled. The late afternoon sun caused shadows from the cypress trees to smudge snaky shadows across the road while at the same time gilding the tops of the trees on the opposite side. In the distance stood hills covered with olive groves, and in front of the hills stretched freshly plowed fields filled with many a farm laborer. The position of the sun in the sky behind them let them know that they had less than two hours before sunset.

"Where are we?" Alex asked Brother Memory.

"We're on the *Via Aurelia*, also known as the Aurelian Way. This road was built by the Emperor Aurelian about eighty years ago." Suddenly, a light went on in Brother Memory's head. "Oh yes, and I've just been reminded of something else."

"What's that?" asked Alex.

"The sun shining behind us just reminded me of it."

"Tell us what it is!" Grant exclaimed.

"Something else the Emperor Aurelian did. It is he who declared December 25th to be the birthday of *Sol Invictus*."

Grant frowned and rolled his eyes. "*Saul Wickus*? Who in the world is '*Saul Wickus*'?"

"No. *Sol Invictus*," he clarified. "In Latin, the letter 'v' should be pronounced like a 'w'. *Sol Invictus* was what the Roman's called their sun god. You see, December 25th is the day of the winter solstice, the shortest day of the year, so Aurelian thought it was logical to celebrate the birthday of 'the undying sun' on that day."

"Oh," the boys uttered rather unenthusiastically. At this point they didn't understand why this fact was really important, but they would soon find out the shocking truth.

As they traveled on, Alex asked, "Where does this road lead?"

"The saying goes that 'all roads lead to Rome,' and this one is no exception," Brother Memory answered. "Soon we'll be entering the city from the west."

As they walked along, Alex became curious about the workers in the fields and asked, "What are they doing out there?"

"Sowing the last of the winter wheat," Brother Memory answered. "Planting must be finished before the celebrations of Saturnalia begin, and those begin tonight. That is why the slaves are in such a hurry."

"The laborers are slaves?" Grant asked.

"Yes," he replied. "Not everyone is privileged enough to be a freeborn Roman citizen, but I'm sure those slaves are looking forward to tonight when slaves and masters will be reversing roles. From the seventeenth until the twenty-fifth of December, the slave will act the master, and the master, the slave. Masters will serve their slaves sumptuous meals while slaves will enjoy ordering their masters about."

"What will happen to the slaves once Saturnalia is over?" Grant asked.

"Everything will revert back to its usual order," he answered. "Slaves will have to return to serving their masters, and masters will return to giving orders to their slaves. Saturnalia is fun for a week, but when the festival concludes, and the fun and games are over, the slaves will have to return to their miserable life."

About that time, Alex caught sight of something in the distance. "What's that ahead?"

"You mean the milestone?" Brother Memory inquired.

"No, further down past the stone marker," he said.

"Oh. Those are the walls that surround one of the suburbs of Rome known as the Trans-Tiber. We shall be going through that part of Rome on our way to the temple of Saturn. That's where the festivities of Saturnalia are being held." After walking a couple of more miles, they saw that the road continued through a gate. "The gate ahead has the same name as the road," Brother Memory informed them. "It is called the *Porta Aurelia*, which means 'Aurelian gate.'"

When they entered through the gate into the city, Brother Memory continued talking. "The suburb we are going through now was settled long ago by people who were neither fortunate enough to be Roman citizens nor unfortunate enough to be slaves. Many who settled here were Jews. See those buildings? They are called '*insulae*', which means 'islands'. The bottom floors have shops of all sorts and places where one can buy a quick meal. Families live on the floors above the shops. These Roman houses are pretty small as you can see. You can find larger ones than these in Rome, but only a few of the big ones can be found in this part of the city. Look at that building ahead on the left side of the road. Do you see anything familiar?"

As the boys drew closer to the building, they noticed that it had an image sculpted on one of its walls.

"That's the image of the Menorah we saw in the Hebrew Temple!" Grant exclaimed.

"Exactly," Brother Memory said. "That building's a synagogue."

"A synagogue?" Alex asked.

"Yes, the place where Jewish people gather to worship," he answered. "There are quite of few of them in this part of the city since this is where the Jewish population of Rome lives. Some, in fact, are descendants of the ambassadors of Judas Maccabeus who came here to seek Rome's help in the war against the Beast, Antiochus the Fourth. This area is special because it was here that Christianity first spread. The Apostles Paul and Peter easily could have preached in some of the older of the synagogues located in this part of the city. When the Roman general Titus, who later became the Roman Emperor, destroyed the Jewish Temple in A. D. 70, many Jews were brought to Rome as slaves. Some of their descendants now live here, too."

Grant looked shocked. "You mean the Temple in ancient Israel where we celebrated Hanukkah was destroyed?"

"Yes, all except for its Western wall," he replied. "Titus robbed the treasury of the Temple and brought it to Rome. Among those treasures was the Temple Menorah. It was probably melted down long ago."

"That makes me so sad," Grant said.

"Me, too," said Brother Memory. "You see, Antiochus the Fourth was not the last Beast to come against the people of Israel. The kingdom established by Judas 'the Hammer' Maccabeus lasted short of one hundred years, just as I told you it would when we took our last journey. Another Beast arose after that and invaded his kingdom, dashing all Jewish hopes that the kingdom he brought in would turn out to be an everlasting kingdom. As it turned out, his kingdom was so short-lived that it couldn't very well have been the kingdom of the Heavenly Man the Jews were expecting."

"Wow! Look in that window!" Alex shouted, pointing his finger toward it. "Someone's lighting a menorah!" He watched as each candle was lit. "But it has nine branches. I thought there were only seven."

"There are eight-plus-one because the miracle of the oil at Hanukkah lasted for eight days. The extra, or ninth candle, was added to light the other eight. It is called the *shamash* or 'helper candle'. If you notice, there are four branches coming out on each side of that central candlestick that holds the helper. The Hanukkah menorahs are now being lit because the sun is setting."

"It's starting to get dark," Grant remarked. "Maybe it's time we used the Advent flash lights Young Nanny gave us so we can see where we're going." When he turned it on, the four branches lit up in rapid succession until the central light brilliantly burst out. Grant shined it at the menorah in the window, and the menorah shimmered like gold.

Alex turned his Advent flashlight on as well and shined it down the street. Other menorahs now were beginning to light up in other windows. The boys continued with Brother Memory down the Aurelian Way. Many a side street meandered between densely packed buildings.

"Just a second," said Brother Memory. "I can add some light on the subject, too." Somehow he turned up the flame on the candle that rested atop his head and said, "That's better. Do you see the road there that heads north?" Brother Memory asked the boys, pointing. "That road leads up to the *Via Triumpalis*, or the Triumphal Way. Until just recently, it was used for victory parades for generals and emperors returning in glory from battle. On the 28th and 29th of September in the year 61 B. C., a parade was held in honor of the Roman Proconsul Pompey. He was the one who brought an end to the kingdom of Judas Maccabeus. The contrast between the celebration of the Romans and the sorrow of the Jews living in Rome at the time was as stark as it possibly could be. Hundreds upon hundreds of horses and chariots, legion after legion of Roman soldiers marching in strict formation and saluting, hundreds of carts filled with the spoils of war and the treasures of conquered peoples, battle standards and banners, blasting trumpets, defeated kings and their peoples in shackles and chains—wave after wave of those parading in this gaudy and garish display stood in marked contrast to the private tears, sorrow, weeping, and wailing of the poverty-stricken Jews of that time. Later, Titus, the one who stole the Temple Menorah, had a similar elaborate parade down the same path just like Pompey before him. In Titus' honor, the Romans erected a triumphal arch. That was his reward for utterly destroying the Hebrew Temple and demolishing the city of Jerusalem in A. D. 70. On that arch is sculpted the triumphal procession that carried the Jewish Temple treasures and the Menorah down Rome's Triumphal Way. That day, too, was a day of tears for the people of Israel."

In time Brother Memory and the boys arrived at a bridge that crossed a river. The reflection from boat lamps, as well as lights on the opposite bank of the river, streaked across the waters, glimmering in the current. The boys shined their Advent flashlights onto the banks of the river and noticed they were lined with large marble slabs.

"The river we're getting ready to cross is the Tiber, and the bridge is called the '*Pons Aemilius*' or the 'Aemilian Bridge,'" Brother Memory explained. "Once we cross it, you will need to stay close to me. This side of the river is pretty quiet because the Jews do not celebrate Saturnalia. In fact, it is not really safe for them to be out because sometimes the pagans force the Jews to do cruel, humiliating, and degrading things."

"What kind of things?" Grant asked.

"Things such as kissing pigs, dressing up like clowns, being made to run down the streets after they have been forced to eat too much food, and much worse. The Roman crowds can easily get out of control during Saturnalia. Unfortunately, Romans' so-called fun is a major cause of Jewish suffering."

"Can't the police stop them?" Alex asked.

"There are no police here as in modern times," Brother Memory replied. "Officials in charge of keeping order could do something, but they usually don't bother. In fact, most of the authorities approve of these abuses because the gods the Romans worship are themselves cruel and merciless. Saturnalia is, after all, a feast honoring the god Saturn. True, as one of the gods of farming he may seem harmless enough, but the Romans also believe that Saturn horribly mutilated his father and ate his own children alive. What can one expect from people who worship a god who is such a terrible example?"

"Are they crazy?" Grant asked.

"Not necessarily crazy," Brother Memory replied, "but without a doubt deliberately evil and morally corrupt. This is why Saturnalia has been such a big problem since Christianity was declared the religion of the Roman Empire about thirty years ago by the Emperor Constantine. The Jews for the most part have learned to hide out while the festival is going on. The church, on the other hand, is trying to do what it can to curb the practices and get rid of the cruelty. Unfortunately, the church is now between a rock and a hard place. When Constantine decreed that his empire would be Christian, this did not mean that the pagan Romans were terribly happy about it. Outlawing Saturnalia would have caused riots. This is still a problem because the government here in Rome is also pretty shaky at the moment. Last year Constans, one of the now-deceased Emperor Constantine's sons, was overthrown by one Magnentius. In March, Magnentius was overthrown by Vetriano. I happen to know that Constantius, another one of Constantine's sons, is trying to get Vetriano removed from power so that Magnentius can be reinstated. So, you see, everything's a big mess here, and the leaders of the church are trying their best to come up with a compromise on Saturnalia right in the middle of it all. Only time will tell if their strategy will succeed."

When Brother Memory and the boys had crossed the bridge halfway, they saw to the north of them shore lights outlining a boat-shaped island in the midst of the Tiber River. "That is the Tiber Island, a place known to have healing properties," Brother Memory said. "When we come to the other end of this bridge, we will be entering the Roman Forum. If you listen closely, you can hear the distant sounds of revelry and celebration."

When they had crossed the bridge, the sounds of shouting and laughter became louder. Occasionally, they would see a young man running through the streets carrying a torch, or a party of drunken revelers walking down the streets with their arms around one another. "We are about to enter the Roman Forum," Brother Memory told the boys. "Stay close to me. I would hate for you to get lost in the crowd."

There was plenty of torchlight now, so the boys turned off their Advent flashlights and Brother Memory turned down his candle. As they walked, they saw a large hill with a temple on top of it. "That is the Capitoline Hill," said Brother Memory when he noticed the boys staring at it. "On its top is the temple of Jupiter."

When they entered the Forum, they could hardly get through the thick crowds. Just ahead, they could see buildings constructed in the classical Roman style and decorated with all kinds of greenery. Garlands of greenery were also strung between buildings and were wound around columns on their porches. "This large building on our left is the Basilica Julia," Brother Memory told them as they walked under the garlands. "And on our right we are coming up alongside the temple of Saturn. When we round the corner, you will see the front of it."

Inside the Forum were throngs of noisy, bustling people wearing red woolen caps that looked like the kind Santa Claus wears but without the white trim. Some people, dressed in what seemed to be swimsuits, were dancing around holding candles and singing goofy songs. Others in colorful clothing sat at tables and feasted on all kinds of exotic foods. The boys noticed that adults and children alike were eating cakes shaped like little miniature men. Meandering among those who were feasting was an occasional loud-mouth drunk. A throng of people had gathered to listen to a man who was standing on a stone platform and addressing them. "You must do everything I say," he shouted. "I, the Lord of Misrule, command it!" Whenever he would order someone in the crowd to do something, like fetch him an apple or carry him a glass of wine to drink, they would immediately obey. Though they played like they were taking him seriously, they were also laughing at him hysterically.

"Who is he?" Alex asked Brother Memory.

"He is one of those unfortunate souls who will not live to see next week," he replied. "That poor man was chosen by the crowd to be 'the Lord of Misrule'. For a month, the pagans have wined him, dined him, and indulged him in all kinds of excesses and pleasures. When Saturnalia concludes, they will sacrifice him to the god Saturn.

Remember that I told you Saturn ate his own children? That is the meaning of the small human-shaped cakes they are eating. They are like gingerbread men. That man who calls himself 'the Lord of Misrule' will become like a gingerbread man that the god Saturn will devour. That is why they have fattened him up and indulged him in all kinds of delights. The superstitious Romans think the death of this unfortunate man will bring them forgiveness for all the bad deeds they have committed over the past year."

"Will they really kill him?" Grant asked.

"Indeed, they will," Brother Memory replied. "But he will not be the only one to die before this feast is finished. Human sacrifices are now pretty normal at this time of year in Rome."

Just then, two drunken Roman men got into a fist fight. Instead of trying to break them up, the others merely egged them on. After several rounds, one of the men was badly beaten and left for dead. Not one spectator, however, tried to help the injured man. Instead, every last one of them laughed at 'the loser' and spat on him as they walked by.

"How can they be so mean?" Grant asked angrily.

"What you see here is merely the surface of Roman meanness," said Brother Memory. "In Roman homes, this sort of abuse goes on all the time. Wives are beaten by their husbands. Children are beaten by their parents. Pets are beaten by the children. Children perceived as weak or different are bullied by other children who think of themselves as strong, and bullying is encouraged by the teachers. Girls have it worst of all, especially baby girls. There's no telling how many infant girls will be thrown out on Rome's garbage heaps before the week is out. The good news, however, is that many of these infants will be rescued by Christians. The Christians and the Jews are the only ones in this city who understand what sympathy and compassion are. The rest haven't got a clue."

Grant decided to turn on his Advent flashlight again and to shine it on the crowd of people. When he did, what he saw caused him to jump backwards.

Alex also turned on his Advent flashlight. "Oooo! They look like flesh-eating zombies!"

In the beam of their flashlights, the people looked as though they had leprosy. Their skin was covered with white patches, and sores festered on their hands, arms, legs, and faces. Their eyes were sunken in and dark.

"They are being haunted by ghosts, too!" Grant said. "Just look around them!"

Sure enough, there were dark, hooded spirits herding the crowds with serpent-shaped staffs. When Grant and Alex shined their Advent flashlights on them, their eyes glowed like the eyes of animals, but they glowed red like hot coals."

"I'm scared," said Alex. "Who are they?"

"Evil spirits," Brother Memory answered. "Though you can see them with your Advent flashlight, none here celebrating Saturnalia know they are even around. The creatures you see are filled with malignant hate. They use hate to herd these Romans and make these Romans do their bidding."

"Could they be the aliens from Saturn we heard about the last time we were in the present?" Alex asked Grant.

"You mean Saturnalians," Grant corrected him. "That would explain why Christmas present was the way it was when we were there last."

"How do we stop the evil spirits from invading the present?" Alex asked Brother Memory.

"Stopping them is exactly what I hope to help you do," he replied. "But you must first learn the secret puzzle piece of the time-wiring-diagram that lies hidden here in fourth-century Rome. We need not stay here in the Forum any longer. I think you have seen enough to know that we cannot allow any part of this evil to follow us into the present and contaminate it. The time has come for us to see what Julius, the Bishop of Rome, is planning to do about this situation. The way will be dark, so use your Advent flashlights. I will turn my candle up again, too."

Brothers Grant and Alex switched on their flashlights and followed Brother Memory as he led them several miles northward through the dark city streets and back across to the Tiber to Rome's west side. In time, they climbed a hill and arrived at a large building. From its windows a pale torchlight shone. Grant and Alex turned their flashlights on the building in an attempt to see what it looked like.

"It's hard to see now, I know," said Brother Memory turning up the candle atop his head as high as it would go, "but that is a new church called the Basilica of St. Peter."

The boys pointed their Advent flashlights in its direction so that they could get a better view of it.

Brother Memory continued. "It was begun by the Emperor Constantine on the very spot where the Emperor Nero once had a garden party, but thank goodness the light you see shining through those windows is not the same as the unholy light that illuminated that party. The memory of that light had the power to make even the most hardened Roman citizen cringe. When it came to finding lamps for lighting, he decided to burn Christians."

Shock flew across Grant's face. "What? They burned people as lamps?"

"To anyone coming from the modern world, it seems beyond belief," Brother Memory said, "but it did truly happen. Nero was a deranged maniac who set fire to his own city. He wanted to clear the slums to make room for his own building project, so he set fire to the city and then looked on and sang as it burned. Believe me, the deep darkness that surrounds us now is much to be preferred to the hellish light that pierced the night Nero sang for joy at his evil accomplishment. After the fire destroyed this part of Rome, he then proceeded to blame and punish the Christians for his horrendous deed."

"I'm beginning to hate Ancient Rome even more than I hate the Beast," Alex remarked. "How could that Nero be so evil?"

"I can't begin to tell you even the half of it," said Brother Memory. "Young ears simply must not be made to hear of the many evils he engaged in. Few older people even have the stomach to hear of it. Nero was one of the wickedest, most depraved people who ever lived on planet earth. This is why that church you see there so highly signifies the triumph of good over evil. Its beacon may seem pale now in comparison to the thick darkness around us, but the light of that beacon will increase over the years until it is more brilliant than the light shining from your Advent flashlights. Indeed, from the fires and ashes of martyrdom, this church has arisen like a phoenix. Inside, the Bishop of Rome, Julius, is now convening a council to determine the future of Saturnalia. It is time for us to go inside and listen in."

The boys followed Brother Memory into the great church and down a central aisle that was lined on each side with columns that reached up to a high ceiling made of timber. Attached to these interior columns were torches that illuminated the nave of the church, and just past them, the boys could see rows of smaller exterior columns joined by Roman arches. Hundreds of candles were spaced in groups around the perimeter of the nave, and with the torchlight added, this made it possible to see the church's interior quite well. Brother Memory and the boys walked past the arches and soon heard conversation drifting out into the hallway through open double doors. They proceeded through the doors into a large, torch-lit room filled with church leaders, churchmen, and prominent Roman citizens. The churchmen were dressed in robes, while the prominent citizens were dressed in fine Roman apparel. On a throne in front of the room sat Julius, the Bishop of Rome.

"Citizens, friends, and brothers," Julius said. "Let us come to order now." The room became silent. "The urgent matter we must discuss here is the future of the festival of Saturnalia that even now is being celebrated in the ancient part of our city where the pagan past still claims victory over Christian humility and charity. The spirit of Saturn, god of butchery and cannibalism, even now flies rampant through our city. We know that he is none other than the Evil One who incited the crowds in Jerusalem over three centuries ago to crucify our blessed Lord. His thirst for blood is not quenched. It grows ever greater even here in Christian Rome, for though the empire may be Christian in name there is still much work to do. I have heard from some of our dear sisters that no less than seven female infants have been rescued from the garbage heaps this very night. However, these dear children of our Heavenly King—as well as others who, no doubt, will appear on Rome's garbage heaps before this festival is over—are to be pitied less than those who must endure the secret cruelty that lives within the walls of many a Roman household. These rescued infants, at least, will be placed under the care of Christians. But what is to be done about the others who cannot be rescued? What can be done for our children who are too easily sacrificed upon the altar of pleasure by those given over to the Saturnalian excesses? I offer a proposal to you that may on the surface seem strange, but I believe it can provide us a way to curb the excesses of Saturnalia and at the same time inspire the people to save their children from misery. I propose that we institute a special 'feast of the nativity' on December 25th, the last day of Saturnalia, and that we celebrate the birthday of our Savior on that day."

Suddenly, rumbling spread across the crowd. Julius raised his hands and shouted, "I know this proposal seems strange, brothers. Please tell me of your concerns, and I shall try to address them."

One of the clergymen stood. "Bishop Julius. This suggestion, I must say, strikes me as extremely odd. As you know, Clement of Alexandria over a century ago speculated the time of Jesus' birth as April 20th or 21st. The Eastern Church and the Church in Armenia celebrates the coming of the magi on January 6, and they suggest that same date as the correct date of Christ's birth."

"I hear you, dear brother," said Julius, "but this does nothing to help us deal with the Saturnalia problem. We Romans have always been a practical people, and we have learned that sometimes, when it comes to minor things, we must compromise. As you know, I have never compromised on major issues of church teaching. I stood firm against those who denied that Jesus was fully God and supported the church's official stance that God was made flesh and dwelt among us. Now we must try to show how the 'true light that enlightens the soul of every man while coming into the world' is greater than the pagan sun-god *Sol Invictus*. As you remember, the Emperor Aurelian instituted his birthday on December 25, calling it 'the birthday of the Unconquered Sun'. Can we not replace this false and erroneous celebration with the celebration of the birthday of the true 'Sun of Righteousness'? Can we not try to cure those still blinded by the dark spell of paganism and turn them toward the true Light of the World?"

Another of the clergy rose up and spoke. "I think I understand what Bishop Julius desires to do, but I wonder if we shall truly succeed in replacing the rites of the pagan winter festivals with Christian ones. We cannot afford simply to whitewash the sepulchers that are these pagan festivals with the name 'Christian' and also expect them to become Christian in spirit and practice. That would be naïve."

A monk with a long beard and a shabby robe arose. "I am against the whole idea!" he shouted. "We have seen enough polluting of the true ways of Christ by the ways of the world! Christians should not be celebrating anything that in the least bit resembles Saturnalia. Instead, we need to practice self-denial, fasting, and prayer, remembering that God is the God who will one day judge the evils of Rome and indeed the whole world!"

"Agreed!" shouted another monk. "Even now the barbarians on our northern frontiers are clawing at the doors of this empire! The handwriting is on the wall! We would be doing the people of Rome a favor if we were to abolish Saturnalia entirely."

Applause could be heard throughout the room, but it was sporadic and unenthusiastic. Then a very old man stood up. "I am ninety-five years of age, and you all know what that means. I was alive when the persecution of Christians came to a head under the reign of Emperor Diocletian. I've seen what the pagan Roman beliefs and practices did to my brothers and sisters. Many a bishop—just like you, illustrious brother Julius—were singled out by the Roman authorities and cruelly martyred for their faith. All that time, it was not our compromise but our courage in the face of death that garnered their respect. Courage is the only virtue the pagan Romans really understand. So, I ask. How can courage ever be demonstrated through compromise?"

Again, rumbling erupted from the crowd.

"May I speak," said Julius. "I indeed agree that courage in those days of tribulation was the way our fathers impressed their Roman superiors. Indeed, if that courage had never been demonstrated, then no Roman Emperor would have ever embraced Christianity as the religion for his empire, and we certainly would not be sitting here having the discussion we are now having. In those days of persecution, however, we were not in a place of authority as we are now. Because now we *are* in a place of authority, now is also the time for clemency. It is time for us to practice what our Lord said, 'Do unto others as you would have them do unto you'. Surely we can afford to be more gracious in victory than Rome ever was in theirs. We can afford to show the people of Rome a better way. We can show them through our actions that loving our neighbors as we love ourselves is superior to the coldhearted and self-indulgent ways of the revelers of Saturnalia. I have heard what my brother monks have said, and I suggest that we follow their wisdom and institute a period of self-denial, fasting, and prayer prior to any celebration of the 'feast of the nativity'. During the period before our holiday, we will try to help the people of Rome see that divine judgment is coming and that every heart must indeed prepare itself to meet God and to give an account of every evil thought, word, and deed. Afterward we can focus our celebration on the way God's forgiveness has come to us through an infant. This will stand in stark contrast to such terrible Roman practices as sacrificing 'the Lord of Misrule' or throwing infant daughters on garbage heaps. We will teach them how the cradle of Jesus leads to the cross he died on. We will tell them of his words from the cross, 'Father, forgive them, for they know not what they do'. This feast will celebrate the abiding joy of self-giving love rather than the fleeting joys of self-seeking pleasure."

One of the Roman citizens rose to his feet. "Father Julius is a wise man, and wise not only in the ways of the faith. He is also wise in the ways of Roman politics. We now are in a time of crisis. Dissenting forces in the empire are working everywhere to turn back the clock to the days of paganism and persecution. These people want the church suppressed, persecuted, and eventually snuffed out. At this moment, any attempt of the Church to crush festivals like Saturnalia as some here may be suggesting would spark rebellion. Those who want to suppress our faith would then rush in to assume political control once again. Who here would want to return their fathers, their mothers, their children, and their friends to the dark times of persecution?"

The old man who had stood up before rose to his feet again. "No one here wishes to return to those times, and I see now what Bishop Julius is suggesting. His compromise now seems to me a reasonable one, especially if by it a new kind of celebration could help save children from the evils of the old one. We should perhaps remember, too, that the feast of St. Nicholas is held in the month of December. All of you here remember St. Nicholas as a wonder-worker, but he was most well-known for his charity to the poor and especially to children. Do any of you remember the legend of how he raised three boys from the dead who had been pickled by an evil innkeeper? Or how he secretly gave money for the dowries of three young ladies so that they could be married rather than being sold off as slaves? Regardless of whether one believes these tales or not, one cannot deny that the many secret acts of charity by Nicholas are perfect examples of what our Lord taught us about the giving of alms, 'Let not your left hand know what your right hand is doing'. What better example could there be to counteract the showy gift-giving and self-indulgence of the Saturnalian revelers."

Applause broke out from the assembly, and the old man raised his hands to quiet them.

"If I may make one further point," he continued. "St. Nicholas is also a good example for us to follow because he suffered like so many of us did under the persecution of Diocletian. In his own life he practiced prayer, fasting, and self-restraint. Honoring his example of holiness would help us remain vigilant and on our guard lest we should end up supporting the very practices that have caused our religion so much trouble in the past."

Another round of applause again broke out, and this time most of the clergy and citizens stood up in support of the old man's suggestions. Julius then motioned for all to sit.

"My dear brother is right, of course," Julius said. "Celebrating our Savior's birth on December 25th and remembering the example of St. Nicholas at this time of year can go hand in hand to provide a Christian alternative to the atrocious Roman feast. Ours is a great and solemn task, however, and we must be on our guard. Love must be tempered with truth, and truth must be delivered in love. This way is difficult, but is the only one that shows any promise. Is there any further discussion on the proposal?"

There was silence.

"What then is the council's pleasure with regard to making December 25 the day on which Christians celebrate the birth of Jesus?"

After each person in the room expressed either approval or dissent, it was determined that a large majority was in favor of Julius' proposal.

"Very well," Julius said. "It seems that the proposal has passed. The official date for the celebration of Christmas will be December 25th. May God grant us grace and wisdom to use this holiday to magnify the true and ever-living God, and may the blessing of God Almighty, Father, Son, and Holy Spirit, be with you now and evermore."

All said, 'amen' at the end of Bishop Julius' blessing.

Grant, Alex, and Brother Memory had watched the debate intently. When it was concluded, Grant said, "Alex, I want us to try something." He took out his Advent flashlight. Alex knew what he was thinking and took his out as well.

"Okay?" said Grant. "Point it at the people and switch it on."

The boys' pointed their Advent flashlights at those attending the council and cycled them on. The brilliant beam shone from them onto the assembly. None there saw the light, but Grant and Alex watched as the light revealed golden halos around virtually everyone assembled there, including Bishop Julius. The faces also glowed with joy in the brilliant light.

Then Alex exclaimed. "Look! There are angels here, too!"

Sure enough, the Advent flashlights revealed angels who were gently guiding the assembly. The Advent flashlights revealed that there were no real enemies, for they saw none of the people with leprosy and sores. Even those who had expressed dissent appeared radiant when the Advent flashlights shone on them, and the boys understood that all the points of view represented at the council were valid and needed to be taken into account.

"So," said Brother Memory. "You have seen the worst of Rome and the best of Rome. These assembled here will have a difficult task, for it is one thing to decide on the date of a holiday, but it is another thing entirely to succeed in making the holiday accomplish what they want it to accomplish. Many prayers will have to be offered up for that to happen. Now," he said, changing the subject. "I must be sure you have the puzzle piece of the time-wiring-diagram figured out before you leave. Follow me. There is something I want you to see."

As the boys followed Brother Memory, Alex asked him, "Is St. Nicholas the same as Santa Claus, and does this mean that Santa Claus is real?"

"Yes and no," he answered. "St. Nicholas was a real person, but over the years, forgetfulness and ignorance have transformed him into something very different in the minds of most modern people from what he was in the days of old. Even his name has been corrupted from what it was originally, for 'St. Nicholas' first became 'Sinterklaas' and then 'Santa Claus'. The modern 'Santa Claus' is really a poor caricature of the real St. Nicholas, and in fact the modern Santa Claus may condone the selfish spirit of Saturnalia more than the spirit of giving that Bishop Julius and his companions wanted to get across."

The boys followed Brother Memory as he led them to a place beneath the cathedral. "This is the crypt," he told them. "Dead people are buried here, but not just any people. There are saints and martyrs in this place, and one of them is St. Peter who died under the reign of Nero, the same one who burned down part of Rome and blamed it on the Christians. There is a scroll in this crypt I want you to see."

Brother Memory led them to the scroll and unrolled it. On it was printed a cross, and under the cross appeared the Latin words, 'in hoc signo vincet'. "Do you boys know what those words mean?"

They shook their heads.

"They mean, 'in this sign conquer'. These are the very words the Emperor Constantine saw written in the heavens when he had a vision of the cross and won a decisive battle that helped him gain control of the Roman Empire. These words, however, are easily misunderstood, and even Constantine may not have fully grasped their meaning. Many will try to adapt the cross to the old Roman ways of conquering. They will use crosses to gain victories over their enemies like the Romans once used tactics of cruelty and intimidation. They will use the sign of the cross to injure, to persecute, to kill, and to sacrifice others. A time will come when they will burn crosses to instill fear in the hearts of people like the Jews who live in the Trans-Tiber region. Those who do such things, however, understand nothing of what the sign of the cross really means. God does not conquer the human heart by force, but by the power of love tempered by truth and truth delivered by love. That is why God made his triumphal entry into this world as a baby born in a manger to peasant people, not as a Roman general or Caesar parading down the Triumphal Way and carrying riches they had plundered from others. That is one reason why the early Christians called Jesus, 'Son of God', because 'Son of God' was first used by the Romans to refer to their Caesars after Julius Caesar proclaimed himself to be a god. No Caesar, however, was a true god or Son of God. The only true Son of God was the one who made his triumphal entry into Jerusalem riding on a donkey, and who was crucified by a mob very much like the one you saw at the festival of Saturnalia. There is an irony when you think about the fact that the true 'Son of God' has managed to conquer Rome! Now, before you return to the present, take a good look at the words again, *'in hoc signo vincet'*. Alex, what do those words mean?"

"In this sign conquer," he said.

"Very good!" Then Brother Memory asked Grant, "Tell me what the word 'sign' refers to?"

"To the cross," he replied.

"Wonderful!" Next, Brother Memory asked Alex, "What does the sign of the cross really mean?"

"God made his triumphal entry into the world as a baby in a manger and died on a cross," he answered.

"Excellent. And remember what Bishop Julius said. Love must be tempered by truth, and truth must be delivered in love. Now," Brother Memory said, changing the subject. "Shine your Advent flash-lights on the scroll."

When the boys did as he said, the words appeared, 'Advent conquers Saturnalia'.

"What does that mean?" Grant asked.

"It's another way of understanding the meaning of the words 'in this sign conquer,'" Brother Memory replied. "When the monks talked about a time for people to fast, pray, and think about the coming judgment of God, they were suggesting the time before Christmas that will come to be known as 'Advent', which in English means 'Coming'. Bishop Julius figured out a way for Advent to conquer Saturnalia when he suggested that the time of fasting, prayer, and reflection on God's judgment should precede the celebration. In that way, the kind of excesses, such as those found in the celebration of Saturnalia, are curbed. In that way, too, the overindulgence that blows the time-fuses and makes the future of Christmas bleak and dark can be avoided."

"Oh, I get it now," Grant said. "The excesses of Saturnalia are like an electric power surge that blows out a fuse. So by using Advent to regulate the excesses of Saturnalia, we can avoid blown time-fuses and keep the lights on in Christmas future."

"Exactly," said Brother Memory. "I think you have learned your lesson well, and the time has come for you to return to the present and put what you have learned to work. But first we must find your mailbox. If we are lucky, we will find it nearby."

The boys followed Brother Memory back through the church, out the doors, and into the churchyard. They had not travelled far down the road when they found the mailbox. Soon, they were inside, and Brother Memory had shut the door behind them.

—Chapter Twelve—

THE PURPLE, THE ROSE, AND THE WHITE

AFTER MAKING THEIR way down the corridor and through the snow-globe portal once again, Grant and Alex boarded Young Nanny's plane. As usual, she was stacking bags of mail for the trip back to the present. The boys greeted her when they reached the plane, and told her of their experiences in Rome.

"Were your Advent flashlights helpful?" she asked them.

"Yes," Grant replied. "Whenever we shined them, we were able to tell good from evil. They also came in handy when we had to walk down the dark streets of Rome."

"Alex, do you know how those flashlights work?" she asked.

"No," he replied.

"Then that is something we ought to talk about on our trip back. Go on to the cockpit, and I'll join you in a minute."

The boys did as Young Nanny asked and buckled up in their seats for takeoff. She soon joined them in the cockpit, buckled herself in, engaged the propellers, and taxied down the runway. In no time, they were airborne, and she began asking questions.

"What was wrong with the way the Romans celebrated Saturnalia?"

"They were really mean," Alex said. "They didn't understand anything about love. They didn't care about anybody but themselves."

"We found out that Saturn, the god they worshiped, was a cannibal," Grant added. "He ate his own children. Now the Romans think it's okay to do like their god and sacrifice their children, too. They even throw away their baby girls like garbage."

"Does anything about ancient Rome remind you of the present?" Young Nanny asked.

The boys thought for a moment. "Yes," said Grant. "Like the Romans at the feast, the Orna folk in Christmas present ate until they couldn't walk. They didn't care about their babies or children either. They were like the Orna folk at the Scrooge stores that trampled other Orna folk and then threw them away just like they did their other trash."

Alex added, "Some of the Roman children got sold into slavery because their parents didn't care about them. The strange crackpot who warned of the aliens from Saturn invading the earth made slaves out of the Orna children, too."

"Like the Romans at Saturnalia, people in the present are also selfish and hateful," Grant continued. "I think this is why the fuses have blown and made the lights go out in Christmas future. The Orna folk, like the Romans, caused a power surge because they just didn't know when to stop celebrating."

"I'm glad you see that," Young Nanny said. "Many of the Romans lived by the rule, 'Let us eat, drink, and be merry, for tomorrow we die'. Remember what you learned about *memento mori*?"

"Yes," Alex said. "Pater Kronos taught us about that."

"Well, the Romans used another phrase, *carpe diem!*" she said. "It means 'seize the day'. They made the most of their time by 'seizing the day', but they did so by eating, drinking, and merry-making at everyone else's expense, including their own children's. They tried to 'live it up' before Saturn devoured them, but in seeking their lives, they lost them. What they didn't expect is that they one day would have to give an account of their behavior before the Judge of the Universe."

"I wonder if that's the reason why the monk at the council we went to wanted to do away with Saturnalia and put prayer, fasting, and repentance in its place," Grant said. "Remember what he said, Alex?"

Alex nodded.

"He wanted the Romans to 'remember death' in the right way," Grant added. "Not like the Romans who celebrated till they blew a fuse because they saw death coming fast."

"I think you're beginning to understand now what makes those Advent flashlights work," said Young Nanny.

"Don't they use batteries?" Alex asked.

"Not exactly," said Young Nanny. "They are powered by five principles, and those are the principles of Advent."

"What is Advent?" Alex asked.

"Here you've been using an Advent flashlight all this time," said Young Nanny, "and you don't know what Advent is?"

Alex shook his head.

"Okay," said Young Nanny. "I'll try to explain. Each of the lights on that flashlight is powered by a different cell. One is called the 'prophecy' cell. In the days of ancient Israel, there were very dark periods—enslavements, captivities, periods when the people turned away from the one the Hebrews called '*Melek ha Olam*', the King of All, who in Arboria is known as Tree King. During those dark periods, prophets came warning the people of their excesses, pointing out how they had mistreated their fellow human beings, warning them of fast-approaching divine judgment, and promising them hope for a better tomorrow if they would but mend their ways and follow the wise edicts of *Melek ha Olam*. In those days, 'earth was waiting, spent, and restless with a mingled hope and fear. You saw how that was true when you visited ancient Israel in 168 B. C. and witnessed the struggles of the people against the Beast. The earth then lay in solemn stillness, waiting for the day when peace would reign over all the earth and would everywhere fling its ancient splendors like the brilliant beam of your Advent flashlights."

"Why are the barrels of the flashlight different colors?" Alex asked.

"Oh, you noticed that," said Young Nanny. "Your Advent flashlight is based on what are known as Advent candles. These are candles that are lit each week for the four weeks leading up to Christmas. Three of the Advent candles are purple, one of them is rose colored, and the central one is white. The same is true of the five barrels of your Advent flashlights. Three are purple, one is rose, and the center one is white. The barrel powered by the 'prophecy cell' is the first purple one."

"Why is it purple?" Alex asked.

"Because purple had a special meaning to the ancient Romans that continues on even to the present time," Young Nanny said. "You're probably wondering how I know all this, but I'm allowed in my spare time to read the postcards on the way to the future. I've learned a lot over the years doing that. When you visited ancient Rome, did you learn anything about the wars the Romans fought against the people of Carthage?"

"No," Alex said.

"Well, there were a series of wars over the years that came to be known as the 'Punic wars.'"

"Puny? Why were they puny?" Grant asked.

"Not 'puny' but 'Punic,'" Young Nanny corrected. "'Punic' refers to the Phoenician people who settled the city of Carthage in North

Africa. The Phoenicians were well known for several inventions. For one, they invented the alphabet. They could say and write their a-b-c's before anybody else. Another thing they invented was purple dye made from sea mollusks. In Latin—the language spoken by the Romans—the word 'purple' and 'punic' started referring to the same thing because of the Phoenicians' reputation for making the purple dye. We also get our English word 'punish' from the word 'punic'. Do you know why?"

The boys shook their heads.

"As you know people usually get purple bruises when they get beaten up. The Romans, of course, were very good at beating people up, and though the Romans made many mistakes, they rarely took the blame for any of them. Instead, they usually blamed innocent people for their evil doings and punished them until they were 'black and blue', or 'purple', if you like."

"Nero!" Grant exclaimed. "He burned down Rome and blamed the Christians. He was so terrible that he used Christians as lamps for his garden party."

"Nero was one of the worst of the Roman emperors," Young Nanny said. "He wouldn't think twice about using people as lamps, but do you know why he would never in a million years light a purple Advent candle?"

"No," Grant replied.

"Alex, do you know why?" Young Nanny inquired.

"Nope," he answered.

"Because lighting a purple Advent candle is a way of saying that you accept responsibility and are willing to take the punishment for your own mistakes," Young Nanny told them. "As you saw when you were in Rome, the pagans had no problem whatsoever punishing innocent people. In fact, they derived enjoyment from it. It never dawned on them that they were really the ones who needed to be punished for all the terrible ways they treated others."

"It's too bad that the Romans worshiped the sun, and the star, Saturn," Grant said. "If they had only known there was a light that never dims, maybe they wouldn't have believed they needed to sacrifice people."

"True," said Young Nanny. "Pagans often sacrificed human beings thinking that the life-force taken from them would rekindle the dying sun, or satisfy the appetite of some god known for devouring everything in sight like Saturn, the god of time, was believed to do. But as bad as the Romans were, the people of Carthage were even worse. They sacrificed their children to the god Baal just like the ancient Canaanites did in the land of Israel during the days of the two wicked monarchs, King Ahab and Queen Jezebel. Jezebel herself was a Phoenician and most likely was blood relation to the people of Carthage who sacrificed thousands of children to their hungry gods. The Christians, however, did not worship a bloodthirsty god, and this made all the difference in how they treated other people. Do you want to know how and why they were different?"

"Yes," the boys replied.

"The early Christians knew the Romans' harsh treatment of innocent people was horribly wrong," Young Nanny continued, "so they willingly accepted punishment for their own wrongful thoughts and deeds by observing a time of fasting and prayer before Christmas. Do you remember how the lighting of the Hanukkah Menorah was a way the Jewish people remembered how *Melek ha Olam* came to their rescue in their time of distress?"

The boys nodded.

"Well, the lighting of candles caused Christians to remember how Jesus was beaten by the Romans and then crucified. The fact that the candles are purple reminded them, as well, that one day they would have to give an account to God for all their misdoings. So lighting purple candles became the Christians' way of saying that they willingly accepted punishment not only for their own mistakes, but lighting them also revealed how willing they were to be persecuted for crimes of which they were innocent. In this, they hoped to be like Jesus who took the punishment he did not deserve in order to teach the world the meaning of forgiveness. During the time of fasting, prayer, and remembrance that came prior to Christmas, the Christians thought deeply about the ways they had both offended others and failed to love others as much as they knew they should. As they lit purple candles, they asked for forgiveness for their offenses and tried to mend their ways. At first, the length of time they spent doing this was as long as eight weeks before Christmas day, but as time passed, it was shortened to four weeks. In the modern world, however, Advent has almost disappeared. As a result, people now have gone to celebrating Christmas in much the same way that the Romans celebrated Saturnalia."

"We saw that with the Orna folk when we were last in Christmas present," Grant remarked.

"Yes," said Young Nanny, "and Christmas future is in danger of being permanently extinguished because of it."

"Why is one of the flashlight cylinders pink and the middle one white?" Alex asked.

"The pink color is actually 'rose', and it stands for the joy that comes when we realize the coming of the Christ child is fast approaching," Young Nanny said. "But the rose-colored candle of the Advent wreath is the third one lit. Before that, on the second Sunday of Advent, a second purple candle is lit. This candle is often referred to as the Bethlehem candle. The lighting of that candle reminds us that Christ was born in Bethlehem of Judea, the City of David, as the prophet Micah foretold. Again, we are to remember what the Christmas carol, 'O Little Town of Bethlehem' says about that place. Bethlehem lies quiet and still, in a deep and dreamless sleep, as the silent stars go by. Then in the dark streets of that little town shineth the everlasting light—in that little town where the hopes and fears of all the years meet."

"I remember the everlasting light!" Alex exclaimed.

"From where?" asked Young Nanny.

"From the Hebrew Temple," he replied. "It was the light that hung in front of the Holy of Holies. But I don't remember what it was called."

"I think I do," Grant said. "the *ner* something or other. The *ner...ner...ner tamid*! That was it!"

"In the hymn, the everlasting light refers to the birth of the Christ child, the one who called himself 'the light of the world' when he was a grown man. The white candle in the Advent wreath, which is called the Christ candle, represents Christ as the light of the world, and that is why the center light in your Advent flashlight shone more brilliantly than all the others."

"But I don't understand why the Bethlehem candle is a purple candle," Grant said. "Shouldn't it be pink, too?"

"No," replied Young Nanny, "and I'll tell you why. Sometimes we take light for granted, especially during the daytime when light is all around us. But have you ever had the lights go out in your house at night and had to stumble around in the dark? If you've ever had to do that, then you know what it is like to be without light. Now I ask you, how can you really appreciate light if you've never been without it?"

"I'm scared of the dark," Alex admitted. "That's when I think there may be ghosts in my closet or monsters under my bed."

"Then you understand how people felt in those days before the light came," said Young Nanny. "They, too, were afraid of monsters, and not just of imaginary ones. Remember that the Beast was anything but imaginary. So it was that in an age of darkness, people were groping about, stumbling over ideas and wrong beliefs, and trying to find their way around in a world full of real monsters just like a bunch of scared kids locked up tight in a pitch-black room."

"So Bethlehem before the birth of Jesus was like a dark room filled with monsters?" Grant asked.

"Yes," said Young Nanny, "and because a small town like Bethlehem was like that, can you imagine what the larger world would have been like? It must have been much worse!"

"I just thought of something," Alex said. "What if the light had never come on?"

"Now that is something to think about," Young Nanny answered. "As you know, the past determines the present, and the present determines the future. So what would the present world be like if Christ had never been born?"

Grant and Alex started thinking about what they had seen at the Saturnalia festival, and then they remembered the council Bishop Julius had convened. If Christ had never come, then that council would never have met. This would mean that the little infants the Romans had thrown on their garbage heaps never would have been rescued. Rome would still be punishing innocent people, and cruelty would have continued on from century to century until the present day. Alex began to cry, and Grant's face became long and sad.

"Now I understand why they lit the rose-colored candle on the third Sunday of Advent," Grant said. "If the candles were only purple, people would get really depressed."

"That's true," said Young Nanny, laughing. "The rose candle is special because it represents the shepherds who first heard the angels singing of the coming of the Christ child. Shepherds were hard-working men, but they were almost considered outcasts in Israel at the time of the birth of the Messiah. Because they worked with animals, shepherds were often considered unclean. They certainly were not the sort of respectable people one might see in church on Sunday mornings. When the angels announced the coming of the Messiah to the shepherds, however, this was the way that *Melek ha Olam* helped the world see that the Messiah would bring light into everybody's darkness, including those on the lowest rungs of the ladder of society. And remember what the angel said, 'I bring you glad tidings of great joy, which shall be to all people, for unto you is born this day in the city of David a Savior who is Christ the Lord'. That is why the third candle is rose colored and is the candle of joy. To light the rose candle is to go against the Romans' idea that the strong have the right to step on the weak. The rose candle takes away despair and depression and replaces it with joyous expectation."

"What does the other purple candle refer to?" Alex asked.

"That candle is often called the 'angel candle,'" Young Nanny said. "It is lit during the last Sunday of Advent, the Sunday immediately preceding Christmas day."

"Why is it purple and not rose colored?" he inquired.

"Throughout the history of ancient Israel, angels were both God's messengers and God's warriors," she replied. "Angels announced to Abraham and Sarah that they would have a child, Isaac, despite the fact that Sarah was barren and could not have children. The angels foretold the destruction of Sodom and Gomorrah by fire and brimstone, allowing Lot and his family to escape that wicked and doomed city. In the Hebrew Scriptures, Jehovah is called 'the Lord of

Hosts', meaning that he is the commander of vast angelic armies and the very starry hosts of heaven. Angels came to the prophets of old and gave them God's word during troublesome times. Often, God's word foretold coming judgment because of the waywardness of his people Israel. The angel Gabriel announced to Elizabeth that she would be the mother of John the Baptist, the forerunner of the Messiah, but because Zacharias, the father of John the Baptist, disbelieved the angel's word, the angel struck him dumb until John the Baptist was born. The angel Gabriel also revealed to Mary that she would give birth to the Christ, and the angel assured Joseph that Mary was with child because the Holy Spirit had caused her to conceive. On the night Jesus was born, the multitude of heavenly angels sang to lowly shepherds of his birth. At the end of time, the archangel Michael will fight against the Devil and his angels and will secure the victory of the people of God against the Evil One. At the last judgment, the Angels will reap the world like a field ripe with grain. They will separate the wheat from the chaff, safely store the wheat, and burn the chaff with unquenchable fire. So you see, because angels can be either fierce or comforting, depending on whether one is an enemy or a friend of God, the candle is purple rather than rose colored."

"When is the Christ candle lit?" Alex asked.

"Usually either on Christmas Eve or Christmas day," replied Young Nanny. "That candle is the largest, purest, and brightest one of all. Its white color stands for the purity of Christ, and though it is the last one lit, it symbolically is the candle from which all the others receive their light."

"Just like the Hanukkah Menorah in the Temple was lit by the *ner tamid*?" Grant asked.

"Exactly," Young Nanny replied. "The light of the Christ candle reveals that the everlasting light shines upon all times and places, including the darkest and most obscure corners of history. This is none other than the eternal light that one day will shine in the Heavenly City, the New Jerusalem. Then there will be no need for the sun, moon, and stars, 'for the Lord God and the Lamb will be the lamp of that city.' Now," she added. "I will give you some initials that will help you remember what power packs are needed for your Advent flashlights PBSAC PPRPW. Try pronouncing it 'pub-sack pepper-paw.'"

"Pub-sack pepper-paw," the boys recited.

"Try it again," said Young Nanny.

The boys repeated it: "Pub-sack pepper-paw."

"Now remember the letters. First, PBSAC: 'P' for 'Prophecy', 'B' for 'Bethlehem', 'S' for 'Shepherds', 'A' for 'Angels', and 'C' for 'Christ'. And second PPRPW: 'P' for 'purple', 'P' for 'purple', 'R' for 'rose', 'P' for 'purple', and 'W' for 'white.'"

The boys repeated the formula.

"Good," said Young Nanny. Just write the first five letters on one line, and the last five letters right beneath them on a second line, and then you will be able to remember the names of the Advent candles and their colors. Just don't get confused by forgetting that 'pepper-paw' stands for the colors of the candles, okay? Now, here some scratch papers. Practice it a few times, and you'll have it down."

The boys did as Young Nanny instructed, and soon they could remember the names and colors of all the Advent candles. Then they practiced with their Advent flashlights, and tried to say each letter as the lights cycled on. At first they were too slow, but soon, they could recite the letters as fast as a gunslinger at the O.K. Corral could draw his pistol.

"You're doing really great," Young Nanny told them, "and because you've learned this so well, I've got special treats for you."

"More sugar cookies?" Alex exclaimed.

"Well, yes, I do have some for you to eat in a moment, but first I've got a special calendar for you."

The boys expected that Young Nanny would have the usual kinds of inexpensive calendars she was well known for giving people at Christmas time, but on this occasion they were surprised. The calendars had little doors for each of the twenty-four days leading up to Christmas that could be opened one at a time. "Do you know what kind of calendar this is?" Young Nanny asked.

The boys shook their heads.

"This is called an Advent calendar," she replied. "In Europe, parents often give these to their children to teach them patience during the Advent season. Each of these little doors has a little piece of scrumptious chocolate behind it, but more importantly, each door has a little scroll of paper that gives you special thoughts or stories about Advent. Now the trick is to open only one of these Advent doors on each of the twenty-four days leading up to Christmas. Now, if you cheat and eat them all in one sitting, then you'll know that you've got some things to learn about keeping the Advent season in the right spirit. However, if you take your time and open only one door each day, then you will learn something about what it means to wait patiently and anticipate the coming of the Christ Child on Christmas Day. So try not to be like the Romans and give in to the temptation to eat them all quickly. If you do that, you will not enjoy the Advent season. Can you promise me that you'll try to take your time?"

Though the boys agreed, Alex, who had a sweet tooth, was not too enthusiastic. To eat only one piece of chocolate a day when he had access to all twenty-four pieces seemed to him too great a temptation to resist. Indeed, Young Nanny had no sooner given them the calendar than Alex was craving sugar cookies.

"Okay," said Young Nanny, taking out her tin and removing the lid. "I think you boys have been pretty patient on this trip." She took out her Nanny stick, removed a couple of cookies each for the two boys, and served them on napkins. "Now," she said, "we're about to land. I will be unloading mail when we arrive, so you boys go on and find out how conditions are in Christmas present."

They soon landed, taxied down the runway, and came to a stop. The automatic stairs rolled up to the door, and Young Nanny opened the cabin door, gave them a hug goodbye, and told them that she would be waiting for them when they were ready for their next flight. The boys ran down the stairs, through the gate and the terminal, and down the corridor to the mailbox door. Alex warned Grant to take his usual precaution before venturing out, in case the Sphinx was again on the loose, so Grant carefully opened the door and peeked outside. He gave the 'all clear', and he and Alex emerged once more into the Tree World of Christmas present.

—Chapter Thirteen—

THE MEANING OF 'HMBG'

THE MOMENT GRANT and Alex climbed out of the mailbox, they saw black and greenish storm clouds boiling overhead. The auroras they had seen earlier were no longer visible because the clouds obscured them. The wind gusted through the trees, bringing the smell of rain into their nostrils.

"Hurry, Alex," Grant shouted. "The bottom is about to fall out."

They scrambled to find cover, and, just in the nick of time, found a shelter at a bus stop. The second after they darted under the shelter, white, marble-sized hail clattered on the roof of the shelter and bounced off the somewhat tarnished looking grass like popping popcorn. An unexpected streak of lightning blazed across the swirling black clouds, cutting through them like a hot knife through butter. A split-second later, a clap of thunder crashed against their eardrums, sending shivers up their spines.

"Gosh, that was close!" Alex shouted.

"It's not safe here," Grant said. "Maybe it would be a good idea to catch the bus when it comes around."

Because of the fierce weather, no one but the boys waited under the shelter. After a few minutes, the barrage of hail ceased, but it was followed quickly by torrents of rain that beat down on the shelter's roof. The howling wind sent sprays of mist onto their faces and their clothes, and soon the cuffs of their trousers were sopping. Though it seemed like they had waited a full hour, only about five minutes passed before an approaching bus's yellow signal light struggled to appear out of the blinding rain. The bus pulled over and stopped at the curb. Then its doors swung open.

The boys darted through the waterfall of rain into the bus, but the bus was far from dry and inviting. Its floor was wet and nasty from the multitude of feet that had tracked in sludge from the sidewalks, and the atmosphere was humid and stuffy. Strange-looking characters wearing what appeared to be wet trench coats sat in seats reading magazines, newspapers, and books. They oddly resembled the crackpot the boys had earlier seen luring Orna children with his 'aliens from Saturn' sign. Many of the odd people had bulging foreheads and thinning hair, wore thick horn-rimmed glasses, and had faces on which permanent frowns had been plastered. As Grant and Alex scrounged to find a seat, the passengers tended to scowl quickly at them over the tops of their glasses and then return to their reading. They seemed perturbed by the fact that the boys had even dared to board the bus, much less that these two urchins were now attempting to find a place to sit. Grant and Alex soon did find a vacant seat across from an elderly woman who seemed to be protecting a pull-cart of groceries like a dragon guarding buried treasure. Next to her, a white-collared clergyman sat reading a newspaper, shaking his head and clicking his tongue as he did. Occasionally, he would stop, slap the newspaper across his knee, huff, and roll his eyes in disgust. Whenever he would do this, the woman would quickly glance at the paper the clergyman had hit his knee with before looking back at her cart. She seemed afraid, however, to go beyond these occasional glances and make eye contact.

The boys smiled at any passenger who might steal an occasional glance at them, but any effort to crack their stony, sourpuss faces was a waste of time. After traveling about ten minutes, the bus stopped. The rain had now let up, so every last passenger with the exception of Alex and Grant got off. The bus driver, too, walked out the door but left the bus idling.

"This must be the end of the line," Grant guessed, so the boys exited as well. They stood in front of a convention center and saw many more of the odd-looking characters arriving in buses, taxis, and shuttles. Across a computerized banner in front of the convention center streamed the words, 'Welcome Members of the National Society for the Prevention of HMBG!'

"I wonder what HMBG stands for," Grant said to Alex. About that time, they heard what sounded like Christmas music. They walked in the direction the music was coming from and found Orna folk dressed up in interesting costumes. Three Orna ladies, dressed as bumblebees, were humming 'The Little Drummer Boy' in harmony while an Orna man dressed like a grasshopper played the drums. The musicians were trying to raise money for charity because in front of them a brightly painted red kettle with a slot in its top to put money through was suspended by three chains from a stand. The strange-looking characters attending the convention walked past them quickly with furious looks smoldering on their faces. Soon, two police officers arrived. One arrested the singers and handcuffed them while the other emptied the red kettle into a canvas bag and handed it to an odd character who seemed to be one of the organizers of the convention.

"We have the right to assemble and the right to free speech!" the Orna man dressed like a grasshopper protested.

"Not here, you don't!" the convention organizer returned. "You are interfering with a public event, and we won't stand for it!"

"Do you want to press charges, sir?" one of the officers asked the organizer.

"Yes!" he replied. "Prosecute them as far as the law will allow!"

"What about the money we raised for charity?" one of the Orna ladies dressed up like a bumble bee asked.

"Since it was raised on public property, you will have to forfeit it to the public treasury," the organizer stated coldly.

"But, officer!" the Orna woman said. "That money was raised to help support underprivileged children. If that man takes it, the money will go to support HMBG prevention among children. That means they will brainwash children to hate Christmas."

The organizer's pupils shriveled to a hateful point. "She just used a forbidden word," he spat. "Since that word is now illegal in this city, I insist upon pressing further charges."

Alex, who was observing, asked Grant, "What word did she use?"

"I think it was 'Christmas,'" Grant whispered. "I wouldn't say it here, though, if I were you."

A police officer proceeded to write up the Orna woman up for saying 'the forbidden word'. "You do know that using that word will mean certain incarceration," the officer stated.

Alex asked Grant what 'incarceration' meant, and Grant explained that it meant 'jail time'.

"Okay, come along," the officer said, and he and the other officer escorted the handcuffed Orna folk to a police wagon to be carried off and booked for their crimes.

A woman, who was standing next to the convention organizer, commented. "It serves those fools right. They should realize that we know better than they how to funnel money appropriately to children's charities. The very fact that they dressed up in those ridiculous bug outfits shows how incompetent they are to know what is best for children. Talk about 'humbug.'"

"Are you here for the convention, madam?" the convention organizer asked.

"Yes, I wouldn't miss it for the world," she replied.

The man and the woman turned to go into the convention center, and Grant and Alex followed them. All around people were holding signs. On many signs, a red circle with a red slash running diagonally across its diameter covered pictures of Christmas trees, manger scenes, Santa Clauses, snowmen, and other reminders of Christmas. Other signs had the words 'NO HMBG' printed on them. Still others read, 'Make Reason Your Reason for the Season'.

"I don't like their signs," Grant remarked.

"Me neither. I wonder what 'HMBG' stands for," Alex asked Grant.

"If you try pronouncing it, it sounds like 'humbug,'" he replied.

"Is that why they didn't like the Orna folk to be dressed up like bugs humming?" Alex inquired.

"Don't be silly," Grant replied. "Don't you remember? 'Humbug' was Ebenezer Scrooge's favorite word when referring to..." Grant held his hand to Alex's ear and whispered, "Christmas."

"Oh," Alex whispered back. "Like 'Bah Humbug', I get it."

"Since they can't use the forbidden word I just whispered in your ear," Grant spoke softly, "I guess they use HMBG instead."

"But if they meant 'humbug' why don't they just say it?" Alex asked. "Why call it HMBG?"

"They are most likely trying to be politically correct," Grant guessed. "Or maybe HMBG stands for something else. If it does, we will probably find out at this convention."

About that time, the doors to a large auditorium opened and the throngs began making their way in and filling up the seats. Grant and

Alex sat towards the back and listened in to some of the conversations going on around them.

"How many Orna folk do you suppose are left now?" A tall, slender woman said to a short, slightly overweight woman. Both women, who were sitting directly in front of the boys, wore the same kind of black horn-rimmed glasses as the people who had ridden the bus. The tall women had salt and pepper hair, and the short woman's hair was orange.

"I hear they are shattering to pieces left and right," said the woman with the orange hair. "Of course, that's to be expected. Just think of what they stand for. Once they're gone, we won't have to be reminded of that horrible holiday anymore."

"You're right, Virginia," said the tall woman. "It's their H. M. B. G. viewpoints, of course. Okay, I'll go ahead and pronounce it! '*HUM-BUG*'! There! Now I feel much better just calling it what it is."

The auditorium lights began to dim, and the stage lights were turned up. The organizer they had seen earlier appeared from behind the curtain and walked across the stage to the podium.

"Welcome," he said to the gathering. "We are happy that you have taken time out of your busy schedules to attend our convention this year. This year's program will feature many notable experts, and I am convinced that your time attending the sessions will be well spent. As you know, we are all about alternatives here, alternatives to worn-out traditional values like marriage, family, having children and bringing them up, and especially superstitious holiday celebrations. As you know, we have conveniently found a way to clump all these outdated values together under the label 'HMBG', which, of course, is commonly pronounced 'HUMBUG'. Those who have attended our meetings over the years, however, know that 'HMBG' actually stands for 'Homogeneous Misanthropic Bigoted Groups.'"

CHAPTER THIRTEEN

Grant and Alex looked at each other curiously and frowned.

The convention organizer continued: 'HMBG-positive individuals', as we like to label them, are persons who think too much alike, who tend not to agree with persons with different ideas like ourselves, and who only approve of persons with strong opinions like their own. You can most easily recognize them because they celebrate the holiday 'Christmas' that now has been outlawed in this city. We no longer use that word, of course, and it bothers me even to speak of it now. In our city, the Anti-HMBG movement has been strongly effective thanks to our members' persistent efforts to use the court-system to their advantage. We hope that soon the whole nation, and indeed the entire world, will come to accept our position, and that all will ultimately cease and desist from propagating further nonsense about 'Christmas.'"

"I wonder what his problem is," Grant whispered to Alex.

Alex shrugged his shoulders. "I don't like what he's saying," he whispered back. "I wonder if there's a way we can leave."

"The doors are shut," Grant said. "Maybe we need to stay just for this session."

The orange-haired woman in front of them turned, scowled, held the index finger of her right hand up to her lips, and went "Shhhh!"

"Our first speaker today comes highly recommended," the organizer went on. "He is a charter member of the Society for the Prevention of HMBG and President of the Society for the Education of the Religiously Misinformed and Superstitiously Confused. He is author of several books, including *Hogwash throughout the Ages, Why I worship the Goddess Reason*, and *Who in His Right Mind Needs to Believe Anything? Hogwash throughout the Ages* is his special book on the history of the holiday commonly called 'Christmas', and that will be the topic he will be speaking on today. Please welcome our guest,

S. J. Pestermante-Doogletarket, as he comes to enlighten us with his marvelous insights."

A storm of applause broke through into the auditorium, and one of the odd-looking characters wearing the horn-rimmed glasses came to the podium.

"A weird name if I ever heard one," Grant uttered to Alex.

Pestermante-Doogletarket started: "Greetings to all who know the truth of the following statements: There is no Tree King, there is no Scrooge cemetery at the end of history to be afraid of, Christmas is a pagan superstition, 'reason' and 'reason alone' is the 'reason for the season', and Bah Humbug to all!"

Laughter erupted from the audience, followed by an enthusiastic round of applause, but Grant and Alex glared at each other with disturbed faces and cried, "What?"

"Point one: There is no Tree King," said Pestermante-Doogletarket. "There are only facts, facts, facts. I stand before you speaking, and that is a fact. Where is Tree King? He is not here standing before you because he is not a fact. There is therefore more evidence for my existence than for the existence of Tree King. Tree King is a superstition made up by ancient people who knew nothing of science. Science is not superstition. Science is truth."

"Plug your ears, Alex," Grant whispered. "I think he may be one of those Scrooges from cemetery plot 'A.'" Alex plugged one ear, but continued to listen with the other.

"Point two: Because Tree King does not exist, we need not fear the Scrooge cemetery that some keep warning us about. The Scrooge cemetery is an illusion based on a superstitious belief."

"Liar!" Grant said. The women in front of them both turned and said, "Quiet!"

"Superstition is not science and is therefore untrue. Only death is a scientific fact. There is nothing else. So 'eat, drink, and be merry' while you are alive, for soon death and science will put an end to everything. Go not forth through this life afraid of monsters that do not exist. It is a waste of time. Forget the past! Enjoy the present! Do not dread the future!

"Everything he's saying is the exact opposite of what Pater Kronos and Brother Memory taught us," Grant whispered to Alex.

"He'd sure believe in monsters if he'd met the Beast," Alex added.

"Third point," continued Pestermante-Doogletarket. "Christmas is a purely pagan holiday. Pope Julius invented it as an alternative to Saturnalia in the year 350. Christ is nothing more than a sun-god! His so-called Father is none other than Saturn, the god of time! The pagans were better off being pagans: It certainly would have been much simpler if they had remained so, and they would have had a great deal more fun."

"Wrong again," Alex whispered. "He wasn't in Rome like we were. How could he know?"

"Point four," the man continued. "'Reason is and ought to remain the 'reason for the season'. To use irrational superstition as a 'reason' for anything cannot be sustained by valid argument. This is why all reminders of Christmas need removing. Replace them with statues of the goddess reason wherever you can! Celebrate the winter solstice, if you will—at least it is more scientific. But do not add unnecessary beliefs like Santa Clause, elves, reindeer, Tree King, mangers with little figurines, or Advent candles—for what can best be explained well using fewer things is explained in vain with more."

Grant just shook his head as Pestermante-Doogletarket droned on, and Alex sat there in disbelief.

"Finally, instead of saying 'Merry Christmas', say 'Bah humbug' as often as you desire," the man urged. "All Christmas baggage is, after all, 'humbug'—bags upon bags of pure humbug—so, clear them out of your closets and attics, set them on your curbs, take them by truckloads to your nearest landfill, burn them to cinders, and finally cover them up with as many tons of dirt as you need to eradicate the memory of them from the mind of every man, woman, and child forever. So I conclude my address to you this evening, 'Bah Humbug' to all, and to all a good night!"

The audience laughed, rose to their feet, and applauded, but Grant and Alex could only sit there shaking their heads and frowning. Just then, the boys felt someone grab them by their collars. They struggled until a familiar voice said, "You boys are in the wrong place. Come with me this instant." They looked and saw Pater Kronos, so they gladly leapt out of their seats and trotted out of the auditorium. Two odd-looking men stood at the doors, staring at them coldly as they exited, but Kronos and the boys, undeterred, walked briskly past them and quickly exited the auditorium. When they arrived outside, they saw the bus they had ridden on, but a fire had started under its hood, and blue-gray smoke was pouring out. The boys caught a whiff of it as they hurried past and recognized the odor to be that of stale 'vampire perfume'. Kronos had brought his motorcycle, so he quickly strapped helmets on the boys' heads, placed Grant on the seat behind him, and hoisted Alex into the sidecar.

"Hold on to me tight, Grant," he said. "We've got to get out of here quick!"

Grant grabbed Kronos around the waist, and they zoomed off. By now, the rain had slacked, but the sky was still overcast so that the auroras were not visible. Kronos carried them back in the direction of the mailbox they had exited earlier. When they arrived there, he looked the boys sternly in the face. "It's my fault that I let you get in with that Anti-HMBG bunch. I got delayed by the weather and lost track of you. Now it's very important that you forget everything you heard at that convention. The people there are masters at distorting facts. They do not understand the puzzle of the Tree World, and none of them knows or cares that the wiring has been overloaded and that Christmas future is in danger of being extinguished forever."

"Why do they hate Christmas so much?" Alex asked.

"Some of them are just angry for no reason at all," Kronos replied. "Others have a reason, but I don't think it's a very good one."

"What reason?" Grant inquired.

"Mainly hurt feelings," Kronos replied. "Instead of having fun pretending about Santa Claus bringing gifts down chimneys as most kids do, they took their belief in Santa Claus way too seriously. As you learned when you were in Rome, the modern idea of Santa Claus is based on the real St. Nicholas who lived many years ago, but the modern idea unfortunately does not always reflect who St. Nicholas actually was and what he stood for. When some of those people attending that Anti-HMBG convention were children, their parents told them that their gifts came from Santa Claus. Other children they knew believed this, too, but when some of these children got more and better gifts from Santa than they did, the kids who got fewer and inferior gifts got jealous. They began to wonder, why did Santa give those kids more than me? Does Santa love them more? Did he give them more gifts because they were better behaved? So these hurt children tried to be very good, but they did something else, too, that they shouldn't have. They kept two lists. One was the list of all their good behaviors. The other was a list of all the bad behaviors of the kids that got more gifts from Santa. Now, when these bad kids still got more gifts than they did, the kids that got less became really angry. Some set out to disprove the existence of Santa Claus by secretly watching for him on Christmas Eve, putting up detection devices, and planting hidden cameras. They tried to prove that all the gifts they received were brought by their parents or grandparents, not by Santa. When these children presented their parents with the facts, sometimes the parents would say, 'Of course you can't see Santa, don't you know he's invisible?' But the children were not convinced. They figured out that Santa was a hoax. Next, they began to think, maybe if there is no Santa then there must be no Creator and King of the Universe—or in this world, no Tree King—either. That's how they started to doubt whether the maker of all things existed. Eventually, they only trusted what they could see. They got to the point that they could only rely on reason and logic to figure out their world. They got angry with all the people who kept the hoax going and referred to their beliefs as 'humbug.'"

"I can sort of understand how they felt," Grant said. "Were they right about Santa?"

"Yes and no," Kronos answered. "First, they were right to conclude that the Santa they had been taught to believe in was unfair. Unfortunately, the Santa they were taught to believe in was not exactly the same as the St. Nicholas who actually lived many years ago. If you remember, St. Nicholas was a real person who performed acts of charity in a world full of needy people. St. Nicholas was born to wealthy parents, and those parents died when he was but a lad. Because that wealth passed to him, Nicholas had the wherewithal to help others who were in desperate straits. Because he didn't want to bring attention to himself, he gave things secretly to the needy when no one was looking. That's where the tradition of St. Nicholas bringing gifts to children in secret came from. As you well know from your visit to ancient Rome, children in those days did not have nearly as good a life as children today. In those times, children sometimes were abandoned on trash heaps, and not just by needy parents. Wealthy parents sometimes did such horrible things, too. The gifts that St. Nicholas brought meant for most who received them the difference between having enough food to eat and starvation, or the difference between freedom and slavery. St. Nicholas did not magically produce the money he gave away either in the way people say Santa magically produces toys. For it is said that St. Nicholas spent everything he owned helping the poor, and especially children. So you see, Santa Claus is not the best imitation of St. Nicholas because Santa brings lots of gifts to boys and girls, many of whom already happen to be spoiled rotten by their parents. These children grow up thinking that such gifts are owed them, and they throw tantrums if they don't get exactly what they want when they want it. For such children, Christmas rarely means learning how to give to others. Instead, Christmas means getting lots of loot. Because their parents overindulge them, such children often turn out to be selfish, ungrateful, and spoiled. In the old days, Santa was often accompanied by a dark elf called 'Pete' who would punish selfish and undeserving children. That idea is rarely found today. Even the idea that Santa makes a list to see who's naughty or nice isn't taken seriously. Because of this, Santa today represents more the spirit of the Roman festival of Saturnalia than he does the true spirit of Christmas. It's no wonder that some of these spoiled children grow up to be cruel bullies just like the ancient Romans whose desires and appetites knew no bounds and whose disregard for the needs and feelings of others knew no limits."

"I just remembered what Brother Memory told us about the meaning of the Latin words, 'in hoc signo vincet'—They mean 'in this sign conquer,'" Grant said. "The sign of the cross helps us control our desires and focus on the needs of others."

"Yeah, and don't forget that 'Advent conquers Saturnalia', too," Alex added.

"Very perceptive," said Kronos. "But the misunderstanding of the true meaning of St. Nicholas is only one problem the Anti-HMBG people have in their understanding of Christmas. Another place where they go wrong is to think of belief in Santa Claus and belief in the King of the Universe as being the same sort of thing. The modern idea of Santa Claus is a legend based on a person called St. Nicholas, but the King of the Universe is the one who created all things, including St. Nicholas. St. Nicholas for this reason is not the same as the one whom we refer to here in Arboria as Tree King. Indeed, if we are to save Christmas future, it is very important to get our thinking straight not only about the true identity of St. Nicholas, but also about the true identity of the King of the Universe—the one the Hebrew people call '*Melek ha Olam*'. We have to be able to distinguish between their true identity and ways that their identity has been misrepresented."

"I think I understand," Grant said. "Are those pieces of the puzzle of the time-wiring-diagram we need to remember?"

"Indeed they are," replied Kronos. "And speaking of the time-wiring-diagram, we have lost another ten years since you boys were last here. All the green mailboxes after the year 2090 have been reconfigured to that date. This means that we are still losing time and losing it rapidly."

"What about the Sphinx?" Alex asked.

"He is trampling out the vintage where the Orna folk are stored," Kronos replied. "But this does not necessarily mean that the truth of Tree King is marching on as a result. As you saw at the Anti-HMBG

Convention, the truth itself is being trampled on. That is why we have very little time to restore truth to the Orna folk so that they will again be able to find the way to the Star at Tree Top."

"Where are the Orna folk now?" Grant asked. "We've seen only a few since we've been here."

"Get on my motorbike, and I'll take you to see," Kronos told them. "But I must warn you. The scene you will see where I'm taking you is gruesome." Alex put on his helmet and climbed into the motorcycle's sidecar. Grant hopped on behind Pater Kronos again and latched his arms around his waist. Kronos sped out and drove them to what appeared to be a city dump. When he turned the motor off, they could hear the distant roaring of the Sphinx. The crushed bodies of Orna folk stretched out for what seemed like miles. Then they saw the Sphinx in the distance crushing the bodies of the Orna with his paws into ever finer shards of glass. Somehow the Sphinx was able to do this without his paws bleeding. As they watched, a police van pulled up close to where the Sphinx was prowling, and more Orna folk were released. The Sphinx immediately saw them, and sprang toward them in pursuit. When the Orna were unable to answer his riddle, the Sphinx mercilessly crushed them with his powerful jaws and trampled them under his feet.

"Are there any Orna folk left?" Alex asked as tears formed in his eyes.

"The few that remain here are in hiding, but they will be crushed, too, if the policies of the Anti-HMBG people prevail," Kronos replied. "Other Ornas, however, are safe because they have managed to escape down the roads that lead in the direction of Tree Top. Those who have not set their hearts on selfishness will be able to pass the tests given them by the angel stars. They will escape the bondage of this present Egypt. We can only hope that someday they will return and restore Christmas to this lost land. At this point, however, the rapid disappearance of the future suggests this may not happen."

The boys soon grew sick of looking at the horrible sight. Kronos recognized that they had seen enough and directed them to get back on the motorcycle. He started the motor, and they soon sped away from the tragic scene. Eventually, they arrived at a red mailbox that had on it the date A. D. 1684. "This will be as good a place as any for you to go next," Kronos told them. "Your job will be to find Christmas. It will be hard, but if you look carefully you will find it. Godspeed!"

Grant opened the combination on the door of the red mailbox, and he and his brother entered. As he usually did, Pater Kronos shut the door behind them, and they were soon on their way down another corridor to the air terminal to meet Young Nanny.

—Chapter Fourteen—

EATING ORANGES IN OLD BOSTON

WHEN THE BOYS ARRIVED at the gate, they saw Young Nanny's red plane outside the window of the terminal, so they proceeded through the snow-globe portal, hurried to the plane, climbed the stairs, and entered the cabin door. Young Nanny was again stacking her bags, but this time she was dressed rather oddly. She wore a plain long black dress with long sleeves, a white pinafore, a white apron, and a white bonnet. She looked like she had just come from acting in a school Thanksgiving play. The boys wondered if she had brought turkey and pumpkin pie along, too, but they couldn't smell anything of the sort on the plane. Instead, when they looked around, they saw only oranges stuffed inside one of the mailbags.

"Greetings, Young Nanny," Grant said, and Alex echoed the same phrase.

"Hello, boys," she said. "I'm so happy you're back. I'm excited about your trip this time. I guess you know that you're traveling to the year 1684, but do you know where?"

"No," they answered.

"Look at how I'm dressed. Does that give you a hint?"

"You look like one of the Pilgrim mothers we saw in this year's Thanksgiving school play," Alex remarked.

"A close guess!" she said. "But the pilgrims arrived at Plymouth Rock in the Massachusetts Bay Colony sixty-four years earlier than 1684 when you will be arriving. As you know, they would have starved to death if it hadn't been for the Wampanoag tribe of Native Americans that taught them how to fish, hunt, work the fields, and prepare for the harsh New England winters."

"I know," Grant said. "I remember the name of that Indian chief. His name was Massasoit."

"Very good!" she congratulated him. "How did you know that?"

"I played him in the school Thanksgiving play," he answered.

"That's wonderful," she said. "But the Pilgrims who landed at Plymouth Rock were not the only English people who came in those early days. They were followed by a larger group known as the Great Migration. These left England to escape religious persecution. They were not, however, the only Europeans to come. There were also Dutch settlers from the Netherlands who formed a city known as New Amsterdam. Later, four English warships sailed into the harbor and demanded the city's surrender. After that, its name was changed to New York in honor of James II, the Duke of York and brother to Charles II, the King of England."

"Will we be going to New York, too?" Grant asked.

"No," Young Nanny replied, "only to Boston in the Massachusetts Bay Colony. We need to leave soon, though, so you need to get buckled in for the flight. Go on, and I'll be with you in a minute."

The boys got buckled into their seats, and soon Young Nanny joined them.

"I'm sure I shall go down in the record books as the first Puritan great-grandmother ever to fly a plane!" said Young Nanny. She engaged the propellers, taxied down the runway, and soon had gotten the plane airborne.

"Oh, drat," she said when they had reached a safe altitude. "I forgot to get those oranges. Grant, will you go back, look in that bag, and bring some up here for us to eat?"

Grant unbuckled his seatbelt, went into the cabin, took three oranges from the bags, returned to the cockpit, and handed an orange each to Young Nanny and Alex, while keeping one himself.

"Thank you," she said. "Now buckle up again. I want to tell you a story."

"Did you get the oranges from Florida, California, or Texas?" Grant asked.

"None of those places," she answered. "These oranges are from Spain. Spanish oranges at Christmas are special because long ago they were brought on ships from Spain to Holland to give to little Dutch children at Christmas. Do you know how the Dutch children believed that St. Nicholas arrived in Holland?"

"I know," Alex answered. "He flew his magical sleigh that was pulled by flying reindeer."

"No," Young Nanny said. "Grant, do you know?"

"Did he come riding a white horse?"

"He did ride a white horse after he arrived in Holland, but that's not how he got there in the first place. According to the traditions, he actually arrived by boat."

"Why by boat?" Alex asked.

"I'm guessing now, but one reason may be that St. Nicholas was the patron saint of sailors as well as children. One legend about him says that he once returned by ship from a visit to the Holy Land when a storm threatened to send him and the crew to a watery grave. St. Nicholas prayed, and the wind and waters were miraculously stilled. Another guess would be that he lived in the city of Myra which was a port city that had many sailors in it. But there may be another reason why he arrived in Holland by a ship coming from Spain. Again, I'm only guessing, but in the days before the Dutch gained their independence, they were ruled by the Spaniards. After independence, they tried to outlaw as many Spanish customs as possible. One of these customs was the celebration of St. Nicholas Day and Christmas. The Dutch tried to get rid of these customs much like the Puritans in England did, but these attempts didn't set well with large numbers of the Dutch people. The Dutch authorities' plan backfired, and they did not succeed in outlawing Christmas. This may explain why the Dutch kept bringing St. Nicholas back year after year to Holland from Spain. It was the one Spanish custom almost everybody loved. In time, the belief developed that St. Nicholas arrived in Holland every year on December 5th by steamboat."

"Why December 5th?" Grant asked.

"Because the following day, December 6th, was St. Nicholas Day," she said.

"Will we be celebrating St. Nicholas Day when we arrive in Boston in 1684?" Alex asked.

"I hate to say it, but you won't," Young Nanny said. "As I just told you, the English Puritans did not celebrate anything having to do with St. Nicholas or Christmas."

"Why didn't they?" Grant asked.

"The reason has a lot to do with the wars that went on between Catholics and Protestants during the 1600s," Young Nanny told them. "You will find out more about that when you get to Boston. But try not to judge the Puritans too harshly. You will see that they had good reasons for their beliefs. Now," she said, changing the subject. "Why don't we eat our oranges?"

After Young Nanny handed them paper napkins so that they would not make a mess in the plane, Grant and Alex peeled their oranges, broke them into sections, and started gobbling them down.

"Hey, these are pretty good," said Alex.

"Try not to eat them so fast," said Young Nanny. "When I was a girl, it would usually take me a whole day to eat my Christmas orange."

"A whole day? To eat an orange?" Alex laughed.

"Yes," she replied. "We savored every bite of our scrumptious Christmas oranges because we had to wait a whole year to get them. When I was growing up, oranges were rare and very expensive. That's why we were given only one orange a year to eat. Sometimes we also got an apple and a few nuts. But these were the only presents we children usually got."

Grant and Alex thought about the many Christmas toys they had gotten in the past, so many that they couldn't remember them all. They were so sad that Young Nanny only got a few pieces of fruit and a few nuts for Christmas that they wanted to cry.

"It just doesn't seem fair," Alex said. "Why didn't your parents give you better gifts?"

"Mama and Daddy were very poor," Young Nanny answered, "and there were five of us children. I think I mentioned before that there was Elizabeth, me, Velma, Leon, and Arabella Priscilla. With so many of us, it was a real sacrifice for our parents to buy those oranges. We children didn't know any better, either, because that one orange was a real luxury. I suppose if we had eaten oranges everyday like people do now, getting an orange for Christmas would not have seemed like such a big deal. But we children never thought about it that way. Christmas was the most exciting day of the year, and all because it was the day we would get our orange. Now, children get so many gifts, they don't seem able to appreciate the value of them. A lot of children grow tired of playing with their toys, even before the twelve days of Christmas are over."

"The twelve days of Christmas?" Grant asked.

"Yes," said Young Nanny. "We will want to talk about that at some point. But now, I want you boys to think about how lucky you are to have an abundance of food to eat. Where you are going, you will see why the Puritans believed that the celebration of Thanksgiving was more important than Christmas. They knew what it meant to be grateful for what they had."

When the boys first received their oranges, they had torn into them and wolfed down the first few segments without thinking. Now that they only had a few pieces left, they thought about what Young Nanny had said about oranges being so precious in the old days. Grant and Alex ate the rest of their orange slowly, savoring each bite, and trying to imagine what it had been like to think of an orange as an expensive and wonderful Christmas present. As they thought about this, they began to know what it was like to feel really grateful for something. This was a new feeling for them, because in the past they were often disappointed when they had opened their presents and received clothes instead of toys. They began to think that maybe they were like some of the spoiled children that Brother Memory had mentioned when he was telling them about Santa Claus.

"You boys are being awfully quiet," Young Nanny said. "Would you like some sugar cookies now?"

In the past, Alex would have been quick to say 'yes', but he remained quiet. Grant did not take up Young Nanny's offer either.

"What's wrong with you boys?" Young Nanny asked. "Don't you like my sugar cookies anymore?"

"I do," Alex said, "but I want to remember how good that orange tasted. Could I maybe have my cookie later?"

"Of course," she said. "What about you, Grant?"

"I think eating one now would spoil the memory of my orange, too. I'll wait till Alex decides to have his."

Young Nanny smiled, and a tear of joy welled up in her eye. She was thrilled that Grant and Alex were learning some important lessons about the true meaning of Christmas. Indeed, for the first time, they were realizing that having everything their hearts desired might not be the most important thing about Christmas.

"Young Nanny," Grant asked seriously. "What was the best gift you ever got for Christmas?"

"When I got older, people began to have more money, and that included my family, too," she answered. "I've received some pretty nice Christmas presents in my time, including jewelry, a washing machine, a dishwasher, and flying lessons. But I've learned over the years that the best gift is the gift behind the gift. That, of course, is the gift of love. It was the gift of love that I felt when my parents gave us oranges they couldn't afford. Those presents were always better than expensive ones not given out of love."

The boys kept thinking about what Young Nanny had told them, so they were rather quiet for the rest of their flight. Soon, they were landing in Boston in the year 1684. Once the automatic ramp had attached itself to the plane and Young Nanny opened the cabin door, the boys gave their great-grandmother a hug.

"Here," she said, handing both of them a couple of oranges each. "Take these with you to snack on."

The boys took the oranges, thanked Young Nanny, and exchanged farewells with her. After they had left the plane, they again found the snow-globe portal and made their way through it and the terminal to the mailbox door.

* * *

On the other side of the door, Brother Memory was waiting for them. He now was dressed like a Puritan minister. His black, broad-rim hat had a buckle on the hatband, and the familiar burning candle was sticking out of its top. He wore a full-length black robe, and two starched white bands hung from his neck down to his chest. "Good morning, lads," he greeted them. "If ye will but follow me, I shall direct you forthwith to Boston Common." Brother Memory turned and began walking briskly, and the boys followed him.

"Why are you dressed like that?" Alex asked.

"This is acceptable clerical garb," he replied, "well fashioned by busy hands and sewn with cloth secured with money well-earned and spent in a spirit of utmost frugality. It is moreover garb most be-fitting a Professor of Divinity and History at Harvard College. Hurry now, lest we squander precious time and be reprimanded for falling into indolence."

"Do you have any idea what he is saying?" Alex asked.

"Not a clue," Grant remarked. "Can you tell us what 'indolence' is?" he asked Brother Memory.

"Laziness, lad, laziness," he replied. "Need I quote you in full Aesop's fable about the ant and the grasshopper? Have you never heard of the deadly sin of sloth? Remember your proverb! An idle mind is a workshop of the Devil! Now follow me that you may learn industry and the meaning of true diligence, and prevent yourselves from falling into the deadly sin of procrastination."

"Pro-what?" Alex asked.

"You, young gentlemen, need to learn the meaning of words," Brother Memory said. "'Procrastination'—the habit of putting off until tomorrow the work you could have easily accomplished today."

"Oh, that's like *memento mori*!" Grant said.

"So, you know a modicum of Latin, I take it." Brother Memory said. "Commendable, but now learn some more so that your vocabulary will improve in tandem."

"What?" Alex asked.

"Really!" said Brother Memory. "Learning more Latin will go a long way in improving your vocabulary!"

"Well why didn't you say that?" Alex replied. Then he changed the subject, "What day is this?"

"This is the day that the Lord hath made," he replied. "Let us rejoice and be glad in it."

"Here we go again," said Alex. "What day of the week is it?"

"Wednesday, December 25th," Brother Memory said.

"So it's Christmas day?" Alex exclaimed.

"Indeed," replied Brother Memory, "and as good a day as any to work for our daily bread. Remember what the Law commands: 'Six days shalt thou labor. But the seventh day is the Sabbath of the LORD thy God: in it thou shalt not do any work, thou, nor thy son, nor thy daughter, thy manservant, nor thy maidservant, nor thy cattle, nor thy stranger that is within thy gates.'"

"But isn't Christmas supposed to be a holiday?" Grant asked.

"There are no holidays in this colony," Brother Memory said. "There are only Sabbath days. In this year, Christmas day is not on the Sabbath, so it is a work day like all others. Children go to school. Farmers plow fields, their wives milk cows and gather eggs. Bakers bake, candlestick makers make, sawyers saw, and builders build. Look at the birds gleaning in the fields. Do they observe pagan holidays such as Christmas? Do they engage in the sins of gluttony, drunkenness, gambling, dancing, card playing, and sport? Not at all! They joyously do the work of their creator and feed themselves 'while it is day.'"

The boys had a difficult time understanding Brother Memory, but every time they would try to get him to explain things to them more simply, he would recite poetry, tell them a fable, quote a proverb, or chide them for trying to make things simpler so they wouldn't have to work hard at understanding. Still, as the boys struggled to understand him, they found themselves understanding enough to get his general drift.

"We are coming now to Boston Common," Brother Memory said. "I realize that you boys were having a hard time understanding me earlier, but I thought it might be a good idea to give you a little taste of what to expect. Because I want you to understand what is going on here, I'll try as hard as I can to help you figure the Puritans out. If you look, you will see cattle grazing on the Common. There used to be more of them here, but the number has now been reduced to seventy and no more. The wooden building you see ahead just there is the State House. Next to it is the market. The Congregationalist Church and the village school are just north of here."

"Everyone seems very busy," Alex remarked.

"True," said Brother Memory. "The Puritans are known as a hard-working people, and they insist that all members of their society strive to cultivate the virtue of industriousness."

"What's that large wooden thing over there with the holes in it?" Grant asked, pointing.

"Those are the stocks," Brother Memory said. "There are three holes. The larger one is for a person's neck, and the two smaller ones on each side are for his wrists. Offenders are put in the stocks for misdemeanors or for breaking various minor laws. They remain in them for a length of time that can vary depending on the gravity of the offense. Ordinarily, you would see someone in there today who had broken the law by celebrating Christmas. But for several years now, it has been illegal, by order of the King of England, to punish people in that way. I can tell you one thing, however: The clergy, the city magistrates, and many upstanding townspeople are none too happy about the King's interference in the governance of the colony. The situation here is very tense because of it. Indeed, matters have been made worse this year because the King has revoked the charter of the Massachusetts Bay Colony. Furthermore, because the laws have been relaxed, non-Puritans are now moving to the colony, too. The Dutch in particular are bringing in unwanted customs such as the celebration of Christmas."

"I don't understand why the Puritans hate Christmas so much," Alex remarked. "They must be Anti-HMBGs."

"What they hate is not so much the idea that Jesus had a birthday," he explained. "They mainly object to his birthday being celebrated on December 25th. They know all about the Roman festival of Saturnalia, and they believe that Julius I was wrong to try to link Christ's birthday to that pagan festival. Though many years have passed since Julius fixed the time of Jesus birth around the time of the pagan midwinter festivals, the Puritans point out that pagan customs associated with these festivals—such as gluttony, drunkenness, gambling, and playing sports—have continued to be practiced anyway. You will often hear Puritan ministers arguing that Jesus could not have been born in December because shepherds were abiding in the fields and keeping watch over their flocks by night. These ministers claim that shepherds would not have been in their fields during the cold of winter, and that Jesus therefore must have been born during a warmer time of the year when shepherds indeed would have had their flocks in the fields. Most of all the Puritans object to the self-indulgent behaviors of people who celebrate Christmas. Such behaviors go against everything the Puritans stand for."

Grant remembered the oranges that Nanny had given them, so he removed one and started peeling it. When Alex saw what Grant was doing, he, too, started peeling his orange.

"Just ahead is the State House," Brother Memory said, pointing to a large wooden building. "The clergy and magistrates meet there regularly on Wednesdays to discuss matters having to do with the governance of the colony. In this colony, the Congregationalist Church and the state of Massachusetts are not separate organizations as they are in modern America."

Brother Memory led the boys into the Statehouse. Around a large wooden table sat a group of magistrates and clergy engaged in a discussion. One of the magistrates was moderating when a man raised his hand. "The chair recognizes the Reverend Cotton Mather," the moderator said.

"Thank you, good sir," The Reverend Mather acknowledged. "As you know, dear brethren, I am a man of science, a follower of Mr. Robert Boyle of Oxford, who in my time has discovered with the aid of Divine Providence the law of the expansion of gases. Having earned my degrees in divinity from Harvard College in the year of our Lord 1678 and again in 1681, I acknowledge without reservation that this same Providence has chosen us, his elect, to work tirelessly toward the redemption of this pagan land which once the Devil and his minions held tightly in thrall. Now that the gospel of Christian light and liberty is preached to the Indians, an assurance is no doubt forthcoming that their election to the Kingdom of Christ will soon crush the Devil's last stronghold that persists in this new land of

Canaan. Yet, despite this colony's successes in turning back the foul tide of pagan superstition, the floodgates have now been reopened. For many a year, that foul tide had washed up on the shores of the Kingdom of Christ. For an all too brief time, we managed to stem that tide. But what now? Now the sovereign of England, his Majesty Charles II, has carelessly and with great affront to the sensitivities of Christians of good conscience, opened those floodgates yet again. He has allowed that foul tide of vile paganism to flood once more the shores of Christ's Kingdom. What is this but the same vile paganism whose turgid waters rushed into ancient Rome, drowning her in her own gross excesses? I speak, of course, of the pagan festival of Saturnalia which hides ravenous and wolf-like beneath the sheep's clothing of Christmas. Still, beneath that borrowed fleece, the she-wolf that nurtured Romulus, founder of Rome, and taught him to sacrifice his brother Remus to build that infamous city, now returns to reteach those ways. I ask you brethren, what are we to do when the kingdom of this world exerts so heavy a hand upon us? How are we to proceed?"

Another hand went up, and the moderator spoke, "The chair recognizes the Honorable Governor, Mr. Simon Bradstreet."

"Thank you, Reverend Mather, for your eloquent and impassioned defense of our colony's ideals. Dear gentlemen, I have always held our Puritan principles in highest esteem, as my own father, a Puritan minister in Old England, preached the gospel faithfully and accompanied by all soundness of doctrine. However, I am more moderate in my sentiments than the Reverend Mather and have during my tenure as governor of this colony opposed the harsh punishment of those outspoken against the magistrates. In answer to Reverend Mather's questions, I suggest that without wavering we hold firm to our own convictions, but as far as trying to enforce previous statutes, now outlawed by the Crown, by exacting public punishments for offenders who celebrate Christmas, I urge caution and encourage leniency. Let us win over our enemies with arguments, not with stocks, beatings, and public humiliations!"

"If I may," the Reverend Mather interrupted. "The kingdom of Satan is strong, my dear sir, and to admit into our midst even the smallest lump of this leaven of ancient paganism will be to choose a course whose end, I fear, will be the searing of our consciences with a hot iron! What then would be next? The open practice of witchcraft? Public worship of the Prince of Darkness himself?"

"I doubt, my good sir," Governor Bradstreet returned, "that citizens of our good commonwealth will venture into the excesses you predict. However, if I might suggest another possible pernicious outcome: If we err on the side of excessive discipline, we might find ourselves easily driving them in such a direction!"

An elderly man raised his hand, and immediately every man present stood and applauded.

"Mr. John Alden, how richly we are blessed by your presence today, sir," said the moderator. "The chair recognizes you with the greatest affection. Please share your wisdom with us."

"Who is he?" Grant asked Brother Memory.

"He was the first man to set foot on Plymouth Rock when the Pilgrims arrived on the Mayflower."

"Magistrates, good reverends, brethrens, and sirs," Mr. Alden began, "Five and fourscore years have I been a pilgrim in this world. Four and threescore of those years I have spent in this good land to which the hand of Providence saw fit to guide our pilgrim band. By trade, I was a cooper for the Mayflower when it was docked at Southampton in Old England."

"What is a cooper?" Alex asked Brother Memory.

"A barrel-maker," he whispered.

"In September of 1620, when I was in my twenty-first year, I was on board that vessel as it began sailing its treacherous three month journey to this New England. I may have been a good barrel-maker. Many have said so. But it was by God's grace that many a barrel, filled to the brim with salted fish, ale, and other provisions, survived that voyage. During one horrific storm, a mate about my age, Mr. John Howland by name, got swept overboard, but with God's help he managed to grab hold of the topsail halyards long enough for us reach him with a boathook and complete his rescue. John and his wife Elizabeth later dwelt close by us in Duxbury. I recall with sorrow how over half who signed the Mayflower Compact died during that first harsh winter. We who survived did so with the help of the Indians, making it clear to us that they—though commonly denounced as pagan—were, just as we, created in God's image. So grateful were we to be alive by the time our first harvest came that we covenanted to observe a feast with the Indians who had helped to save us from what would have been certain starvation and death. Unlike the feasts some of us had known in Old England, in which sobriety and propriety were thrown like caution to the wind, this feast was observed in a spirit of austere reverence. In the Old World, feasts all too often occasioned excesses of gluttony, drunkenness, dancing, card-playing, dice-throwing, gambling, and other frivolities. Our solemn observance, however, knew nothing of these excesses but was instead seasoned with prayer and thankfulness to God for his bountiful provisions. Now, as an old man, I see evidences of our turning aside from the pilgrim way. True, we are threatened again by Old World paganism, but wherefore? Is it that grace, forgiveness, and a grateful spirit no longer guard us? Is it that we have abandoned these better guardians for the taskmasters of strict regulation, harsh punishment, and mean-spirited treatment of others? Can we do better than show compassion towards others who share this New World with us as well, whether Indian, Dutchman, German, and whether Puritan, Baptist, Quaker, or Church of England? Graciousness, I predict, will more easily win over our enemies than any rigid rule enforced in a spirit of spite."

Grant and Alex had been eating their oranges, watching the Reverend Mather to gauge his response to the words of John Alden. His face was stone-like, his lips were pursed, and his eyes were squinted.

"It's time for us to leave here before things turn nasty," said Brother Memory, so he led the boys out of the Statehouse back into Boston Common. "I hope you enjoyed your oranges. Children here in Boston will not even get that for Christmas. Do you need for me to explain to you what was going on in the State House?"

"That Reverend Mather reminds me of the monk we heard when we were in Rome," Grant remarked. "He wanted to get rid of Saturnalia just as bad as Reverend Mather wants to get rid of Christmas."

"They very much have the same idea," said Brother Memory. "But I want you to understand that the good Reverend's approach, while well-meaning, will have some disastrous effects. In the year 1712, he will preach a sermon that will urge people to be charitable towards others with whom they disagree, but by this time, the tide of history will have turned against him. When William and Mary will come to the English throne in the autumn of 1688, an edict of toleration will be signed that will outlaw religious persecution in England and the American Colonies. As time goes on, persons who are not Puritans will begin to settle in Massachusetts as well. Some, like the Dutch, will bring in their traditions about *Sinterklaas*, which is the Dutch word that 'Santa Claus' comes from. *Sinterklaas* is the Dutch nickname for St. Nicholas. '*Sinter*' means 'saint' and '*Klaas*' is short for

'Nicholas'. But when the Dutch pronounce '*Sinter*', it sounds like 'Santa.'"

"Oh, yeah. I remember Young Nanny telling us about him," Alex said. "He's the one who brought oranges by boat from Spain."

"That's how the legend goes," said Brother Memory. "But I haven't finished my story about the Reverend Mather. Do you want to hear the rest of it?"

The boys nodded.

"It wasn't just on the Christmas issue where he and some other Puritan clergymen overstepped their bounds. They also went too far when they allowed innocent people in Salem, Massachusetts to be accused and convicted of practicing witchcraft."

"I'm scared of ghosts, vampires, and Scrooges," Alex said. "Please don't tell me there are witches here!"

"I doubt there are," Brother Memory assured him, "but the Reverend Mather certainly believed there were. In the year 1692, a number of innocent citizens in Salem were accused by a bunch of hysterical girls of witchcraft."

"Hey, I know some girls like that from my school," Grant said.

"Well, before you go calling girls 'hysterical', I think you ought to know that there may have been a good reason why the girls in Salem were that way."

"Why?" asked Alex.

"Some scientists think a kind of blight on grain may have caused them to hallucinate," Brother Memory explained. "If that is true, then I'm sorry the Reverend Mather, who in many ways was a man of science, had no way of knowing it. After all, the Reverend did, among other things, successfully inoculate people against smallpox. In doing so, he saved many from an untimely death."

"So why did he believe people were witches?" Alex asked.

"In 1689 he wrote a book entitled *Memorable Providences, Relating to Witchcrafts and Possessions* in which he claimed that he had found several instances of witchcraft being practiced in New England. The book became very popular among other Puritan ministers, and by 1692, reports of witchcraft began to crop up everywhere. Actually, the Reverend Mather was not as extreme in his prosecution of witches as some other Puritan clergy, but he did believe that these instances of witchcraft and possession by evil spirits were real. When the hysterical girls began to accuse innocent citizens of witchcraft, things went way too far. The hysteria spread. Soon innocent people were being jailed and threatened with hanging if they did not confess their involvement in witchcraft and repent of it. Since the innocent people who were falsely charged had not really practiced witchcraft, they had nothing to confess. Indeed, if they had confessed it, they would have been guilty of lying, and for a Puritan lying is also a sin. Because they refused to lie, some of these innocent people ended up being hung by the neck until dead. Sadly, one of the persons accused of witchcraft was John Alden, Jr., the son of the kind old gentleman you heard speaking at the town council."

"The Reverend Mather sure had a hateful look when Mr. Alden spoke," Grant said. "Was he trying to get even with Mr. Alden?"

"I don't know about that," Brother Memory said. "One thing is certain. The harsh penalties imposed on others by some of the Puritan religious leaders did leave a bad taste in the mouths of a lot of people. Over time, the children and children's children of the Puritans abandoned Puritanism and went in the opposite direction. Some of them turned against religion entirely."

"I wonder if some of their children's children could have been the Anti-HMBG people we saw when we were last in the present," Grant said.

"It wouldn't surprise me," Brother Memory replied.

"They did have the same mean spirit," Grant said. "And they both believed Christmas was nothing but a superstition."

"There are people who, as the saying goes, are willing 'to throw the baby out with the bathwater,'" Brother Memory commented. "Such people are just as responsible for the lights going out in Christmas future as the Saturnalians."

"Could they be related to the Scrooges in any way?" Alex asked.

"Nothing could be more certain," Brother Memory replied. "When Charles Dickens wrote *A Christmas Carol* a couple of hundred years later, there were still people in England who kept the Puritan attitude toward Christmas going. Ebenezer Scrooge was typical of that attitude. However, the Puritan attitude of people like Ebenezer Scrooge was even worse than what it had been in places like New England, for now rich employers merely used it as an excuse to exploit their underpaid and overworked employees. The fact that Ebenezer Scrooge wouldn't let poor Bob Cratchit celebrate Christmas with his family was just a symptom of a much bigger problem, and that was the total lack of compassion and charity on the part of many well-to-do citizens toward the poor and the underprivileged. Children—especially handicapped children like Tiny Tim Cratchit—could be nothing but victims in such an unfeeling and uncompassionate world."

"Then the Scrooges don't care much more about children than the Romans who sacrificed children during Saturnalia?" Grant asked.

"Correct," said Brother Memory. "Remember what Ebenezer Scrooge said before his change of heart about poor people who would rather die than have to go to the poorhouse: 'If they would rather die, they had better do it, and decrease the surplus population.' So you see, there is really no difference between the Saturnalians and the Scrooges at all. Whether they celebrate by overindulging their desires at the expense of their children, or decide to be stingy and miserly by hording their money, the result is exactly the same. Children suffer."

"But what about the children who are spoiled because they get too many presents," Grant asked. "Isn't that a problem, too?"

"Of course it is," said Brother Memory. "And the Puritans knew this because they believed in a Providential God. Unfortunately, this is one of the Puritan truths that didn't quite get through to people in the present. For some today, God is like a mean old ogre who enjoys punishing people. Their idea of God reminds one of the Emperor Nero. For others, God is like the genie in Aladdin's lamp. He is at their beck-and-call and is only there to satisfy their selfish whims. The Puritans avoided these extremes and understood that God gave his people what they needed without spoiling them rotten. However, they also understood that God also disciplined his people without making them cower in fear, just as wise parents discipline their children in a spirit of love. Do you boys understand what I'm saying?"

"I think so," Grant said, but Alex shrugged his shoulders.

"That's okay, Alex," Brother Memory said. "You will understand more clearly in time. But now, we have to find the pieces to the time-wiring-diagram puzzle for you to remember. Follow me as we go on a covenant hunt."

—Chapter Fifteen—

TWO KEYS
TO THE TREASURE CHEST

"WHAT KIND OF A HUNT?" Alex asked.

"A covenant hunt," Brother Memory said. "But don't get the wrong idea. A covenant is not an animal of some sort. Follow me, and I shall try to explain."

Brother Memory started taking them down a road that led to the north part of Boston.

"Where are we going?" Grant asked.

"To the church where the Reverend Cotton Mather's father ministers," Brother Memory replied. "His name is Increase Mather."

"Why there?" Alex wanted to know.

"That's where the covenant is," he answered.

"Are we looking for a treasure like the lost Ark of the Covenant?" Grant inquired.

"You could say that," Brother Memory replied. "Like the lost Ark, the covenant I'm talking about has been lost in modern times, but not in the same way the Ark of the Covenant of Ancient Israel was lost. We won't be looking for a box with angels on its lid, if that's what you're thinking."

"So what will we be looking for?" Alex asked.

"We're looking for some old documents that belonged to a man named John Winthrop."

"Who was he?" Grant asked.

"He was one of the founders of the Massachusetts Bay Colony," Brother Memory replied. "Now, just ahead is Clark Square. The North Church is that wooden building there. As you can see, it's a rather plain building as buildings go. It is sometimes called the 'second church' because the first building burned in 1677 when a great fire spread through this part of the town. The Reverend Increase Mather's house unfortunately was burned, too, along with the houses of some of Boston's most prominent citizens."

The main part of the church itself featured two rows of five windows each. At its front, which was on the church's east side, there stood a tall square tower with vertical rows of windows. There were four windows each on its north and south sides, one window on the west side where the tower attached to the front of the church, and three windows on the east side beneath which was the church door. The tower was crowned with a high peaked roof topped by a weathervane.

"The Puritans believed in the ideals of plainness and simplicity," Brother Memory continued, "and these ideals are reflected in the way their church buildings were fashioned. As the Puritans highly discouraged adornment in their clothing styles, they discouraged the same in their church buildings. You will see that this church is really more of a meeting house than anything."

Brother Memory opened the front doors to the church and led the boys inside. There were rows of pews separated by aisles. The ceiling and walls were plain white. At the front of the church was a raised platform with a pulpit at the center made of dark walnut.

"See, everything inside is plain and simple, too. The windows are not stained, but plain, glass. You will find no paintings and no objects like crosses in here. The Puritans thought of those things as idols that God's people were forbidden to have."

The boys followed Brother Memory through a side door of the church into an adjoining building. In it was a library with shelves inside cabinets having glass doors. Most of the books were bound with fine leather. Brother Memory opened one of the doors, took out a chest, sat it on a desk, and opened it.

"These are letters and writings of John Winthrop," he said. "These letters hold the clue to a piece of the time-wiring-diagram puzzle you are collecting. What you will find here is John Winthrop's description of the situation in Old England. Many people that made up England's lower classes were hopeless. The upper classes were taking advantage of them and saw them as a burden and a nuisance. Even though the servants did virtually all the work for the upper classes, they were treated harshly and with contempt. Children were generally seen as a burden and a nuisance as well. Winthrop writes that in this new colony of Massachusetts servants and children will be seen as divine blessings, not as burdens to be endured or eliminated."

Brother Memory sifted through the writings in the box.

"Is the chest you're looking through the covenant?" Grant asked.

"No," he replied, "but we are getting warm. I know that it's inside here somewhere. Oh!" he exclaimed. "Look here!" Brother Memory removed some of the papers. A title page read, 'Modell of Christian Charity'. "This is one of John Winthrop's sermons," Brother Memory told them. "Listen to his words, 'For we must consider that we shall be as a city upon a hill. The eyes of all people are upon us.' In this he argues that the success of this city will depend upon all of the members of that society keeping 'the Golden Rule'. Do you know what that is?"

"Yes," Alex replied. "Do unto others as you would have them do unto you."

"Exactly right," said Brother Memory. "In this sermon, Mr. Winthrop mentions that the principle by which the golden rule is lived is 'Love'. Look here at what he says! 'Love' is the ligament that binds the body together!' That's what I've been looking for! This is the special thing that will make John Winthrop's covenant work!"

"I don't understand," Grant said. "What is a covenant anyway?"

"Yeah," said Alex. "We don't have a clue."

"Oh, my dear boys, I am sorry," he replied. "Maybe the best way to explain it is to tell you a story. Would you like to hear it?"

They nodded.

"Once, long ago, the people of Northern Europe were being attacked by a vicious foe. This foe, like thousands of wild bears, rushed down from the far northern lands at a time when the weather in Europe was warmer than usual. At first, the foe attacked the coastlands of England and Ireland. In those days, beautiful monasteries had sprung up along the coasts, great places where both faith and learning were kept alive. One monastery, which lay on an island called Lindisfarne, housed great treasures. Among these were books of ancient learning going back to the days of the Roman Empire and beyond. Now, when the invaders from the north arrived, no one expected them. Everyone was surprised, because nothing like this had ever happened. Because they were unprotected, many monasteries were looted and destroyed. Over time, the fierce invasion forces traveled up rivers, pillaging and burning village after village. Again, the people in these towns were unprepared for what had come. They were, after all, simple farmers unschooled in the ways of war and defenseless against so powerful an enemy. As time went on, the amount of fear in Europe became intolerable. Never had they met such fierce and relentless invaders."

"Who were they?" Alex asked.

"The Vikings," Brother Memory answered.

"I read about them in school, but I didn't know they were so bad," Alex said. "Why did they do such mean things?"

"They knew nothing of love," said Brother Memory. "They believed in loyalty to their superiors, yes, but unfortunately this loyalty did not include any sense of right and wrong any more than those gangs of bullies you sometimes meet at school know the difference of right from wrong. The Vikings did know how to band together, though, and this is one of the things that made them so strong. When the people of Europe saw how effective the Vikings were in banding together to commit acts of evil, they decided that they would figure out a way to band together, too. One group of people learned how to fight and protect the other group of people. Those who learned how to fight were eventually called knights. The rest of the folks would continue farming and would give part of their crops to pay these knights to protect them. To be sure everyone would do their jobs properly, the people would swear oaths of loyalty or 'fealty' to the knights, and the knights would promise to be loyal to the people they had agreed to guard and protect. As time passed, the knights organized the people to build castles where everyone could go to be protected in case of a Viking invasion. The system worked very well at first, but over time, the people who farmed the land got the short end of the stick. They woke up one day only to find that they had simply traded one enemy for another. It all happened when the knights who had sworn to protect them started treating them like sheep and cattle. As livestock are herded, fleeced, milked, butchered, and eaten by their human masters, these poor people found themselves being exploited by their masters, too. There was nothing these poor people could do, either, because they did not know how to fight, and they had no weapons to fight with. Now, I want to see if you boys remember, what was the main thing that bound the Vikings together into a group and bound the people and the knights to one another?"

They didn't answer, so Brother Memory probed them.

"Grant, do you know?"

"No."

"Alex, do you?"

"Not really."

"Okay, I'll give you a hint," said Brother Memory. "It starts with the letter 'L.'"

"Oh, I think I know now," Grant said. "Loyalty?"

"Yes!" Brother Memory replied. "Loyalty is the bond that keeps the band together. But what does it mean to be loyal? Suppose that one of your friends went and told on you for something you did wrong. Would that be a loyal friend?"

"No," said Alex. "I hate tattletales."

"But what if you knew a wrong thing your friend had done that would put him in very great danger," asked Brother Memory. "What if he went exploring a cave that he had been told not to go into, and fell to his death? And suppose that he had done this several times before this accident happened, but you said nothing about it to anyone because you didn't want to get him in trouble. Would you feel bad about not telling?"

Alex hung his head. "Yeah, I guess I would. I didn't think about it that way."

"Now suppose that you had a friend who got mixed up in a gang," Brother Memory said. "And suppose that friend joined that gang and turned out to be a loyal gang member. Would you call his loyalty to that gang a good kind of loyalty?"

"Not really," Alex replied.

Brother Memory looked at Grant. "So what would be a good kind of loyalty?"

"I guess a kind of loyalty that is always looking out for the other guy," he replied.

"Now, with the Vikings, let me suggest to you that their loyalty was misplaced," Brother Memory continued. "The loyalty of the Vikings to one another is really no different from the kind of loyalty gang members have for one another. Both kinds of loyalty are based on fear. The members of the band or the gang are afraid of what will happen to them if they are disloyal. Maybe they will lose an eye or a finger. Or maybe they will even lose their life if they betray the group. Would you say that kind of loyalty is a good thing?"

The boys shook their heads.

"Now," Brother Memory went on, "was the kind of loyalty the farmers and the knights had for one another a good kind of loyalty?"

"Yes," Alex said. Then he immediately changed his answer, "I mean 'no.'"

"I know," Grant said. "At first the loyalty was not so bad because the agreement the farmers had with the knights helped everybody."

"That is a kind of agreement that is mutually beneficial to the parties making the agreement," Brother Memory clarified. "Do you understand what I mean by that?"

"I think so," Grant said. "It's like trading baseball cards. Sometimes trades are equal. But one time I traded away one of Dad's cards that was worth a lot of money for a card that wasn't worth anything."

"So you got taken," Brother Memory stated.

Grant looked angry. "Yeah! That's right!"

"So it didn't make you happy?" Brother Memory asked.

"No!" he answered. "My dad had to go to my friend's dad to get the card back. I got in trouble for trading it, too."

"Now think how those poor farmers felt when they got the raw end of the deal," Brother Memory said. "Alex, do you think those farmers would go above and beyond the call of duty when those knights required something of them?"

"I sure wouldn't," he answered. "I would try to find a way to get out of the work if I could."

"At least you're being honest," Brother Memory said. "But suppose the situation were different. Suppose someone who had authority over you did all kinds of good things for you. Suppose that person bought you clothes, fed you, gave you a roof over your head, bought you toys at Christmas to play with, and then asked you to do something like mow the yard. Suppose then that you refused to do it because you were lazy or wanted your own way. Would that be a good thing?"

Grant hung his head, because he had done exactly this.

"Grant, what do you think?" Brother Memory asked.

"I think I understand what you're saying," he replied. "For the bond between people to be strong, they need to be sure they don't take advantage of each other."

"Yes," said Brother Memory. "But the fact is that all of us at times take advantage of others. That means we need to ask others to forgive us. Now let's go back to the Vikings. Do you think one Viking would forgive another for betraying the group?"

"No," Grant said.

"Alex, what do you think would happen to that Viking?"

"He probably would be punished: Maybe even killed."

"I think you're right," Brother Memory said. "And if a knight caught a farmer goofing off, do you think that the knight would forgive him?"

The boys shook their heads.

"Nor do I," Brother Memory said. "The poor farmer probably would be beaten, or worse. So, what makes the kinds of agreements we've just talked about any different from the kinds of agreements the Puritans made with each other? Again, I'll give you a hint. The word starts with an 'L.'"

The boys thought, and finally Grant said, "Loyalty?"

"Sorry, Grant, but you've already used that one. The answer is 'Love.' This was John Winthrop's great discovery. If love, not fear, is the main ingredient that makes the bonds of the covenant strong, then the result will be a better society, or, as Winthrop said, a 'city on a hill' that all the world will wonder at."

"But if the Puritans love each other, why are they so strict?" Grant asked.

"One thing a real Puritan agrees to do when he enters into a covenant with other Puritans is to be strict toward himself. This means that he willingly holds himself to a higher standard and has high expectations of himself. He expects others to do the same too, of course, because he knows that in entering into a covenant with one another they have agreed to do the same thing. So, he holds them accountable for their actions, just as he expects they will hold him accountable. He is also willing for others to hold him accountable and bring him back to his senses if he should err. If a Puritan errs, he will ask forgiveness of the others, but he will also change his behavior because he loves the others in his group. Now, do you think the others will forgive him if he asks, or will they treat him the way the knight might treat a farmer, or the way a Viking might treat a traitor?"

"Forgive him?" Alex asked.

"Yes," Brother Memory said.

"But what about the innocent people who were hung as witches?" Grant asked. "Those people were killed."

"That's true," Brother Memory said, "and it an example of what happens when trust breaks down. Love best survives where there is trust and mutual respect, and these are things the Puritan clergy lost sight of. As the people allowed fear and mistrust to get the better of them, they stopped respecting one another. Soon they forgot that 'perfect love casts out all fear.' The hanging of those innocent people as witches frayed severely the covenant that had been put in place here in Massachusetts. Even the relationship between Increase Mather and his son, Cotton, was tested to the limit. After the witchcraft trials, Cotton Mather wrote *The Wonders of the Invisible World*, a book in which he tried to vindicate his belief that witchcraft was being practiced in the Colony. His father read it and disapproved of it so heartily that he burned a copy of it in Harvard Yard. This story only goes to show that to open up the secret treasure of the covenant one needs two keys—both shaped like an 'L.' One key simply will not do. Those two 'L's' are 'Loyalty' and 'Love' as I have said. But as with ancient treasure chests that had more than one lock and had to be opened by as many as two or three people, the treasure chest of the covenant cannot be opened unless both keys are used. Now watch as I write down the two 'L's' and show how they form a square when placed together like a mirror image."

Brother Memory traced out on some parchment the two 'L's' to reveal a square.

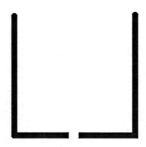

"But it has no top," Grant observed.

"That is good, because it is shaped like the Holy of Holies of the Hebrew Temple which contained the Ark of the Covenant," Brother Memory explained. "The Holy of Holies had no ceiling but was open to symbolize the fact that God, who is infinite, cannot be boxed in."

"That makes sense," said Alex.

"Loyalties that are forged with love rather than fear are the only loyalties that will abide the test of time," Brother Memory continued. "All other kinds of loyalties are destined for the Scrooge cemetery. You must remember this."

"Okay," said Grant. "But what will we find in the treasure chest of the covenant? Where is it, and when can we open it?"

"Follow me outside, and I will tell you about things yet to be here in Boston," he said.

After Brother Memory had closed the chest, he led the boys outside into the square. Then he said to them, "Do you see the church across the street?"

"No," they replied.

"That's because it hasn't been built yet," he told them. "But it will be built about forty years from now on that spot right there. It, too, will be called the North Church, and it will be in the Church of England. And from this 'city on a hill' that John Winthrop spoke of two lights will one day swing in the tower of the church that is not yet there. The man who will swing those lights will be a friend of a patriot by the name of Paul Revere who will be born here fifty years from now and will live in this square. When Mr. Revere sees those two lights from across the Charles River, he will know as he makes his midnight ride to tell the Patriots through the cities of Medford, Lexington, and Concord, that the British will be invading by sea. So the two lights that will swing in that church will play a major role in the success of the American Revolution. One could say that those two lights will beam forth the image of the two 'L's' that will foretell the defeat of the invading British. After that, this treasure chest known as 'America' will begin to be opened, and as long as the ideals that began with the Puritan covenant remain strong, the riches in that treasure chest will greatly multiply. However, if the ideals of the covenant are lost, and this is what seems to be happening in Christmas present, then those treasures will dwindle and the future will look bleak and empty. This is why you must remember this piece of the time-wiring-diagram puzzle when you return to the present. Will you boys promise not to forget?"

Alex nodded, and Grant said, "Yes, the two 'L's', 'Loyalty' and 'Love', that together form a square."

"Then it's time we returned to the mailbox so that you can travel back to the present," Brother Memory said. "I have a feeling that the knowledge you have gained here will be badly needed by now."

Brother Memory led the boys back through Boston, and eventually they returned to the mailbox they had arrived in. After they went back inside the mailbox, Brother Memory shut the door behind them, and soon they were on their way down the corridor to the gate and through the snow-globe portal to hitch a ride with Young Nanny.

—Chapter Sixteen—

INVASION FROM A SINKING LAND

WHEN THE BOYS HAD once again boarded the plane, they found Young Nanny stacking bags of mail as usual. She no longer had on her Pilgrim clothes but now wore a green square-dancing dress with white ruffles. She was listening to square-dance music on the radio and practicing her dance moves as she worked with the mail. The man singing on the radio was named 'Tex' something or other, and the boys listened to him give the dance commands as a bluegrass band played 'Turkey in the Straw'. "Swing your partner, do-sa-do, turkey in the hay and turkey in the straw, allemande left, now allemande right, and put on a tune called Turkey in the Straw."

"Young Nanny, what are you doing?" Grant shouted over the music.

She rushed to turn the radio down. "Land sakes! You caught me! I was practicing my square dancing. I'm glad you boys are back. How was your visit?"

"We learned about the Pilgrims and the Puritans," Grant said.

"Yeah," said Alex, "and we went on a covenant hunt."

"Well, that's a new one on me," remarked Young Nanny. "Did you have a good Christmas in Boston?"

"They didn't celebrate Christmas," Alex replied. "They don't really celebrate much of anything there."

She scrunched up her face and shook her head. "Of course. I knew better than to ask you that question. I just wasn't thinking. What about Thanksgiving. They did celebrate that, didn't they?"

"Technically, no," Grant replied. "'Celebrate' is the wrong word. They *observed* Thanksgiving."

Young Nanny slapped herself on the forehead. "What's wrong with me! My mistake again! You're right, Grant. 'Observed' is the word I should have used."

After a brief period of silence, Grant asked her, "Are you on your way to a square dance?"

"Yes. I'll be off to the Christmas square dance shortly after we land in the present. I know you didn't find any Christmas square dances in Boston. Am I right?"

The boys nodded. "The Puritans don't believe in dancing or any other kind of entertainment," Grant confirmed. "They were pretty strict and serious."

"I figured as much," she said. "Well, there is a time and place for being strict and serious. But remember: All work and no play make Jack a dull boy."

"Who is Jack?" Alex asked.

"Oh, Jack could be anybody," she said. "'All work and no play' is just an old saying. It means that he who does not know when it's time to play becomes so boring nobody wants to be around him."

"For the Puritans, having people not want to be around you would be bad," Grant said. "They did put a lot of emphasis on loving one another and being part of their group."

"Those are good things," said Young Nanny, "but sometimes people get so serious they forget how to laugh. There is a time to be serious, but there is also a time to laugh and have fun with family and friends."

"Is that what you plan to do at the square dance?" Grant asked.

"Yes," she replied. "Square dancing is good exercise, and the body needs exercise. It's also good for the mind because you've got to remember the commands and follow them at the same time. Doing both isn't as easy as you might think."

"Have you always square danced?" Alex asked.

"Not always," he replied. "I remember that on one Wednesday night my sister Elizabeth and I sneaked out of church and went square dancing. My father gave us both a stern talking to not just for leaving church, but also for going dancing. He and mother did not approve of dancing at all."

"I'll bet he was a Puritan, then," Alex stated.

"Well, the Puritans were our ancestors, and that explains a lot," Young Nanny said. "But just remember that spending too much time having fun can be as bad as having none at all. I limit my time square dancing for that reason. I don't want to go overboard with it. I've known friends who have, and they get to the point that they don't have time for anything else."

Young Nanny stacked the last of her mailbags and said, "Okay boys, let's head to the cockpit. It's time for takeoff." They followed her and got buckled into their seats. Young Nanny engaged the plane's propellers, and soon they were airborne. When they reached their cruising altitude, Young Nanny said, "I've made a fresh batch of sugar cookies. Would you boys like some now?"

"Yes! Yes! Yes!" Alex exclaimed, and Grant said, "Me, too!"

Young Nanny took her cookie tin from the compartment, removed the lid, and used her Nanny stick to serve the boys their cookies.

"Tell me," she said. "What was the one thing you enjoyed most when you were in Puritan New England?"

"Oh, that's easy," said Alex. "The oranges you gave us."

"What did you miss most while you were there?"

"A good nap," Grant answered. "I've never seen people work so hard in all my life. It made me tired just to watch them. And to see them have to work on Christmas day? Well, that was pretty depressing."

"I guess so," said Young Nanny. "Why don't you boys take a long nap if you're tired? I'll let you know as soon as we land, okay?" The boys closed their eyes and about ten seconds later were fast asleep. When they landed, the boys were still dead to the world, so Young Nanny went to fetch something for them to eat. She returned with a bucket of fried chicken, some rolls, and corn on the cob.

"Okay, boys, it's time to wake up. I've got food for you."

"Gee, thanks, Young Nanny," Grant said.

"Yeah, thanks, Young Nanny," Alex echoed. "Where did you get the chicken?"

"I fried some up earlier. I brought it out because I figured you were hungry."

"We were," Grant said. "This looks really good."

"I was planning on taking that chicken to the square dance," she said. "We'll be having a potluck dinner tonight, too. I always like to take fried chicken and corn on the cob because it reminds me of the wonderful church picnics we used to have when I was a girl. We would always have the best time eating. Afterward, we would gather for a sing-along. Sometimes people were too stuffed to sing and just sat around in chairs fanning themselves!"

"Aren't you going to eat any chicken or corn on the cob?" Alex asked her.

"I'm afraid I'll mess up my pretty dress," she replied. "Don't ask me why I make such messy food when I'm wearing my good clothes. It doesn't make a lot of sense."

"I know why you make it!" Alex remarked. "Because it tastes so good!"

"I suppose you're right," she said. "Now, when you boys are finished, I need some help carrying a few of those mailbags. They're heavier than normal."

"Why is that?" Grant asked her.

"They are full of lengthy contracts," she answered. "Mail from Puritan New England is always pretty heavy because of them. But I suppose they are important."

"Will they go to the dead letter office like the Christmas mail?" Alex asked.

"The contracts? No, I don't think so. For some reason those always get through. That's one thing the Puritans started that people still seem keen to hang on to today."

"Have you read any of them?" asked Grant

"Most of them are labeled 'confidential,'" she replied. "But I have read a couple that were not private."

"What did the contract say?" Grant asked.

"Oh, it is way too complicated to try to explain," she answered. "Those contracts are filled with scads of minute details, legal jargon, and fine print. The words are defined very precisely, and the terms of the contract are so rigid, there's virtually no wiggle room left for people to get out of them once they're signed. People simply have to abide by the terms or suffer the consequences. It reminds me of the time my brother Leon and I were playing Cowboys and Indians, and he tied me up so he could 'scalp' me. He knew all those Boy Scout knots, of course, and he could tie them so tightly and so well that nobody could get out of them. My mother gave him a thrashing for doing that to me. Of course, he really never intended to scalp me."

"Grant tied me up once," Alex said.

"Grant! I'm surprised at you!" Young Nanny said.

Grant smiled.

"But it was okay," Alex said. "He didn't try to scalp me either."

Soon, the boys had finished eating, and they helped Young Nanny carry the mailbags to the letter office. After that, they exchanged goodbyes and returned to the entrance of the mailbox. When they opened it, Pater Kronos was waiting for them.

"I'm so glad we didn't have a rainstorm this time," he said when he greeted them. "And you will be glad to know the Sphinx is not here in these parts either. You've arrived at a safer place than you did when last you were here. But this doesn't mean we don't have an important job to do. We've lost another five years off Christmas future, so it's time that we started working on it."

"But don't we have to have the time-wiring-diagram puzzle put together first?" Grant asked.

"I know we don't have all the pieces, yet," he replied, "but I do think we have enough of them to get started. In order to do that, however, we are going to have to convince the Orna folk to help us. The puzzle cannot be put together, and the repair of the time-wiring cannot be started, without their help."

"I thought all the Ornas got eaten up by the Sphinx," Alex remarked.

"A lot did, but not all of them," said Kronos. "The ones you saw crushed in the land-fill were the ones who wasted their time seeking pleasure rather than wisdom. They were lazy and refused to heed the wisdom of the angel stars in the schools along the road to Tree Top. Most of the Ornas who are left behind there now are the younger ones. The man you heard speak at the Anti-HMBG convention, S. J. Pestermante-Doogletarket, has taken most of them in because their parents died and they had no one to turn to except for him and his group. Doogletarket and his followers are now brainwashing the young Ornas with Anti-HMBG propaganda. There are many other Ornas, however, some young and some old, who have been able to press on toward higher levels. These are the ones who used their time wisely by preparing for their examinations and passing them. When these Ornas succeeded in passing their tests, the angel stars let them travel up the road to the next level of the Tree World."

"What about the Anti-HMBG people?" Grant asked. "Are any of them here?"

"Not yet, but they will be," Kronos replied. "They are gathering south of here. Would you like to know what they are planning now?"

The boys nodded somberly.

"The Anti-HMBGs are using their propaganda to turn the young Orna folk into bombs," he said. "They have brewed up a very explosive substance that they give the young Ornas to drink. The substance is not poisonous, but it is highly volatile like nitro-glycerin. The least little movement can cause the young Ornas to explode. Once the Ornas are loaded, the Anti-HMBGs convince them to get close enough to the angel stars to carry out their assault. The Anti-HMBGs have managed to explode one angel star already using this tactic."

"Why in the world would they want to explode the angel stars?" Alex asked.

"So they could get past them," Kronos replied.

"But couldn't they just do that by learning their lessons and passing their tests?" Grant asked.

"They could, of course, but they won't because they hate the wisdom the angel stars teach too much," Kronos replied. "They hate it because it is also the wisdom of Tree King, whom they despise. They don't even want to hear his wisdom, much less try to follow it. Instead, they want to crush it and rely on their own flawed strategies to do things their own way. Now, because the Anti-HMBGs are on the march, this region of Arboria where the Orna folk have found temporary safety will not protect them for long from what the Anti-HMBGs are planning."

"Why not?" Grant asked. "What are they planning next?

"A massive invasion of each and every region of Arboria," Kronos replied. "Exploding the angel star is their first line of attack. Because the Anti-HMBGs don't want to get their hands dirty, they are merely using the young Ornas as pawns to carry out their strategy. Unfortunately, exploding the angel star was a bad idea from the start, and it has caused them trouble they were not expecting."

"What kind of trouble?" Grant asked.

"The region of Arboria where they are now is sinking down," he replied. "Now, in addition to launching an invasion, the Anti-HMBGs are trying to find a way of escaping the catastrophe they themselves are responsible for causing."

"Where is that region of Arboria sinking down to?" Grant inquired.

"Do you remember the lava streaming from the volcano in the cemetery of the Scrooges?" Kronos asked.

"Yes," Grant answered.

"The bomb that exploded the first angel star was not intended to help the Anti-HMBGs escape from anything," he continued. "Their intention at first was to invade the higher lands and wage their war in those places. However, the detonation of that angel star unexpectedly started a volcanic fault to open. That is why the regions south of us have begun sinking down."

"Is this part of Arboria we are in sinking down, too?" Alex asked.

"Unfortunately it is," Kronos answered, "because this part is supported by the regions beneath. Right now, the Orna folk are escaping like survivors fleeing a sinking ship. The only thing that can be done is to stop the sinking. However, the Anti-HMBG strategy will not prevent that."

"Why won't it?" asked Alex.

"They wrongly believe that the only way they can escape is to explode more angel stars, but every time they do this, they only succeed in making Arboria sink faster. In fact, the Scrooge cemetery you saw in Christmas future will be located at Tree Top if the Anti-HMBG people have their way. Furthermore, if they succeed, the lava will one day start erupting from the highest peak of Arboria, where the Star at Tree Top is now located, and where Tree King dwells. The Star at Tree Top in Christmas future will then be transformed into an inferno, and instead of a glorious river of light flowing out from under the throne of Tree King, only fire and brimstone will issue out from under it."

"Can anything still be done to stop the sinking and prevent this terrible future?" Grant asked Kronos.

"Yes, but the Orna here and in the regions above will need to be rallied to go back," he answered. "They and they alone will be able to reverse the curse that is playing out there. But rallying them will be hard to do."

"Who will rally them?" Grant asked.

"That's where you and Alex come in. You will need to start teaching them the lessons you've learned on your trips. You will have to convince them to return, and then prepare them to do just that."

"But how will we do all that?" asked Alex.

"First, you need to pinpoint what the main problem is," he answered. "The Ornas know virtually nothing about Christmas past. The Anti-HMBG conspiracy has succeeded in getting rid of most information about Christmas history. You will need to teach the Ornas what the Anti-HMBGs have been keeping from them."

"I remember most of what we saw on our trips, but not everything," said Grant.

"As you also know, the dead letter office is full to capacity with undelivered mail," Kronos reminded him. "Most of the traditions you have learned are recorded in the undelivered letters and cards waiting there."

"We can help deliver it!" Alex exclaimed.

"Good," said Kronos. "You will have to bring the Ornas that mail if the traditions of Christmas past are to be carried on into Christmas future. The lack of knowledge is why so many of the Ornas became like the Saturnalians, and that is why they ended up being trampled by the Sphinx in the landfill."

"We'll try to get the mail delivered," Grant said.

"Remember that time is of the essence," Kronos reminded them. "If you fail for whatever reason to enlighten the Orna folk, then there can be little hope for the Tree World either now or in the future. But do not forget that you will be facing many obstacles. Many of the Ornas enjoy the comforts of their present safety too much, so they won't want to go back. Most know that if they were to go back, then they would also have to confront the Anti-HMBGs as well as the Sphinx. That not only seems dangerous; it also seems too big an effort. What you need to help them understand, however, is that if they refuse to make an effort and go back, they will merely be delaying the sure and certain end of Christmas future. The Anti-

HMBGs are coming, and so is the Sphinx now that his job in the regions to the south is almost finished."

"Will the Sphinx be coming soon?" Alex asked. "He really frightens me."

"Just remember what you learned before about courage and the *memento mori*," Kronos reminded him. "Courage is always the best way to face the Sphinx and to keep him from eating you. Speaking of the Sphinx, we are wasting precious time. Are you boys ready? The first thing we will need to do is start our recruitment efforts, and I have the hunch that the best places to start will be at the angel star schools that line the roads leading to Tree Top."

—CONTINUED IN —
THE MAILBOX TREE PART II,
The Riddle of Time

About the Author

RANDALL BUSH is a Professor of Philosophy and the former Director of the Interdisciplinary Honors Program at Union University in Jackson, Tennessee. An ordained Baptist minister, he holds a Bachelor of Arts degree from Howard Payne University in Brownwood, Texas; the Master of Divinity and Doctor of Philosophy degrees from Southwestern Baptist Theological Seminary in Fort Worth, Texas; a Doctor of Philosophy degree from the University of Oxford in England; and studied at the University of Texas; and for a brief time in Germany. For five years, he was a Professor of Bible at his college alma mater where he also served for one year as Vice President for Student Affairs. Upon returning from his doctoral studies in Great Britain, he served as Rockwell Visiting Theologian at the University of Houston before coming to teach at Union in 1991. He also taught ninth-grade English at Lamar High School in Houston, Texas, and served as an adjunct Professor of Philosophy in the Houston Community College and the North Harris County College systems. He is the father of two grown and married children, Chris and Laura, and now resides in Jackson, Tennessee with Cindy, his wife of 36 years.

Bush's other life experiences have included attending the Houston Conservatory of Music, playing first-chair first trumpet in his high school band, hymn-writing, extensive travel, doing mission work in the Houston inner city, living on a West Texas ranch, and serving as a part-time minister in a British Baptist church. He has also served numerous churches as a Sunday School teacher, a church pianist, a church organist, a minister to youth, a minister of music, a minister of education, and an interim pastor.

CPSIA information can be obtained at www.ICGtesting.com
Printed in the USA
LVOW081720021212

309724LV00003B/124/P